The Fall of
Lord
Drayson

The Fall of
Lord Drayson

RACHAEL ANDERSON

HEA Publishing

Cover image credit: Lee Avison/Arcangel images

ISBN: 978-1-941363-16-4

Published by HEA Publishing

Oh, what a tangled web we weave
When first we practise to deceive!
—Sir Walter Scott, *Marmion*

OTHER BOOKS BY RACHAEL ANDERSON

Regency Novels
The Rise of Miss Notley (Tanglewood 2)
The Pursuit of Lady Harriett (Tanglewood 3)

Contemporary Novels
Prejudice Meets Pride (Meet Your Match 1)
Rough Around the Edges Meets Refined (Meet Your Match 2)
Stick in the Mud Meets Spontaneity (Meet Your Match 3)
Not Always Happenstance (Power of the Matchmaker)
The Reluctant Bachelorette
Working it Out
Minor Adjustments
Luck of the Draw
Divinely Designed

Novellas
Righting a Wrong
Twist of Fate
The Meltdown Match

Miss Lucy Beresford, the late-vicar's daughter, had been instructed by her loving parents to always tell the truth. It was the good and moral thing to do, and Lucy doted on them, so she had striven to follow the wise counsel. The last time she had fibbed to her parents was at the young age of eleven, when she had returned home quite disheveled after a disheartening grasshopper race.

Young ladies of good breeding did not catch, race, or wager on grasshoppers with the farmer's sons. That would be most unseemly, as Lucy well knew, which was why she explained to her mother that she had found a small bird stuck in a marsh and had muddied her skirts in an attempt to free it. The lie worked beautifully until Johnny's papa had dragged Johnny to the vicarage to force an apology and return the guinea Lucy had wagered and lost when her grasshopper decided it would rather sunbathe than hop.

The lie thus exposed, Mr. and Mrs. Beresford did not scold or exact any sort of punishment. Mr. Beresford had merely looked upon his daughter with a sad countenance and said, "I am deeply disappointed in you, Lucille."

He had used her full name—he *never* used her full name—and Lucy had never felt more awful. From that

1

moment on, she had determined to refrain from telling another falsehood as long as she lived.

Eight years later, at the ripe age of nineteen, Lucy prided herself on holding true to that promise, although certain situations did require some creative truth-telling. Such was the case the day Lucy spotted Mrs. Manning emerging from the milliner's wearing a new bonnet. The creation had an exceptionally large poke that fanned around Mrs. Manning's thin and angular face, and with the added variegated blue feathers splaying out in all directions, the woman looked a bit like a peacock on display.

She spotted Lucy and rushed to her side. "What do you think of my new hat, Lucy? It only just arrived from London, where it is all the rage, I hear."

Rather than tell Mrs. Manning the thing ought to be sent back to London straightaway, Lucy responded with warmth. "It is quite sensational, Mrs. Manning. I'll wager you will be the center of attention wherever you go."

Beaming, Mrs. Manning patted Lucy's hand. "You are always such a dear." She pranced away, wearing a ghastly bonnet and a radiant smile.

Lucy continued on with a smile of her own, happy in the knowledge that she could still be counted among the truthful. Her father, had he still been alive, would have been proud.

Not two days later, on a dreary March morning, Miss Lucy Beresford had the misfortune of encountering a gentleman who provoked Lucy into doing something that would greatly distress her mother and cause her father to roll over in his grave.

For the first time since Lucy had made her vow eight years prior, creative story-telling wouldn't do, nor a little white lie either. No, what came out of Lucy's mouth was nothing less than a plunker.

"SELL?" ERASMUS GRAHAM, THE long-time bailiff of Tangle-wood, abruptly pulled on the reins, bringing his grey to a halt. His bushy eyebrows mashed together over bulging eyes. "You want to *sell* Tanglewood, my lord?"

"I believe that is what I said, yes." Colin Cavendish, the fifth Earl of Drayson, pulled the brim of his beaver hat lower over his forehead to better protect his face against the freezing rain. Even through his heavy riding coat, his body began to chill. Perhaps he should not have sent his valet ahead to London earlier that morning. If the skies had not looked so welcoming only hours before, he would not have done so. Wet clothes were deucedly difficult to remove without assistance.

Colin sighed and looked out over the vast estate, wondering what his grandfather had first seen in the austere and unwelcoming property. Under the thick smothering of clouds, the massive stone edifice, Tanglewood Manor, glistened in the drizzle between overgrown trees. The picture it created suffocated him, and Colin felt the sudden need to loosen his necktie.

No wonder his mother had insisted on raising her

children in the family's charming country estate in Danbury, Essex.

"Sir, this house has been in your family for four generations. Your father once climbed those trees and fished from the streams yonder. And now you wish to sell?" Erasmus continued to gape, even though his hat offered little protection from the rain.

"It is not entailed, so yes, that is precisely what I intend to do." The earl gestured to the manor house. "The few servants we have retained are not able to keep it up, the estate is only barely profitable, and Yorkshire is a far cry from Essex. No one in the family has lived here in ages, and the neglect is obvious. We need to sell while we still can."

"You could return for a time and renovate," the bailiff tried.

"For what purpose? So it can remain vacant for twenty years more?"

"What of The Honorable James? Or Lady Charlotte or Lady Harriett? Do none of your siblings wish to retain it?"

The earl smiled grimly at the image of Charlotte ensconced here—a two-day drive from London. She would consider it the worst sort of entrapment. "Charlotte and James prefer the polish and glamour of the city, and Harriett, like our mother, enjoys Danbury."

"If Lady Harriett prefers the country, perhaps—"

"My mother would never hear of it, Erasmus. It is too far from Danbury. And surely you remember Lady Drayson well enough to know how convincing she can be. It was her persistence, after all, that removed my family from Askern in the first place. It is of no use arguing. Like it or not, Tanglewood will soon be sold and off my hands."

Erasmus shifted in his saddle and heaved a heavy sigh. "I was certain you had come with happier tidings, my lord. Why make such a long trip only to instruct me to sell?"

The earl's Arabian danced to the side, no doubt anxious to be out of the rain as well. "I had some business in Lancashire, so it wasn't too arduous a journey. And, as you stated before, this place meant something to my father and grandfather, so I suppose I wanted to see for myself if it inspired any sympathetic stirrings. Unfortunately, one glance was all it took to convince me that I'm right. Tanglewood has served its purpose in my family history, and it is past time to see that it stays there. For your sake, I truly am sorry, but I'm certain I can convince the buyer to keep you on. You have served our family most faithfully."

"If I had done a better job, perhaps you would not be so anxious to be rid of it."

The earl was ready to leave the rain behind and move this meeting indoors. "Come now, Erasmus, do not add to the dreariness of the day with such self-pitying thoughts. You could have done nothing more for this place, as you well know."

The man swiped a soaked sleeve across his forehead, smearing the rain and sweeping his eyebrows into miniature Brutuses. "It is not myself I'm sorry for, my lord. What of Mrs. and Miss Beresford? What will become of them?"

The names meant nothing to Colin. "Who?"

"The late vicar's wife and daughter. They are currently occupying the dower house."

"What?" Colin's Arabian whinnied, making its impatience known, but the earl no longer cared about the cold. He pulled on the reins to keep his horse steady. "Who authorized such an arrangement?"

"Two years past, when the reverend contracted a disease of the lungs and died, your father offered the dower house to his widow and daughter. They have been residing there since."

"Why have I not heard of this before?" Colin said.

"My apologies, my lord. I assumed you already knew. Your father—"

"Was a sentimental fool," inserted Colin, more than a little annoyed by this latest development.

"Sir." The bailiff's tone was one of reproof.

The earl dismissed the rebuke with a wave of his soaked glove. "You know as well as I that everyone was fond of my father, including me. But these six month's past I have been tidying up a rather large mess he left at my door, and when I begin to think it is finally at an end, I discover he has let out the dower house of a property I wish to sell as soon as humanly possible. Even a saint would be vexed, Erasmus, and I am no saint."

"I understand, my lord."

The earl sighed as he considered his options. This news certainly complicated matters. The Beresford family would have to take up residence elsewhere before the estate could be sold, but how long would that take? "What sort of agreement did Mrs. Beresford make with my father? Is there a written contract of some sort?"

"No, my lord. Your father gave only his word as a gentleman. He journeyed from Danbury for the funeral, and I shall never forget the sight of him taking Mrs. Beresford's hand in his and saying, 'As long as I'm alive, you will have a home in the dower house at Tanglewood.'" The bailiff stared at a copse of trees that the earl could only assume hid the dower house.

The earl let out a breath. Finally, some good news. "So nothing in writing then."

Erasmus swung his gaze toward the earl, seemingly indifferent to the water dripping in his eyes. "You intend to give them the boot then?"

"Unless you can find a buyer who is willing to purchase a home with tenants in the dower house, I see no other option."

"I shall do my best to find such a buyer, my lord."

The earl let out a humorless laugh. "I was only jesting, Erasmus. A buyer like that could take years to find, and I am unwilling to dedicate that sort of time. I have made my decision. The Beresfords will need to make other living arrangements as soon as possible. You may tell them they have a month to vacate the premises."

"A month! But, sir—"

The earl lifted his hand. "Two months then, and there shall be no further argument on that."

The bailiff shook his head slowly but forcefully. "I will not do it, my lord. I will not be the one to tell Mrs. Beresford and her daughter they must find somewhere else to live." The set line of his jaw told the earl that he meant what he said.

Colin cast him a warning glance. "My father spoke highly of you when he was alive, Erasmus. Do not give me a reason to give you the sack."

"I will give myself the sack before I will deliver such news, my lord."

The earl blew out a breath as his horse danced anxiously beneath him. "Very well. I am bound for London once we have concluded our business. When I arrive, I will have my barrister draft a letter to—"

"You are here now, my lord," said the bailiff. "Why not speed up matters by delivering the news yourself? Your father made the agreement in person. I would think it only right to break it in person."

Colin considered the bailiff's words. It would be a disagreeable conversation to be sure, but not the first he'd

7

experienced. And, as much as the earl hated to admit it, Erasmus was right. The Beresfords deserved to hear the news from him.

"Very well, Erasmus," said Colin. "I will deliver the news myself." Surely, once the earl explained, they would understand why he must sell and why they must move. The matter would be well in hand by nightfall, and he would be that much closer to finally gaining the upper hand on all his newly-acquired holdings.

ON HER HANDS AND KNEES, Lucy scrubbed a particularly stubborn spot on the kitchen floor when the only servant the Beresfords could afford to retain breezed through the back door. Petite and rail-thin, with her blond hair tucked under a worn straw bonnet, Georgina had always been more of a friend than a maid.

Georgina immediately set down the basket of food she carried and rushed to Lucy's side. Her skirts were soaked from the rain. "Miss Lucy, you shouldn't be doin' that!"

Lucy sat back and drew in a deep breath, filling her lungs with air that tasted like it had been stuck inside the kitchen far too long. "What should I be doing, Georgy? Pretending to care about needlepoint or the pianoforte? You know as well as I that I have no drawing room talents, and one person cannot be expected to do everything around here. You work much too hard. It is only right that I should help out once in a while." Besides, thought Lucy, it was rather interesting to play at being a maid, especially on such a dreary morning as this when she was trapped indoors. With her mother off helping a sister during her confinement, Lucy could do as she pleased, for though Georgy attempted to tell her to behave, she could not insist on it.

9

"I work nah 'arder than anyone else in me position, Miss," said Georgina, "and you 'ave plenty of drawin' room talents."

Lucy raised an eyebrow. "Such as?"

Georgina stood and pulled Lucy to her feet, no doubt attempting to come up with at least one of Lucy's so-called "talents."

"You always like a good book, Miss," came the answer after a time.

Lucy pressed a finger to her lips in a teasing way. "Shh, Georgy. Do not go spreading that around. I would so hate to be considered a bluestocking."

Georgina extracted the scrubbing brush from Lucy's grip and tossed it on the table. "Better a bluestockin' than a maid, Miss. And that stain 'as been there since before I came 'ere. It will not budge, nah matter 'ow 'ard you scrub. Na take off that apron and cap and try ter be'ave proper-like for once. Word in town is that you're ter expect a visitor soon. Mr. Graham told me 'isself."

Lucy left the apron tied around her waist and rested her palm on the table. "Oh, what fun. Is it a rich, long-lost relative, do you think?"

"Nah."

"A constable on the hunt for an outlaw?"

Georgina giggled at that. "I think not, Miss."

"Perhaps an eligible man who has heard all about my, er . . . talents and delightful personality and is coming to pay court? Yes, I am sure that is it," Lucy teased as she dusted off her apron. "I think it best to let him see me as I really am, don't you, Georgy?"

"We can agree on that, Miss," said the maid as she pulled the cap from Lucy's head. "You always be forgettin', but you're the daughter of Mr. and Mrs. Beresford."

Lucy sighed. "You make me sound very dull indeed."

Georgina smiled and patted Lucy's cheek. "You're anythin' but dull, Miss. Na take off that apron. I'm off to fetch some fresh milk from the McCallisters, so mind your manners whilst I'm away, and don't let anyone in before I get back."

"I thought you are to take orders from me and not the other way around," said Lucy.

"Not wif your ma away and me the only grown up 'round 'ere." Georgina's lips quirked into a grin before she stepped out the door and pulled it closed behind her, leaving Lucy alone in the kitchen.

Almost instantly, Lucy felt a return of her earlier boredom. She leaned forward, resting her elbows on the counter and her chin in her palms. What now? Perhaps she could walk to the neighboring estate and visit Mr. Shepherd. He was always good for some interesting conversation, although lately he seemed preoccupied with the science of etymology, having recently read a book on the subject, and Lucy had no desire to learn the Latin or Greek origins of words like "candid" and "procure."

A loud knock echoed through the house, startling Lucy. Was the mysterious visitor here already? She patted the sides of her hair as she strolled out of the kitchen and down the hall. In the foyer, she drew in a deep breath before pulling open the heavy, wooden door, only to discover a man standing in front of her.

His eyes caught her attention first. Under the brim of a black beaver, and sandwiched between trimmed side whiskers, they were blue and intelligent, brimming with complexity and mystery.

He doffed his wet hat, revealing thick and wavy hair the color of molasses. Lucy studied his person, wondering who he was and what business he had with her family.

"I'm here to see Mrs. Beresford, if you please." The deep timbre of his voice matched the depth of his eyes, and Lucy was sure she had never beheld such a handsome creature. Tall and broad-shouldered, he was dressed impeccably, from his traveling coat and simple cravat to his perfectly shined riding boots—a sharp contrast to her own untidiness.

Aware that she was practically gaping at him, Lucy forced her gaze back to his face, where she found a hint of an amused smile.

She cleared her throat. "Mrs. Beresford is away, I'm afraid. Perhaps I might be of assistance?"

Apparently he didn't care for that answer. His jaw tightened, and his lips became a straight line. When he didn't respond right away, Lucy glanced past him through the sleet, to where a beautiful black Arabian stood tethered to the post.

"Is that your horse, sir?" she asked, ready to offer the use of the stables as shelter for the poor animal.

He followed her gaze before turning back to her. In a dry tone, he said, "I have never seen that animal before in my life."

Lucy's lips twitched. "You are bamming me, sir. Is this your way of pointing out the silliness of my question? You know as well as I that the animal is, indeed, yours."

"You should never assume anything about a stranger," he said.

"Are you a stranger?" she countered, her curiosity growing by the second.

"Perhaps," was all he said.

Unperturbed, Lucy nodded toward the horse. "Does the animal have a name, or is that a silly question as well?"

The man studied her for a moment, as though assessing whether or not she was worthy of knowing such information, before answering. "Darling."

"Pardon?"

"His name is Darling."

She studied him for a moment. There was a hint of humor in his eyes, as though he was challenging her to believe him. "I do think you are serious."

"I am."

"Surely not. No respectable man would name his horse Darling."

"Perhaps I am not respectable."

"I'm beginning to think that might be the case."

His lips twitched a moment before settling back into a straight line. "If you must know, I experienced a moment of weakness when I promised my mischievous niece that she could name my next horse. Once decided, there was no talking her out of Darling. I should probably forget my promise and give the animal a name more suited to his sex and disposition, but alas, I am a man of my word. So I must either sell it, which would be a pity, or call him Darling."

Charmed by the fact that he had a soft spot for his niece, Lucy said, "You could always omit the L and call him Daring, or something a little more masculine."

He pressed his lips together as though considering it. "Not a bad idea. Perhaps my niece would allow Darling to be his surname instead."

"And Daring his Christian name?"

"Exactly."

"Daring Darling?" Lucy laughed. "That could twist one's tongue, couldn't it?"

"Ah, but therein lies the genius of it, as my niece is vastly fond of alliteration. And with a name like Amelia Applegate, how could she not be?" His expression was now relaxed and somehow more handsome than before.

"I must adjust my earlier judgment of you, sir. Any man

who dotes on his niece in such a way must be at least a little respectable."

The praise had a perplexing effect on him. Instead of smiling, his lips straightened. In an instant, he became the formal and stiff gentleman who had first appeared at her door.

"You give me too much credit, I'm afraid," he said. "Now, if you would be so kind as to tell me when I might expect to find Mrs. Beresford at home?"

"A fortnight."

"A fortnight!" If he had not been displeased before, he certainly was now. Apparently two weeks was far too long for Lucy's mother to be away.

Her mouth lifted into an impish smile, and she gestured inside. "Would you care to wait for her?"

He blinked for a moment, obviously taken aback by such an offer. "Surely you jest."

"Of course," Lucy said with a laugh. "As diverting as this conversation has been, I think it would be most unseemly to allow you entrance into our home when neither my mother nor our maid is present."

His eyes widened, and his gaze swept over her appearance in a show of surprise. "Are you Miss Lucy Beresford?"

She dropped into a quick curtsy. "How do you do, sir? Did you think me the maid?"

He did not try to pretend otherwise. "Of course I thought you the maid. You answered the door and are wearing an apron, for heaven's sake. And your hair is . . . ahem, never mind." At least he had the presence of mind to refrain from finishing that sentence.

Lucy's insides were positively whirling at what he must be thinking. It wasn't every day a handsome man mistook one as the maid, but she refused to let his obvious shock at her appearance and lack of propriety unsettle her. She lifted her chin instead, holding out her palms for his inspection. "Have you noticed the deplorable state of my hands as well? They are red and blotchy from scrubbing the kitchen floor."

He continued to stare at her, his mouth opening and closing a few times before finally speaking. "Are you in such dire straits as that?"

Pity or concern was the last thing Lucy wanted from this man. She dismissed his question with a wave of her hand. "No, of course not. I was simply bored, is all."

"You scrub floors to stave off boredom?"

"Only when the alternative is embroidery or practicing the pianoforte," she said, her eyes dancing merrily.

Once again, his lips twitched and quirked, but the stubborn man refused to smile. Perhaps it was for the best. Lucy's heart would likely turn to jelly if he became any more attractive.

"You have me at a disadvantage, sir," said Lucy. "Apparently you know me, and yet I haven't the faintest notion of who you are."

He cleared his throat, perhaps attempting to gather his wits about him. "My apologies for not introducing myself in the beginning. I am Colin Cavendish, the Earl of Drayson and current owner of Tanglewood."

Lucy's forehead wrinkled. He appeared to be quite serious, and yet . . . "I find that very interesting, sir, considering I have met Lord Drayson not two years ago, and you look nothing like him."

"I should hope not," said the man. "My father was bald and portly, with a ruddy nose. I, fortunately, take after my mother's side."

All humor faded from Lucy's being as an otherwise

nondescript, three-letter word captured her attention. "Was?" she asked, her voice barely above a whisper.

"He passed on last summer, I'm sorry to say."

Lucy's palm flew to her mouth. She didn't know why she found the news so distressing—she had hardly known the man—but the late Lord Drayson had been so kind to her family after her own father had passed away. The earl had journeyed all the way to Askern for Mr. Beresford's funeral and, upon learning that the widowed Mrs. Beresford had been left only a paltry income, had offered them the use of the dower house. Since that time, Lucy had held him in high esteem and was saddened greatly by this news. Her mother would find it even more upsetting, no doubt.

"I am sincerely sorry for your loss," she managed to say. If anyone knew what it felt like to lose a beloved parent, it was Lucy. "I was not aware—nor was my mother—or I daresay she would have informed me. Goodness, he seemed so young and in good spirits . . . but then so did my father before . . ." She lifted sad eyes to his. "Life can be unpredictable in dreadful ways, can it not?"

"Yes." Lord Drayson didn't look at all comfortable at the turn the conversation had taken. He cleared his throat again and looked away from Lucy's face. "I had hoped to speak to your mother, but I cannot stay in Askern for an additional fortnight to await her return, so I fear I must relay my message to you instead."

"Message?" Lucy's mind was still far away, recalling memories of a firm handshake, kind words, and the promise that her family could live in the dower house as long as they pleased.

"As the new Earl of Drayson, I have been looking into and making necessary changes to some of my family's holdings. There is no easy way to say this, but I must inform you that the Tanglewood Estate is to be sold as soon as possible."

The words "Tanglewood Estate" and "sold" effectively jerked Lucy's thoughts to the present. "I beg your pardon?" she said. "You plan to sell Tanglewood?"

He fiddled with his hat, not meeting her gaze. "It will be listed as soon as you and your mother can make arrangements to live elsewhere. I am hopeful that two months should give you enough time."

Lucy's breath caught. *Other arrangements? Two months?* "But this is our home, my lord. How can you—"

"Forgive me," he said gently, "but I believe it is *my* home."

"No." Lucy was determined to make him understand. "This is your *house*. It is *our* home."

His dark and mysterious eyes finally lifted to meet hers. Though his tone remained gentle, it was also firm. "But you do not own this so-called home, do you?"

If Lucy's face reddened, it was not because she was mortified at being taken to task. It was because her veins began to pulse with both fear and anger. Lord Drayson made it sound so easy. Make other arrangements, as though penning a quick note and sending it off to a close relative would do the trick. But the few relations the Beresfords had left were no better off then they, and Lucy and her mother would never sink to asking for help from those who could not afford to give.

Which left what alternative?

Already, Lucy's mother mended clothing for a pittance, and Lucy, an adept gardener, sold her prized roses during the warmer months for a pittance more. It was the only way to keep Georgina, the horses, and food on the table. Without this house, the meager earnings the Beresfords brought in would barely cover the rent of another, far lesser home. How would they ever manage?

Apparently the new Earl of Drayson was in every way the opposite of his father—both in looks and disposition—for he did not seem to care that in two month's time a widow and her daughter would be without a home.

Lucy lowered her pride enough to plead, "Your father gave us his word that we could live in this house indefinitely."

"My father never mentioned you or your mother to me, and from what I understand, you have signed no contract."

"No," Lucy reluctantly agreed, feeling her spirits wither by the second. "It never occurred to us to ask for a contract. A gentleman's words seemed more than sufficient at the time."

"And yet that particular gentleman is no longer among the living."

Lucy's eyes sprang to his. How could he be so unfeeling? His father had been wonderful, and even his mother was said to be all that was good and kind. "So you will not honor the promise of your father even though you claim to be a man of *your* word?"

"It was his promise, not mine."

"I see," said Lucy, though the only thing she really saw was a despicable man who cared more about his purse than a person.

Lord Drayson sighed. "Surely you have noticed that Tanglewood Manor is going to ruin. It does not turn nearly the profits it would take to restore the house to the immaculate condition it ought to be in. Yes, advances could be made to increase profits and make it lucrative once again, but why should I dedicate time or money to a property that my family no longer takes an interest in? This estate should

The Fall of Lord Drayson

have been sold when my family relocated to Danbury, but it wasn't, and now I have been handed a property that will bring in much less than it is worth because of its current, worsening state. Surely even you can understand my predicament."

"Not as much as I understand my own, my lord," said Lucy woodenly.

"I am sorry for it. Truly, I am. But I have made up my mind. Tanglewood will be sold."

"And," Lucy added, "despite your father's promise, my mother and I have only two months to find another place to live."

Lord Drayson fiddled with his hat and looked away. "If it would help, my man of business can locate a new residence for—"

"Thank you, sir, but we are perfectly capable of finding our own home," said Lucy. Her pride refused to allow her to accept one ounce of help from this man.

"I'd consider it an honor if you would allow me to help you in some way."

What shred of self-control Lucy had left evaporated. "How can you speak of honor when you so obviously have none? You have shown your true colors, sir, and I will not assuage your guilt by accepting any help from you or anyone else in your family. So please, take your leave and be on your way."

His body stiffened, and his jaw tightened. He said nothing for a moment before giving her a curt nod. "Very well. Good day, Miss Beresford."

"Not at all, my lord," Lucy muttered before closing the door with a hearty shove. Her fingers clenched into fists, and she stormed into the parlor to pace off her frustrations, adding more wear to an already worn carpet. Concern after

19

concern flew through her mind, fueling her anger and frustration. The beastly earl had failed to see anything beyond his own perspective. He hadn't asked what would become of the Beresfords—only assumed that he was merely inconveniencing them with a move. Had it ever occurred to him to wonder why she and her mother were living on the charity of others? It was a most unusual arrangement, to be sure, and any person of substance would at least attempt to understand the circumstances before threatening to remove a family from their home.

Yes, Tanglewood needed improvements, but the fact of the matter was that Lord Drayson had money and therefore options. He could improve the property. He could try to find a new owner who would allow the Beresfords to remain in the house. He could be the sort of man who did everything in his power to take care of a family who had once offered a service to his.

The Beresfords, on the other hand, had no options. But had Lord Drayson cared to consider that? No. He did not want to be bothered by anyone's plight but his own. He viewed Tanglewood as a noose around his neck, and the Beresfords as the knot that held that noose in place. The sooner he could cut them off, the sooner he would be free.

And the sooner Lucy and her mother would be out on the streets.

Colin swung into the chilled, wet saddle and gathered the reins in his gloved hands. He clicked his tongue, and Darling responded immediately, carrying his master away from the house and the difficult woman inside it.

Now that he had finally met the young Miss Beresford,

Colin could understand why Erasmus had rather quit his job than confront the chit with bad news. She had obviously been raised with no notion of propriety or she would not have appeared as a maid, spoken to him with such frankness, or transformed into a spoiled child who accused him of having no honor.

Had she accepted the help he had offered? No. Had she tried to be understanding? No. Had she, at the very least, remained civil? No. She had been brash and curt and blind to the fact that no one should be required to retain a useless piece of property for the sake of two tenants.

And now, because of her lack of self control, Colin was made to feel like a veritable cad.

"Blast it all," he muttered under his breath, urging his horse to a faster pace. The sooner he could be rid of Yorkshire the better. Colin had done what Erasmus could not. He had delivered the news, and, like it or not, his bailiff could take it from here.

Colin leaned low over the horse, willing it to move even faster. As they rounded a bend in the drive, Darling cut into the turn, but his hooves hit a slippery patch, and the horse stumbled off the road and into some deep mud. Colin's body flew sideways, and he experienced a brief moment of shock before his head crashed into something solid.

"MISS LUCY, MISS LUCY, COME quick, come quick!" Georgina's shrill voice echoed through the sparsely furnished room, where Lucy still paced angrily, thinking of all the ways she could do away with the new Earl of Drayson.

Picking up her skirts, she rushed to meet her maid, who clung to the banister, appearing as gray as the clouds.

"There's a m-man," Georgina stammered. "D-dead, in the road. 'E's so p-pale and blue. Looks as though 'e's been there a while. And—"

Lucy didn't wait to hear anymore. She bolted out the front door, not bothering to don her coat or bonnet or even some boots, and ran down the carriage path. The sleet slapped against her face, feeling like hundreds of needle pricks and making it difficult to see. Her slippers soaked up the water, chilling her feet and toes, while pebbles dug into the soles. Still she continued on, running as fast as she dared on the slippery path.

A few bends in the road later, she finally saw the man and stumbled to a stop, her eyes wide. It was as she'd feared. Lord Drayson lay sprawled across the road in a limp and awkward position. The bluish hue of his skin did, indeed, make him appear dead—the exact fate Lucy had wished on him only moments before. Not far from his person lay his hat, now sodden and mashed.

Oh no. One hand rested against her queasy stomach while the other covered her mouth. Had she caused this? Surely God knew that she hadn't really meant such a fate to happen to anyone, even to someone as horrid as the earl.

What now?

Lucy had no idea what to do. The cold seeped into her body, triggering a fit of the shivers. First her chest, followed by her arms and legs, and finally her lips. As she stood there in shock, a slight movement captured her attention, and her breath caught in her throat. She took a few steps nearer, watching the earl's chest closely. Sure enough, his chest rose and fell ever so slightly, indicating that he was somehow still breathing. Lucy let out the breath she had been holding. He wasn't dead. Her dreadful wish had not come true.

Thank heavens.

Lucy's relief was only momentary, however, for while she *was* grateful that Lord Drayson was still among the living, she had little desire to help him—he, who had caused her so much distress. Why couldn't he have tumbled from his horse far enough away for someone else to find him?

Speaking of his horse, where was Darling? Lucy looked around, not seeing the Arabian anywhere. Perhaps the animal had gone for help and would soon lead a more willing rescuer back here.

Lucille Beresford, how can you think such wicked thoughts! she chided herself. She must remember her papa's favorite sermon about the Good Samaritan and help this man, but coming to the aid of someone she did not care for at all was an extremely unpleasant prospect.

Georgina arrived out of breath at Lucy's side and wrung her hands, clearly agitated. "'E's dead, isn't 'e? Oh, Miss, wot should we do?"

"Calm yourself, Georgy," said Lucy. "I am afraid that he is not dead. See? Still breathing."

"Afraid?" Georgina widened her eyes at Lucy. "Why would you wish a stranger dead, Miss? You, the daughter of a vicar!"

"He's no stranger to me, and I really do not wish him dead," said Lucy. "But I have no wish to help him either. Still, something must be done, mustn't it? We cannot leave him here to die." Lucy folded her arms and began rubbing them in an attempt to warm her body while she gave the matter some thought. Should she send Georgina for the doctor? No. Even if her maid saddled Zeus and rode him to town, it would take hours for them to return. They could not leave Lord Drayson out here in this wretched weather until then.

"Should I go for 'elp?" Georgina asked, still wringing her hands.

"Perhaps after we get him inside."

"Get 'im inside? 'Ow do you s'pose we do that?"

"By dragging him, of course," said Lucy. "There are two of us and only one of him. I am sure we can manage. Come now. You take that arm, and I shall take this one."

Georgina didn't look overly convinced this was a good plan, but she moved to do as Lucy suggested. They each grabbed an arm, hefted the earl's upper body, and pulled and exerted, maneuvering him closer to the house one painfully cold step after another.

When they had made it about halfway, Lucy's muscles gave way. She dropped the earl's arm and collapsed on her knees, breathing heavily.

"Merciful heavens, he's quite weighty, isn't he?" Lucy said. "What has he done, lined his pockets with lead?"

Georgina fell to her knees across from Lucy and ran her palm along the arm she still held. "Lined wif muscles, more like," she said, studying the earl's face. "'E's a 'andsome one, ain't 'e?"

Lucy glared at the maid. "Georgy, don't you dare find anything to admire about this man. He is odious, I tell you. Odious."

"Even odious men can be 'andsome, Miss."

Fueled by her mounting frustration, Lucy stumbled back to her feet, grabbed hold of the earl's arm and began pulling again. It took another twenty minutes or so, but they eventually managed to drag him up the stairs and into the house, where they deposited his body on a large rug in front of the fire.

Exhausted, both women sank onto the sofa to regain their breaths, not caring at all that they were drenched and filthy.

"Wot na, Miss?" said Georgina, looking like a shivery wet bird. "Should I fetch the leech?"

"Gracious no," said Lucy. "At least not until the weather has cleared and you are dry and well rested. I will not sacrifice your health for this man's." That, and Lucy truly despised visits from the doctor. She had suffered through one too many of them when her father had taken ill and was not anxious to have the doctor cross her threshold again. It was bad enough the earl had to do so.

Georgina didn't look convinced. "Are you sure, Miss? 'Is skin don't look 'ealthy at all. I would 'ate for 'im ter catch a fever on account a me."

"And I would hate for us to catch a fever on account of him," said Lucy firmly.

"But we can't just leave 'im on the rug, can we?"

"I am not as heartless as that," said Lucy with a sigh, almost wishing they could leave him there. "We shall get him out of his wet clothes, tend to his scrapes, and deposit him on the bed in the empty room off the kitchen. Will that suffice?"

"Aye, Miss, but—" Georgina stopped talking and bit her lip.

"But what, Georgy?" said Lucy with a hint of impatience in her tone.

The maid's voice dropped to a whisper. "Wot if 'e awakens whilst we're undressin' 'im?"

Of all the things to be worried about! thought Lucy crossly. "Then I shall whack him with that candlestick and put him back to sleep."

"Miss!"

"I am only teasing, Georgy," said Lucy. Goodness, where was her maid's usual sense of humor? "Truth be told, I will be glad if he awakens. Then we will excuse ourselves and allow him to finish the job himself."

Georgina didn't look appeased. Her forehead crinkled with worry even as her body shivered from the cold. "Mrs. Beresford will not like this at all. Two women alone wif a man. We should fetch Mr. Shepherd. 'E'll know wot ter do."

"We are not going to fetch anyone right now," said Lucy. "This man will be gone before Mama returns, so there will be no need to tell her about him at all." Mrs. Beresford would never leave Lucy on her own again if she learned of this situation, and Lucy had rather liked feeling independent.

Georgina was shaking her head. "I don't know, Miss. That would feel like a lie, and your papa used ter say—"

Lucy heaved a sigh of frustration. "I never lie, Georgy, and I wouldn't ask you to take up the habit either. If my mother asks if we were required to rescue a gentleman and tend to some scratches and bruises, we will answer that we did indeed, and you may have my leave to tell her everything. But if she does not ask, it is not a lie to say nothing, now is it?"

"I suppose not, Miss."

"Good, then we are agreed." Lucy pushed herself up from the sofa and cringed at her filthy skirts. "Let us change into something dry, and I will see about finding the odious man something to wear. Together, I am certain we can get him dry, dressed in clean clothes, and off to bed. How does that sound?"

"Like somethin' a proper vicar's daughter would say," said Georgina. "Except the odious part, that is. 'A do you know 'im, anyway? I 'ave never seen 'im before. I would 'ave remembered that face for sure."

"His name is Colin Cavendish," said Lucy, offering no further information than that. "And you can take my word that he is, indeed, despicable. As soon as he wakes up, you shall see for yourself."

Lucy forced her tired body up one flight of stairs to her bedchamber where she quickly changed into a worn blue morning gown and tied her hair back with a ribbon. Then she ascended two more sets of stairs to the attic, where she paused in front of one of her father's old trunks and eyed it with misgiving. It had taken her and her mother months to muster the fortitude to carefully fold all of his clothes and stash them in these trunks. They had recounted many memories while doing so, shed many tears, and folded many clothes that day. When it came time to close the trunks and leave them behind, Lucy had never felt heavier.

Memories were tricky things. They could play with one's heart, twirl it around the way her father used to twirl Lucy around, and then drop it in the dirt to be stepped upon, never to feel the same again.

Lucy's heart had been trodden upon too many times, and she knew from experience what the cost would be if she opened that trunk. But what other choice did she have?

Dress the earl in one of her gowns? She almost giggled at the thought. If only one would fit him, she might be tempted to do it. But alas, he was too large. The only clothes that would work rested before her in this dark and dusty room.

Drawing a deep breath, Lucy knelt in front of the trunk, unhooked the latch, and hefted it open. She had hoped to smell the scent of sandalwood that she had so often associated with her father, but sadly, that scent had departed, replaced by the unfriendly odor of must and old wood. She picked up the white shirt on top and breathed it in, hunting for sandalwood and not finding even a hint of it.

She set it down and sighed, feeling a renewed sense of loss. It was for the best, she tried to tell herself. If her father's scent was still intact, it would be much harder to share the clothing. Yet the memories were as vibrant as ever. Her father, wearing this shirt as he exited the church after giving a wonderfully inspiring sermon. The people in his parish had flocked around him, wanting a word, and yet his eyes had sought out his wife and daughter. When he saw them, his mouth lifted into a smile and his hand rose in greeting. Lucy's mother once told Lucy that she would never have to wonder if they came first in Mr. Beresford's eyes because he would prove it to them every Sabbath after service.

And he had. At least until the day he no longer could.

Tears pooled in Lucy's eyes, and she quickly blinked them away. She dug into the trunk, determined to find something for the earl to wear that would not reduce her to a watering pot every time she glanced his way.

Near the bottom of the stack, she finally found a soft, pink shirt and dark green trousers, both of which her father had worn once and never again. Given to him by a sweet, elderly woman with poor eyesight and poorer judgment, her father had put them on one day only to immediately remove them when his wife made the comment, "You look like a pink rosebud."

The memory caused Lucy to smile, for Lord Drayson surely deserved to look like a pink rosebud. Perhaps the new attire would inspire a new, prettier disposition.

Thus satisfied, Lucy slammed the trunk closed and trotted down the stairs, where the air became easier to breathe.

It took some work to free the earl from his sodden clothing, especially since Georgina insisted on covering the man with a quilt while they worked, but they eventually finished the job. By the time darkness encased the house, the earl, outfitted like a pale flower and ensconced in bed with his scrapes cleansed and dressed, continued to sleep quite soundly.

Lucy, on the other hand, did not sleep a wink, which did nothing to help *her* disposition.

"*CUM DILECTIONE HOMINUM ET ODIO vitiorum,*" Lucy murmured to herself as she descended the staircase the following morning. She repeated the phrase while helping Georgina in the kitchen. Her maid had long since stopped protesting Lucy's efforts to aid with the cooking, for it did no good.

"Wot does that mean?" Georgina asked when Lucy repeated the Latin phrase yet again.

Lucy glanced up from the broth she was stirring. "It's from St. Augustine. It means 'with love for humanity and hatred of sins.' My father quoted it often in his sermons."

"Wot did 'e mean by it?" said Georgina, busy punching out scones from dough.

"It means that whatever wicked sins a person might commit, we must separate out the bad and find a way to love him in spite of his wickedness. It is a beautiful idea, is it not?"

"Aye."

"And much easier said than done, I'm afraid," added Lucy. "For I cannot think of one thing to like about that man."

"You mean Mr. Cavendish?"

The spoon stilled in Lucy's hand as she thought about how to answer the question. Colin Cavendish was not *Mr.*

Cavendish. He was The Honorable Colin Cavendish, Earl of Drayson, come to take their home away. Should Lucy correct her maid and explain all, or would that only complicate matters by causing Georgina to fret as well? Lucy had no way of knowing whether or not they would be able to keep a maid on once they left. If only her mother were here to help shoulder this burden and tell Lucy what they should do.

"Why do you find 'im so odious, Miss?" Georgina asked. "'As 'e done somethin' horrid ter you?"

Again, Lucy hesitated. Perhaps it was best to keep the whole situation as contained as possible until she had time to give the matter some more thought.

"He named his horse Darling," offered Lucy as her excuse.

Georgina's hands stilled on the cutter, and her brows furrowed in confusion. "Darlin'?"

"Yes," said Lucy. "What sort of man would name a male animal such a name, I ask you? It is not to be borne."

Georgina blinked at Lucy three full times before she burst out laughing. Her body quaked as she leaned over the dough and laughed and laughed. When she finally recovered, there were tears in her eyes. "Oh, Miss Lucy, yer a strange one ter be sure. I figured 'e'd made improper advances on you or somethin' of the sort. I'd about made up me mind ter go for the constable, whether you liked it or not."

"In that case, I am glad I told you," said Lucy. "The constable would have thought us most silly, indeed. Naming one's horse Darling is certainly not a crime, after all."

"It seems it is ter you, Miss." Georgina laughed again, her smile bright. Through the window behind her, a ray of sunshine glimmered through the clouds, lifting Lucy's spirits. Sunshine in March was a good omen and gave Lucy reason to hope. Perhaps once the earl awakened, he would be so grateful for the service she and Georgina had rendered him that he would find it within his heart to consider an alternative to forcing them out.

It could happen, she insisted to herself. Even ogres had hearts, after all.

Lucy was tipping a spoonful of broth down Lord Drayson's throat when he coughed and spluttered and opened his eyes, only to squeeze them shut again with a moan. "Oh, my head."

Lucy wasn't surprised by his moan. He had a nasty lump at his temple with a dark bluish hue to it.

His eyes blinked open again, more slowly this time. He flickered a glance to the right and to the left before settling his gaze on her. His forehead creased in confusion. "Where the devil am I?"

She lowered the bowl of broth to her lap, not appreciating his tone at all. "Askern, Yorkshire, in the dower house at—"

"Yorkshire?" the earl said, cutting her off. "What the deuce am I doing in Yorkshire? And at a dower house, no less?"

Lucy wasn't about to remind him. He would remember soon enough, and she was determined to keep the conversation as civil as possible until that time. She stood from where she had perched beside him on the bed and set the bowl on a small bedside table. "You fell from your horse and smashed your head on a rock. My maid and I—"

"That is absurd. I never fall from my horse." He paused and frowned. "Or, I don't think I do. No, I'm quite sure I don't. That's preposterous."

"Well, you did," said Lucy, feeling more and more cross. He had rudely interrupted her twice now in order to proclaim his own self-importance. What conceit.

"Who are you?" He peered at her for a moment before lowering his gaze to his hands, which he lifted and turned over, examining his palms thoughtfully. "Even more perplexing, who am I?"

Lucy's brows drew together. He must have hit his head harder than she'd imagined if he could not recall his own name, though sometimes head injuries had that effect on a person, did they not? She was certain she remembered reading about that somewhere, or perhaps Mr. Shepherd had told her as much. He did so love reading medical journals.

"You do not know who you are?" asked Lucy, curious. How long did it usually take for one's memory to return?

"Of course I do," he said sharply. "I just . . . can't recall my name at the moment."

"What about your mother's name?" Lucy tested. "Can you recall that?"

His forehead furrowed a moment before he pressed the heel of his hand against it and groaned. "What did you do, strike me with a mallet?"

Lucy couldn't help but think that she would very much *like* to strike him with a mallet. "I have already told you. You fell from your horse and struck your head on a rock."

One light eye opened and he glared at her. "And I told *you* that I never fall from my horse."

"How can you be so sure? You can't even recall your name," she countered.

"Because I *am* sure about that. I can't explain why, I just am, like I'm sure I detest broth."

Lucy eyed the bowl on the table and shrugged. "To be fair, I cannot say for sure that you fell from your horse, as I wasn't there to see it happen. All I know for certain is that I watched you ride away, and when I next saw your person, you were lying in the path, unconscious. Perhaps a highwayman rode up behind you and clubbed you on the back of your head—not that I have heard of any highwayman around these parts, but you never know. Or mayhap you ran into a low-lying branch. Or a monkey swung out of a tree and frightened you off your perch." Lucy barely refrained from describing it as a "top-lofty" perch.

"A monkey? In Yorkshire?" he asked. "Did you fall and hit your head on a rock, too?"

"Ah, so we finally agree that is the most sensible conclusion, is it not?" Lucy smiled, feeling oddly triumphant.

He answered with a frown and groaned again, tenderly touching the back of his head. "How did I come to be in . . . Askern, did you say? Or in this house? I am quite sure I do not make a habit of visiting dower houses in Yorkshire."

"Where would you be if not here?" Lucy probed.

His forehead creased again, and he clamped his eyes shut. Moments later, he opened them again, and he shook his head in defeat. "Perhaps you could be so kind as to tell me. We can begin with who you are and go from there."

Lucy watched him closely, feeling a hesitancy to explain anything. She merely said, "My name is Lucy Beresford," and left it at that.

He did not appear the least bit enlightened. "That name means nothing to me, nor does your face. Who are you in relation to me?"

His domineering tone made her hackles rise yet again. Yes, it would be maddening to not remember one's name, but had he paused to consider, even for a moment, the effort it must have taken to drag his body down the path and into this house? Or the kindness it had taken to clothe him or

35

pour broth down his ungrateful throat? Lucy had exerted a great deal of goodwill on his behalf, and now she suddenly wished she could pour the broth over the top of his puffed-up head.

More than ever, it irked her that he was wearing her father's clothes, even if they had been his cast-offs. Lord Drayson was the complete antitheses of all that was good and kind. Earl or not, the man could lend an ear to one of her father's lovely sermons about humility and benevolence.

As could you, came the pestering thought. *Lest you forget the tale of the Samaritan.*

"Good grief, woman, will you not answer me?" barked the earl.

Lucy glared at her patient, thinking the man the Samaritan had helped had surely been more gracious than Lord Drayson.

"No, I think I will not," said Lucy in defiance.

His eyes widened as though unused to such treatment. "You cannot be serious. It is not a difficult question to answer. How did you come to be acquainted with me, or are we even acquaintances? I am beginning to think we could not possibly be."

The airs he put on! Lucy wanted very much to throttle this man.

"How did *I* come to be acquainted with *you*?" Lucy repeated. "How do you know it was not *you* who became acquainted with *me*? Or is that something you simply 'know' the way you know you detest broth, even though someone spent hours preparing it on your behalf so that you would not expire from hunger or thirst."

He stared at her incredulously, as though she had escaped Bedlam. "Are you in your right mind, woman?"

Lucy leaned forward and planted her palms on his bed

so that her eyes were level with his. "My name is Lucy Beresford. I have lived in Askern all my life. I'm the sole daughter of a vicar and a seamstress who lived most happily despite their differences in station. When my father passed away, I came here, to this dower house. So yes, I am in my right mind. It is you who are not."

The earl's jaw clenched, and Lucy took some pleasure at the sight. Perhaps he would come down off his high horse and show at least a small amount of kindness or respect.

"I may not know who I am or where I came from," he finally said, "but at least I do not feel the need to tell tales."

"Tell tales?" Lucy gaped at him. Was he accusing her of telling untruths? *Her*, of all people? What untruths? How dare he!

Lord Drayson glanced down at his fingers, frowning when he spotted grime under his nails. He began to scrape it out as he spoke. "Claiming to be the daughter of a vicar and seamstress is all very romantic, but it cannot possibly be the truth."

"And why not?" she asked.

His gaze returned to hers. "In my experience, the daughter of a vicar would behave with more decorum, would know how to make a palatable broth, and would never allow herself to be alone in a room with a man who is not her relative. If there is one thing I know with absolute certainty, it is that you are no relation of mine."

Lucy's jaw clenched as she fought to control the rage building inside her. Ever so slowly, she pushed herself up to standing and glared down at the earl. "You are correct in thinking I am no ordinary vicar's daughter. I do not love unconditionally. I show decorum only when I wish to. And I despise those who care for no one but themselves. But I do *not* tell tales."

He actually chuckled, but it was more of a scoff than a show of humor. "Did you learn those traits from your father?"

"Do not speak of my father."

"I would prefer to speak of myself, but you do not seem to share that preference, so perhaps we should speak of your father instead. Where is he, by the by? I would very much like to meet him."

Lucy's fingers became fists while her conscience became a battleground between all that was good and evil inside her. It was a short battle, with evil making a quick triumph.

Ever so slowly, her body still trembling with anger, she lifted her chin. If he was going to accuse her of telling tales, then tell them she would. "Very well, Collins. If you must know, I am your employer. And though you may not remember me, or this house, or your position in it, or the fact that you are perfectly susceptible to coming off a horse, just like any other human, I still expect some kindness and respect from you."

"What on earth are you talking about? What position?"

There was not a hint of hesitation in her voice when she answered. "You are a servant in this house."

"A *servant*?" He scoffed as he said it, as though it were a great joke, which it wasn't. Not to Lucy. Not now. She had never been more serious about anything. Or unrepentant, for that matter.

"You are a man of all work. You fulfill the role of butler, footman, and coachman." This lying business came much easier than it should after so many years of disuse. It was both exhilarating and lowering at the same time. Lucy's father would be vastly disappointed in her.

"That's absurd," said the earl. "No one person would agree to fulfill all those duties, and I would know if I were someone's *servant*."

38

"You always did give yourself airs," said Lucy.

"I beg your pardon."

"No, I beg yours," said Lucy. "You lie in our home, making demands like you are the Prince Regent himself, when what you ought to be doing is thanking me. Georgy and I found you half-dead on the path, dragged you a fair distance in the freezing rain, changed you into dry clothes, and poured warm broth down your throat. You have always had a disagreeable nature, but this is beyond anything, even for you . . . Collins."

He inspected his hands before turning them palm-side up for her inspection. "If I am, indeed, a servant, why are there no calluses on my hands?"

"Because you are a slothful servant."

"Then why retain me?"

Lucy thought quickly, recalling to mind a novel she had recently read with a plot that would fit this situation nicely. "Because you came to this house with nothing and begged me to take you on in exchange for food and a room. And I . . . well, I suppose I felt pity on you. I am not sure why now. The moment you are well, I shall give you the boot directly."

At some point during her speech, the earl must have stopped attending for he was now examining the pale pink cuff of his sleeve with extreme distaste. He touched it briefly and quickly drew his hand back as though the fabric had defiled him in some way. "What the devil am I wearing?"

Lucy was more than willing to oblige him with an answer. "Your favorite shirt, of course."

"No. This most certainly is not my favorite shirt, if it can be called such a thing. It is hideous."

"You have no idea how happy I am to hear you say that," said Lucy. "At least one good thing will come from this trying day."

"And what is that?" he said crossly.

"You have finally realized that you have deplorable taste in clothing."

LUCY WALKED INTO THE EMPTY kitchen and collapsed on the nearest barstool, feeling weak and shaky. She leaned forward, dropping her head to the palms of her hands as she tried desperately to regain control of her breathing.

She had just told a peer of the realm—the owner of Tanglewood—that he was her servant. *Servant!* And not just any servant. He was now her butler, footman, and coachman. The Beresfords did not even own a coach, only a small cart.

An eight-year-old vow was now broken to bits and pieces with no way to put it back together. Even if Lucy strode back into the room and confessed the truth, she had still lied. What had she been thinking to lose her temper in that manner and say such things? It went against everything her parents had taught her and everything she wanted to be. Even worse, as soon as the earl recalled his true identity, he would not hesitate to send them packing immediately.

Of all the idiotic, reckless, and foolish things she had ever done.

The side door opened, and Georgina walked inside, smiling as though all was right with the world. "Mornin', Miss. It's a beautiful day today. I can almost see the sun— why, wotever's the matter?"

Georgina set down the pitcher of water she carried and

clasped Lucy's hand. "Don't say Mr. Cavendish died durin' the night."

If only that were the case.

Wicked, wicked girl! Lucy chided herself yet again and immediately wished back the evil thought. It had only been two days since her mother had gone, and it were as though Lucy had opened the door and ushered Lucifer himself in to play.

"Don't worry, Georgy. He is still very much alive." Lucy met the gaze of her maid with a cringe. "But you are going to scarce believe what I have just done."

"Wot 'ave you done, Miss?"

"I told him that he is my servant."

"You told 'im wot?"

There was nothing for it but to tell Georgina the complete truth and pray the sweet girl could help her set everything right again.

"Colin Cavendish is not Mr. Cavendish. He is the fifth or sixth or something Earl of Drayson," Lucy said.

Georgina gasped, covering her open mouth with the palm of her hand. Then she slowly lowered it, frowning in confusion. "I don't understand. Why does 'e fink 'e's your servant if 'e's an earl?"

"Because he does not remember who he is or anything about himself. His memory has vanished for the time being, and . . . oh, Georgy, he said the most insulting things to me. I am afraid I quite lost my temper and told the most monstrous of tales."

Georgina gaped at her. "Oh, Miss, you didn't."

Lucy dropped her head into her hands again. "How could I have behaved so foolishly? What is to be done?"

"I'll tell you what's ter be done," said Georgina. "You must march back in there and tell 'im the truf. Say you was only jestin' before and didn't mean anythin' by it."

"Georgy, you don't understand. If I tell him the truth now, we'll be out on our ears before dark."

The maid's eyes widened. "Out on our ears? 'A can 'e do that?"

Lucy sighed, deciding it was past time to explain. In a pained voice, she told Georgina all about the earl's visit, about the distressing news he'd imparted, about the way she had yelled at him and slammed the door on him.

"That is why I think him so odious," she finished. "Though his horse really is called Darling, so that was not a fib—not that it matters anymore." The weight of the day suddenly felt too heavy to bear any longer, and what was left of Lucy's nerves began to unravel. "I broke my promise, Georgy. I told myself I would never lie again, and today I have spun the most abominable tale ever. Papa would be so disappointed. That is the worst bit in all of this."

Georgina sank down next to Lucy and wrapped an arm around her shoulders. "After all you 'ave been through, it's nah wonder. Your papa would understand."

Lucy chuckled mirthlessly. "No. I do not think he would, sweet Georgy. But I thank you just the same."

Georgina rubbed Lucy's arm absentmindedly as she chewed on her lower lip, her brow puckered in worry. When she glanced at Lucy again it was to ask, "Am I ter be out of a job in two months then?"

"Possibly." Lucy nodded sadly. "Or sooner. Possibly whenever his lordship comes to his senses."

"Oh, Miss Lucy, this is sad news for sure. I could never find another family like yours."

Lucy clasped the maid's hand in her own and gave it a soft squeeze. "You are a dear, Georgy. I think of you more as a friend than a servant, you must know. You are all that is sweet and good and—"

Lucy stopped talking as the words echoed through her mind. Her thoughts began to spin and churn, calling to mind all the kind people she had known in her life. Her father. Mother. Mr. Shepherd. So many friends from town. The shopkeepers. Mr. Shepherd's servants. Georgina. Especially Georgina.

Every single one of them had one thing in common—they cared for others more than themselves. For some it was by choice. Others, necessity. But still they cared, and it made them a better person in the end.

"Georgy," said Lucy slowly, thinking out loud now. "Why are you so fond of Mother and me?"

Georgina thought a moment before responding. "You 'ave never treated me like a servant, Miss Lucy, and Mrs. Beresford neither. It is me 'oo 'as ter remind you of our differences in station."

"Exactly," said Lucy. "We care for each other because we respect each other—not as servants or mistresses, but as people. I have learned to respect you because I have worked at your side and have seen firsthand what you do for us and your own family every day."

A blush appeared on Georgina's cheeks, and she was quick to wave aside the praise. "Miss, yer too kind."

"Do you not think, Georgy, that Lord Drayson might benefit from being a servant for a day or—"

"Oh, Miss, nah. You cannot be thinkin' that," blurted Georgina.

"Only for a few days," said Lucy. "Perhaps, if we are lucky, the experience will serve to change his outlook on life and on people."

"But if'n it don't, 'e'll be so angry." Georgina was wringing her hands.

"No angrier than he will be if I tell him the truth now."

"Oh, I fink 'e'll be a mite bit angrier, Miss."

Georgina was probably right, Lucy conceded, but it did not sway her. "Either way, we will be evicted the moment he does learn the truth, so why not do everything in our power to bring him around before then?"

Georgina was shaking her head again, her eyes wide and frightened. "I don't know, Miss. Wot if 'is memory don't come back? I fink we should tell 'im the truf and fetch the leech, then pray 'e 'as a forgivin' nature."

Lucy scoffed at the notion of the earl having a forgiving nature. Her brief acquaintance with the man had already shown her that he had nothing of the sort. "I'll wager you my first rose in bloom that he doesn't," she said. This would seem like an insignificant wager to most, but Lucy considered her first rose of the season the most special of them all. It showed more stamina and fortitude, clawing its way to life before all the others, thus proving its mettle. It always had a special spot on her fireplace mantle next to the picture of her father.

"Oh, nah, I could never take your first rose," said Georgina.

"Of course you couldn't," answered Lucy. "Which shows you how confident I am that we will be out on our backsides by sundown if we tell Lord Drayson the truth now."

This had a sobering effect on Georgina. She fretted over her lower lip and twisted the fabric of her apron before finally nodding slowly. "Only a few days?"

"A week at most, assuming his lapse in memory lasts that long," promised Lucy, not that her promises held much weight any longer, she thought sullenly.

Georgina pushed herself up from the chair. "Wot sort of servant is 'e ter be?"

"A butler, footman, and coachman," answered Lucy. "And cook's assistant, if needed."

"Oh, Miss, you can't be serious," protested Georgina.

"I am quite serious," said Lucy. "Beginning tomorrow, we will teach Lord Drayson—er, I mean Collins—how wonderful it feels to think of another's needs ahead of his own."

"But 'a can you pay 'im, Miss? You cannot expect 'im to work for nah wages."

Lucy's lips lifted into a mischievous grin, having already come up with a plan. "In that, we need not worry, Georgy. For I have already thought up a past that will suit him nicely."

Georgina looked more concerned than intrigued. "Past?"

"Yes," said Lucy. "Collins appeared on our doorstep a fortnight ago with naught but the clothes on his back. He had no references, nothing to recommend him, and was willing to do any sort of labor for shelter and food. Although hesitant, I recalled the tale of the Samaritan and did what any proper vicar's daughter would do. I took pity on the man and agreed to let him stay on for a short time. He has been a most dreadful servant, however, always putting on airs, but instead of giving him the boot, we have decided to give him one last chance for redemption. So you see, it isn't all bad."

Georgina immediately looked to the heavens, drew a cross over her chest, and muttered something under her breath. Lucy took the opportunity to escape the kitchen and grudgingly ascended the stairs again to the attic, where she had the unhappy task of finding the ugliest clothes amongst her father's old things. She would also need to locate some other necessary items—like boots (which she prayed would fit), a shaving kit, a brush, and of course some unmentionables. If Lord Drayson was to be a servant in this house, he would need a room outfitted to look as though he had been an occupant for a time.

COLLINS LOOKED AROUND THE STERILE room, feeling like he had awakened from a bad dream, only to discover that it was not a dream at all. He was still lying on an uncomfortable bed in a white room with only a single painting on the wall— a rocky landscape with a forlorn-looking tree growing out of a crack and bending almost in half from the wind. Why would someone choose such a painting to adorn a wall? It only added to his discomfort, reminding him of his own pathetic state.

He furrowed his brow in an effort to recall something of his former life, but his head felt so cloudy and irregular. How much laudanum had the woman given him? What had she called herself again? Lucy? Yes, that was it. Lucy . . . Beresford. At least he could remember that. He furrowed his brows and blinked a few times, attempting to find additional clarity.

Collins. Collins. Collins.

The name echoed in his mind. That is what she had called him. It had been laughable at first, thinking of himself as a servant, but he couldn't deny the familiarity of the name. It sounded right and felt as though it fit. And there was no denying the conviction in those hazel eyes when she'd proclaimed, "I do *not* tell tales." But everything else she had spoken made very little sense. It was quite vexing, and he cursed Miss Beresford for drugging him into this stupor. He hated laudanum. See? He knew that with certainty. Just like he knew he wasn't fond of Askern, no matter how welcoming the morning sunlight felt through the small window adjacent to his bed.

And yet he was in Askern, and according to Miss Beresford, had lived here for a short while . . . as her servant. And that is where the doubts began. For at that point, the conviction in Miss Beresford's eyes had been replaced with brilliant flashes of anger, flashes that had ignited her eyes and stirred another forgotten memory somewhere deep in the recesses of his mind.

Blast his forgotten memories! Collins despised being at Miss Beresford's mercy, or anyone's mercy for that matter.

The door swung open, and in breezed a small woman, not much older than Miss Beresford, carrying a tray. A worn, white apron was tied about her tiny waist, and her blonde hair, though held back, frizzed around her face as though she had been up long before the sun.

"Oh, you're awake, m—I mean, Collins. Such a happy sight ter see." She set the tray on the side table and clasped her fingers together in a nervous fashion.

Collins didn't miss the fact that she had stumbled over his name, nor did he oversee the nervous twitches of her hands. He studied her, attempting to find something familiar about her, but . . . nothing. The woman was as foreign to him as this horrid room.

"I made you some toast and . . . chocolate. I hope you like it."

Collins finally found his voice. "Would you not already know what I like, er . . . my apologies. I cannot remember your name."

Her hands detangled, re-clasping behind her back. "It's Georgina, but most folks call me Georgy. And yer right. I know that you like chocolate, Collins." There was a tremor in her voice that bespoke uncertainty.

"Yes, I do," he agreed, taking a sip. "I do not, however, like toast."

Her answer came without hesitation. "Toast is easy on the stomach. You should see 'a it settles before you try somethin' more ter your loiking."

"And what is more to my liking?" he quizzed.

She lifted her chin, but her eyes didn't quite meet his. "Anythin' but toast, I would say. You 'ave a 'ealthy appetite."

Collins hid a smile. She had neatly dodged his questions without giving anything away, and yet it was clear she was hiding something. What man didn't have a healthy appetite, after all? He took a bite of the dry toast and another sip of chocolate to wash it down. "I thank you, Georgina. I must be famished because the toast tastes quite good."

She blushed, either at the use of her full name or the compliment, he couldn't tell. "Are you feelin' more like yourself?"

"My head no longer aches, if that is what you are asking."

She offered him a tentative smile. "Miss Lucy was hopin' that would be the case. I'm ter show you ter your room if'n you like."

"And where is my room?" he asked.

"Below stairs."

"Of course it is." Collins sighed and glanced over his shoulder at the small window, needing one last look before he said goodbye. Then he brushed a few crumbs from his hands and leaned forward, sliding his legs over the side of the bed. The room spun for a moment then righted. He took that as a good sign and stood. Every muscle in his body ached as he followed the maid out of the room and down the stairs, to a damp and dreary floor that smelled of must. One door down on the right, Georgina pushed it open with a creak and lit a tallow candle on a small chest. Then she stood back to allow him entrance.

The room was tiny and drab. There were no windows and no forlorn paintings to adorn the gray walls, only a chest of drawers and a single bed. It was as unfriendly a place as it was chilly, and Collins could not imagine that he had ever called this place home.

On the chest sat a bowl, a pitcher, and a shaving kit, reminding him that he was probably in need of a shave. He scratched at the growth along his jaw, suddenly anxious to be rid of it. "I have no pictures? No mementos of my former life?" he asked.

"You didn't come 'ere wif much," said Georgina. "I don't know more than that."

Next to the candle rested a piece of parchment. Colin picked it up and frowned as he began to read the words written with an elegant hand. It was a list of tasks, containing such things as polish the silver, clean the flue in the yellow salon, and tend to the horses. There were about a dozen demands in all. He lifted an eyebrow and glanced at Georgina, who was quick to clear her throat.

"Your duties," she explained. "When you're feelin' up ter them."

He sighed. "May I clean myself up and have a decent breakfast first?"

Georgina bobbed her head. "I will be in the kitchen if you need anythin'." She disappeared, and her footsteps trod quickly down the hall as though she could not get away fast enough.

Collins shut the door and walked over to the chest, where he pulled the top drawer open. Inside were a few pairs of stockings, along with some small clothes and nightclothes. The second drawer contained three white shirts—no more pink, thank heavens—and the last contained two pair of trousers and a pair of tan buckskins. The clothing was definitely not in the first stare of fashion, but not as deplorable as Miss Beresford had led him to believe.

Not wanting to linger in the chilly, damp dungeon of a room, or in clothes that belonged on a ridiculous dandy with a novice tailor, Colin made quick work of shaving and changing. Then he returned to the kitchen, where he found a plate filled with ham, eggs, and bread slathered with marmalade. It smelled so good it made his stomach rumble, and he glanced around for Georgina. She was nowhere to be seen, so Collins sat down and helped himself to a meal that tasted like heaven itself. Once finished, he downed a mug of ale and picked up the list of chores once again. Although his body still ached, his mind felt clearer and he was anxious to see if any of the tasks came as naturally to him as shaving had.

LUCY WALKED INTO THE YELLOW room just as a billowing cloud of ash and soot descended from the flue and cascaded over the top of the earl. He emerged from the haze coughing and spluttering and filthy. Lucy raised her forearm to cover her nose, along with the smile that rose to her mouth.

"How long has it been since this flue has been cleaned?" the earl demanded the moment he saw her.

Lucy ignored the question. "I realize you do not care for white shirts, Collins, but this is a very silly way to go about dying it."

His glare had no effect on Lucy. She was too busy trying to contain her laughter at the black smudges on his cheeks and nose. A giggle escaped and she was quick to cover her mouth with her fingertips.

He tossed the brush he had been carrying at the fireplace and gestured down at his ruined clothes. "You find this amusing?"

She walked forward and touched the tip of his nose then pulled her finger back to show him the residue. "You look like a very tall chimney sweep," she said.

"Exactly," he said. "Not a butler, footman, or coachman, but a *chimney sweep*. Do you not find that peculiar?"

Lucy had to admit, she was impressed that he had chosen the most onerous task to complete first. She had assumed that he would scoff at the thought of cleaning the flue and take to polishing the silver instead, if he did anything at all. But here he was, covered in ash and soot and looking quite handsome despite everything.

"This is no ordinary household, Collins," explained Lucy. "We do what must be done even if the job varies from what is expected of a certain position."

He appeared ready to argue then clamped his mouth closed, no doubt thinking a myriad of uncharitable thoughts about Lucy. But he kept those thoughts to himself, which was something he would not have done yesterday.

She smiled again, delighted by the fact that he was beginning to understand that his place was not to argue but to do as he was told.

"Well," Lucy said, clasping her hands in front of her. "I suppose we had best get this room tidied up, and quickly too. I was in town this morning and bumped into Mrs. Bidding, who insisted on paying a visit this afternoon. She will be here shortly, and we certainly do not want to send her away looking like a chimney sweep as well."

The earl rolled his eyes—a gesture not lost on Lucy as the whites of his eyes practically glowed against the charcoal of the surrounding skin. But as before, he held his tongue and said nothing.

"Oh, and I also saw Dr. Short as well. I took it upon myself to ask about your . . . condition." Not that Lucy had told the good doctor about the earl. She had merely inquired about head injuries in a universal, for the sake of curiosity, sense.

"And?" said the earl.

"He said that memory loss is quite common after a head injury and that most regain their memory at some point."

"Most?" he asked.

"I thought that sounded better than 'few,'" Lucy answered.

The earl sighed. "Did he happen to mention when I might expect my memory to return?"

"He couldn't say," said Lucy. "Each case is different. Sometimes a few days. Sometimes months."

"Months!"

"I'm afraid that is the truth of it," said Lucy, withholding the fact that he would discover his true self in less than a fortnight, whether or not his memory returned.

"Blimey, wot 'appened in 'ere?" Georgina said, standing on the threshold and gaping at the soiled room with a mixture of shock and dismay.

"Collins happened," Lucy answered, as though that explained everything.

"No," said Collins, apparently unable to hold his tongue any longer. "What happened was a severe case of neglect on the part of the owner. You do realize that flues should be cleaned more than once a century."

Lucy nearly pointed out that he was the owner and not the Beresfords, but she swallowed the retort. "Collins, you forget yourself." *Which happens to be the actual truth of it,* she thought with amusement.

His mouth clamped shut again, and his jaw tightened momentarily before he was able to pull himself together. With an edge to his voice, he said, "Do you know where I might find a broom, Georgina?"

The maid nodded and left to fetch some cleaning supplies. As soon as she was well away, Lucy said, "She prefers to be called Georgy."

"And I prefer to call people by their rightful names, don't you?" There was a hint of challenge in his expression that Lucy could not ignore. Guilt pestered her, but she held her ground.

"Not when one's friend prefers to be called something else," said Lucy.

"Friend?" asked the earl with a lift of an eyebrow.

"Yes, *friend*."

He watched her for a moment, his expression a mixture of skepticism and perhaps a little respect. "What about me, Miss Beresford? Am I a friend as well?"

She did not have to think about that answer. "Not yet."

The earl's lips quirked into a bit of a smile. "So there is hope for even a dreadful servant such as I."

"Lest you have forgotten, I am a vicar's daughter," she reminded him. "My father taught me to believe there is hope for everyone."

His gaze captured hers in a look of interest and intrigue, as though her answer had both surprised and pleased him. Lucy found herself quite disarmed. He was far too handsome for her peace of mind.

"Where are these elusive parents of yours?" he asked suddenly. "You speak of them often and yet I have not been introduced to either."

It was Lucy's turn to arch her brow. "You'll have to forgive my lack of manners, Collins. I had no notion that the masters of the house are to be introduced to the servants."

The earl nodded and let out a breath. "Touché," he allowed. "I must apologize for forgetting myself again. It is becoming a bad habit, isn't it?"

Lucy smiled. "Yes, that is your primary flaw of late."

He chuckled, and the deep, melodious sound sucked some of the chill from the room. If a fire had been blazing in the hearth, despite the ash and soot, the yellow room would feel downright cozy.

Georgina returned with a broom, a handful of rags, and a bowl of steaming water. She handed the broom to Lord Drayson. Lucy was quick to reach for one of the rags, but before she could dip it in the water, Georgina's hand clasped hers. "Oh, Miss Lucy, you mustn't! This is nah work for a gentlewoman."

"Georgy, this argument is wearing on me. When are you going to learn that in my mother's absence, I am in charge and not you?"

"Your dress will be ruined," she said, trying a different tactic.

Lucy smiled. "You and I both know how 'gentle' I am not, and I have always hated this shade of lavender. Mama talked me into it ages ago, and you know how she hates any expense to go to waste. The only reason I even wear this silly gown is to wear it out, and if I can speed up that process by scrubbing away some of this grime, I shall gladly do it."

Georgina squeezed Lucy's hand gently, and her voice softened. "Your father loved that dress too, Miss, which is the real reason you wear it," she said quietly. "If you insist on 'elpin', please put on somethin' less meanin'ful."

Georgina was far more perceptive than Lucy gave her credit for. Though she did not love lavender, this dress did remind her of her father. Perhaps she should go change into something else. Lucy glanced at the earl to see if he had overheard the exchange, but he continued sweeping, showing no sign that he had.

With a quick nod, Lucy dropped the rag. "You're right, Georgy. I'll change and be back in a moment."

She scurried out of the room, and as she ascended the stairs, she overheard the earl say, "So Mr. Beresford is . . ."

"No longer with us," Georgina confirmed.

"And Mrs. Beresford?"

"Gone as well," said Georgina, then rushed on to say, "But not gone, gone. That is ter say, she's off to 'elp 'er sister with the birfin' of her babe and will be back Thursday next."

Lucy hesitated on the landing, waiting for his reply. But when it didn't come, she clutched the folds of her gown and quickened her steps, feeling an unaccountable sadness settle over her. She had already mourned her father's death. She had worked through her feelings, allowed them to bleed out of her in a painful way, and had finally been able to set them aside to move on with her life. Why then, did she ache at the sight of the earl in her father's clothes or feel near tears now, simply because a question had been asked about him? Why did this lavender gown suddenly seem more precious than any of her others?

There was something about the earl that made her miss her father's comforting arms about her more than ever, and she was stumped as to why.

COLLINS SWEPT UP A PILE of ashes and dumped it into the metal bin. His muscles ached and his head was beginning to throb again, but that was nothing compared to his urgent desire to wash and rinse away the grime that covered his body. Unfortunately, a servant could not ring for a warm bath whenever he chose.

He arched his back and glanced over his shoulder in time to see Miss Beresford polishing the silver candelabra. Smudges dotted her face, hands, and dress, but her expression was happy and content. They had been working for over an hour, and Miss Beresford had not once complained or made her excuses to find something more amusing to do with her time. Instead, she had scrubbed, wiped, polished, and hummed cheerful tunes.

When she was not humming, Miss Beresford had entertained Georgina and him with stories of her youth, telling them of the time that she and a neighboring farmer's boy had buried a small box filled with treasures somewhere in the woods behind the house. They had drawn a map and presented it to her father, who agreed that it sounded like a great game. He had even taken the time to don his treasure-hunting boots.

Together, the three of them followed the map and tromped into the woods, only to discover that the map was sadly out of proportion and the children had covered their tracks all too well. They had searched for hours to no avail. When Mr. Beresford asked about the contents of the box, and Miss Beresford informed him that his prized pocket watch was one of the treasures, he didn't think it such a great game any longer. Her punishment had been to read and rewrite all of Exodus 20, and she was to help her mother in the garden for the next month of afternoons, rather than fritter away her time burying other peoples things.

"Did you ever find the box?" Georgina asked.

Miss Beresford shook her head. "No. But it was probably for the best."

"Why?" said Georgina.

"Because Ben thought it would be great fun to add a snake he had found in the woods, along with my pet toad. And well, I've since learned that snakes eat toads, so . . ." Miss Beresford shivered, her expression one of revulsion.

Collins chuckled, realizing he had not minded the work as much as he had thought he might. He grudgingly admitted that it likely had something to do with Miss Beresford's presence, for it was easy to see why Georgina respected her employer so much. When not on the defensive, Miss Beresford had a likeable way about her. She had taken charge of the situation in a kind-hearted way and had even rolled up her sleeves as well. There were many who would look down on her for doing the job of a servant, and yet Collins could not find fault. It felt as though he'd just been taught a valuable lesson—one that he could put to good use when . . .

When what? Collins frowned. It was errant thoughts such as these that made him certain that he was used to being the master and not the servant, but . . . who was he, exactly? Did Miss Beresford know? Or was he really the equivalent of a runaway—hiding behind Miss Beresford's skirts like a coward?

The thought didn't settle well with him, for he was *not* a coward.

"I think that ought to do it," said Lucy, examining the room with a critical eye. "Collins you are never to clean flues again."

"Say it isn't so," he said dryly, making Miss Beresford laugh. It was a lovely sound, and he found himself wishing she would do it again.

Instead she gestured to the door. "Georgy, why don't you wash up and get a bite to eat before Mrs. Bidding arrives? I would so hate for our conversation to be disturbed by a rumbling stomach. You too, Collins."

Collins was both surprised and not surprised by her thoughtfulness. Mostly though, he was grateful, for he was feeling quite filthy and famished, and a wash and food sounded wonderful.

"Would you like me ter draw you a bath before I go down, Miss?" Georgina asked.

"A bath sounds heavenly," said Miss Beresford, "but there isn't time for that now. Later, perhaps."

Georgina dipped into a quick curtsy. "I'll be back ter attend ter you quick as a wink."

"But not before you have had some luncheon," said Miss Beresford. "I am quite capable of washing and dressing myself."

"Aye, Miss." Georgina grabbed the rags and the bowl of grimy water before rushing from the room.

Miss Beresford watched her leave before looking back at Collins. "She won't eat, you know. Georgina will wash and change, only because she does not want to soil my bedchamber. But she will not eat until I am ready to receive Mrs. Bidding and she has prepared something to serve us."

"Then she is a good, loyal maid," said Collins, wondering why Miss Beresford appeared sad.

"Oh, Georgina is the most wonderful of maids. But she also works herself to the bone, and sometimes, well . . . I wish she didn't feel the need. Someday, I will make her my companion, pay her a proper wage, and see that she finds some enjoyment in life."

Collins walked toward Miss Beresford, still carrying the broom. "That is not the way of things, Miss Beresford, as you well know. Companions are ladies of genteel birth, not—"

"Not what, Collins?" Miss Beresford eyed him sharply. "Georgy may not sound genteel, but she is every bit as well-mannered as I, probably even more so."

"Forgive me," he said, unable to look away from her dark eyes. In them he saw fierce loyalty and kindness, along with a dislike of the ways of society. She intrigued him. Miss Beresford had a youthful face, and at times, an almost childlike demeanor, but other moments, when her chin lifted just that way and her eyes sparkled with conviction, she blossomed into a fiery woman. With her dark hair curling around her face, Collins found himself drawn to her like a wave drawn to land. He took another step nearer and caught a whiff of spring.

"Forgive me," he said again, quieter this time.

She nodded, though her chest rose and fell rapidly, betraying that she was as affected as he by their closeness. The silence tightened around them, squeezing the air from the room. Collins couldn't resist lifting his thumb to touch a smudge on her cheek, and as he did so, her breath caught.

His eyes continued to hold hers. "I may not remember

who I am or how I came to be here, Miss Beresford, but I am quite certain I am not a butler, a footman, or a coachman by trade. I feel no hesitancy in meeting your gaze, touching your cheek, or challenging your views." His gaze drifted to her rosy lips.

"Collins . . ." Her voice shook slightly and held a hint of warning, and his hand dropped to his side.

"I forget myself yet again," he said.

"Yes."

Collins passed the broom from one hand to the other and nodded at her on his way out. In the foyer, he paused and looked back. "In what way might I be of service when Mrs. Bidding arrives? Other than answer the door and show her into the parlor, that is."

"Oh, I didn't think—" Lucy looked surprised by his question, even discomfited. She hesitated a moment before saying, "I think I shall have Georgina answer the door this once. The stables are rather . . . untidy, and your services would be put to better use there."

"But I am a butler first and a coachman third, am I not?" said Collins. "I can attend to the stables later."

Miss Beresford approached him hesitantly, her hands clasped tightly in front of her. "If it were any other visitor, I might agree. But Mrs. Bidding can be a bit . . ."

"Of a gossip?" he guessed.

Her eyes shifted to the side as though the word was not the one she intended to use, and then she cleared her throat. "I was going to say a bit much to take."

"I am to assume that you do not wish her to know that you have acquired an addition to your staff—especially when that addition cannot recall his own name, let alone his past. She will have questions that neither you nor I can answer."

Lucy let out her breath, appearing relieved. "Precisely. I am glad we understand each other."

He nodded. "Very well. I shall go and clean myself up a bit—but not too much as the stables are sure to wreak additional damage on my attire. Perhaps I should change into the ghastly pink shirt and . . . how did you put it? Speed up the process of ruination by rolling around in the muck."

Miss Beresford's charming smile appeared, along with an adorable dimple on her right cheek. "Why on earth would you wish to ruin your favorite shirt?"

"It is not my favorite shirt, Miss Beresford, which I am inclined to believe you already know. You seem to take great delight in teasing me."

"Perhaps," was all she said, though her eyes sparkled with mirth.

His lips lifted, and he could not help teasing her as well. "Have a care for what you sow, Miss Beresford. Your day of reaping is sure to come."

He had meant to elicit another laugh from her, but some of the sparkle disappeared from her eyes, replaced with a bit of guilt and a scrap of concern. How interesting. If only Collins could enter her mind and have a glimpse of her thoughts. He was sure he would find them most enlightening.

"Good day, Miss Beresford," he said.

"Good day," she responded in turn.

Collins sensed her stare following him down the hall, and as he rounded the corner and disappeared from her view, he immediately felt her absence. He paused a moment to reflect on this and quickly came to the realization that although he was far more fond of horses and stables than chimney flues, he'd likely choose to clean the latter if it meant another afternoon spent in Miss Beresford's company.

10

"LUCY, ARE YOU ATTENDING?" a brusque voice intruded. "I have asked you the same question twice now with no reply."

Pulled from her thoughts, Lucy's eyes snapped to Mrs. Bidding's. Even though they were both seated in the yellow salon, Lucy had to look up to meet the woman's gaze. She was incredibly tall with mousy brown hair and a face that could easily be mistaken for a man's if not for the elegant gowns and hats she wore. Mrs. Bidding had a commanding presence about her—one that had always intimidated Lucy even though she attempted not to show it. "I do apologize, Mrs. Bidding. I find myself a bit distracted today."

The woman's beady eyes squinted at Lucy for a moment before she sighed and tapped a napkin against the corner of her mouth. "What sort of trouble have you landed yourself in now, Lucy? I told your mother that I didn't think it wise to leave you here alone with only your maid to look out for you, but would she listen to me? No. She was quite adamant that you would get on fine for a fortnight."

"And I am." Lucy was quick to defend herself. "I am simply missing Mama, is all."

Mrs. Bidding's expression softened, and she patted Lucy's hand in a motherly way. "Not to worry, my dear. I have taken it upon myself to check in with you often. Why do you not dine with us at Eggington tonight? And every night, for that matter? I am sure Mr. Bidding would not mind at all."

Lucy berated herself for not being able to think of a less sentimental reason behind her distraction. She had no notion Mrs. Bidding would be so concerned with her welfare. "You do me a great honor with such an invitation, Mrs. Bidding, but you know how I feel about horses, and Eggington is a long walk on foot."

"I would never ask you to walk," Mrs. Bidding rushed to say. "Of course I will send our carriage to collect you and bring you home safe and sound."

Oh dear, Lucy thought frantically, *this won't do at all.* Supping every night with the Biddings would be torturous indeed. Mr. Bidding was altogether too fond of telling the same story again and again. "You are a great deal too kind, Mrs. Bidding, but I could never impose on you in such a way. I am fine. Really, I am. I have Georgina to keep me company, and I am expecting a letter from Mama any day now. I'm sure as soon as I read her words, I will be greatly comforted."

Mrs. Bidding did not look at all convinced, but she did not press the issue. She merely set down her teacup, rose to her full, towering height, and pulled on her gloves, signaling an end to their conversation. Lucy rose as well, though it did little to make up the difference in their heights. She practically strained her neck to look up at the woman.

"Thank you so much for coming, Mrs. Bidding. You are so kind to think of me in Mama's absence."

Mrs. Bidding's mouth dipped into a frown as she looked past Lucy to a painting of a Grecian vase hanging on the wall adjacent to the fireplace. She walked over to it and ran a finger across the frame, pulling it back to reveal a dark spot on her pristine glove.

"Good gracious, does Georgina not know how to properly dust a room? This painting is filthy!"

Lucy grimaced. The painting was her least favorite in the entire house, and she avoided looking at it whenever possible, so of course she had missed seeing the dusting of ash around the frame. Lucy attempted to conjure up a reasonable falsehood to explain away the dirt, only to berate herself for her desire to lie yet again.

How quickly I have fallen, she thought sadly. Thus humbled, Lucy squared her shoulders and answered the question. "We had a bit of a mishap with the chimney flue earlier, Mrs. Bidding. We thought we had scrubbed the room all clean, but apparently we overlooked one painting."

"We?" Mrs. Bidding gaped at Lucy, her expression one of shock and disapproval.

Lucy realized her mistake and quickly amended her explanation. "How could I be sure the room would be up to Mama's standards if I had not stayed to supervise the cleaning of it?" There, that wasn't a lie, was it?

Mrs. Bidding seemed to accept the explanation, for she nodded and glanced at the painting once again. "It seems, my dear, that your supervisory skills could use some work."

"I could not agree more, Mrs. Bidding," said Lucy. "Thank goodness you are here to point out my lack of observation. I will ask Georgy to clean that painting immediately."

Appearing mollified, Mrs. Bidding nodded. "Do have a care, Lucy. You are no longer a child. It would do you well to learn to behave like a competent young woman. Your poor mother will never find you a suitable match otherwise."

"Yes, Mrs. Bidding." Lucy was all too aware of her unsuitability and didn't appreciate the reminder.

"Cheer up, now," said Mrs. Bidding, patting Lucy on the head the way a mother would a child even though she had just proclaimed Lucy otherwise. "I have a wonderful plan to see you married as soon as possible. It may even involve a ball," she whispered conspiratorially, her eyes bright with excitement. "When your mother returns, I shall bring her into my confidence. You may take comfort in the knowledge that I have things well in hand."

With that, she bustled out the door, leaving Lucy in the most uncomfortable state she'd been in since her mother's departure. She pictured herself being wedded to a tall, tall man who looked at the world through a quizzing glass.

No. Mrs. Bidding might mean well, but Lucy would never agree to marry a man chosen by her.

And a ball? Lucy frowned. She had attended a few country dances in the past and had not liked the experience at all. They had made her feel like a fraud. Dressed in a beautiful gown with her hair styled in a lovely coiffure, Lucy appeared like a demure and prettily behaved young woman. She knew how to act the part well, but any attachment formed at such an event would be doomed from the start, for Lucy was far from demure and only sometimes prettily behaved.

It wasn't that Lucy was opposed to falling in love. She often fancied herself meeting a suitor in the woods surrounding her beloved Tanglewood. He would stumble upon her as she climbed to the top of her favorite elm, and instead of being shocked by her hoydenish ways, he would find her charming and fall immediately under her spell, accepting and loving her wholeheartedly as the wild and untamed creature she was.

Deep down, Lucy knew it was a silly fantasy. No eligible

man would ever desire a woman like her for a wife. In her heart, Lucy knew that she was destined for spinsterhood.

But what a glorious and freeing spinsterhood she was determined to have.

"These horses are in sad shape, Miss Beresford," was the first thing out of the earl's mouth when Lucy stopped by the stables to look in on him. He was brushing down Athena's tan coat with long, gentle strokes. "Do they never get exercised?"

Lucy was in no mood to be rebuked yet again. "Not often, Collins. My mother will hitch one to the cart whenever she goes to town, but I prefer to walk."

"Walk?"

"Yes, walk," she snapped. "It is when a person places one foot in front of the other to move oneself along. Even the most dignified of people do it now and again."

Lucy noticed that despite his threats, Lord Drayson was wearing another white shirt, which was surprisingly clean, considering he'd been out here for hours already. He brushed the animal a few more times before giving it a final pat.

"We really ought to take them on a ride this afternoon."

Athena seemed to stare at Lucy with an amused gleam in her eyes as though saying, "I dare you to mount me."

Lucy took an inadvertent step back and cleared her throat. "I am . . . otherwise engaged this afternoon. Perhaps you could exercise Athena first and come back for Zeus later."

"Zeus and Athena?" The earl laughed. "Who gave these poor creatures such impressive names? I'll allow that they're good, sturdy hacks, but that's the extent of it. Better suited names would be Daisy and Bouncer, or, seeing as how you are a vicar's daughter and their manes are in need of a good trimming, Samson and Delilah, perhaps?"

Lucy had to bite her tongue to keep from pointing out the earl's hypocrisy by allowing his own Arabian to be called Darling. "Do you think, Collins, that a person, or a horse, can become what he or she is called?"

"If you are implying these horses have the potential to become a Greek god and goddess, Miss Beresford, then no, I do not," he replied.

Lucy nodded toward the animals. "These 'hacks' as you call them were at one point ornery beasts because their previous owner beat them for their stubbornness. My father purchased them from the horrid owner and brought them home to retrain. He explained that a horse behaved only as a horse was treated, and so he named the female Athena, so that she would become a wise warrior, carrying us wherever we needed to go in safety, and Zeus, so that we could command the weather as well." She smiled softly at the memory. Command the weather indeed.

Lord Drayson rested an arm on Athena's back. "And did you always have cheerful weather when Zeus was at the head?"

"Cheerful weather is in the eye of the beholder, Collins. Rain can be considered cheerful if one wishes for it to rain, after all."

The earl watched her for a moment before setting down the brush. He took Athena by the lead rope and stepped nearer to Lucy, bringing the horse with him. With the animal so close, Lucy felt the anxiety she always felt around large animals, and she retreated farther. She tried to convince herself that her discomfort was because of Athena's close proximity and not the earl's.

"What does the name Lucy mean, I wonder?" the earl asked quietly, his gaze fixed on her.

"Light," Lucy answered. Despite the chill in the air, warmth settled around her, and she felt her cheeks redden. *What sort of person are you?* she wanted to ask. Lucy had thought she knew him, or at least enough about him to ascertain his true character, but now she was beginning to wonder if there was more to his character. He had a heartless side to him, one that placed business before people, and yet she was beginning to see another side as well. A softer side. A kind side. But how much of him was kind and how much heartless?

Perhaps this kindness was a recent development, blossoming from his newly humbled state the way a rose blossomed from thorns and twigs. Or perhaps not. Deep down, a feeling troubled Lucy's conscience, reminding her of something Mr. Shepherd had once said, that it was not fair to pass judgment on a book from the title or even the first chapter or two. One must get to know the book in its entirety before one could declare it a good book or not.

The same was true with people, no doubt. Lucy had only read the first chapter of Lord Drayson, and it had left her with a bitter taste in her mouth and a strong desire to slam it shut and never open it again. But now that she had been forced to read on, so to speak, she found the taste not quite so bitter and rather thought that further reading would not be so punishable as she had first thought.

A strong breeze swept through the stables, chilling Lucy and pulling some strands of hair free from her bun. She quickly swept them back. "I should go," she said.

"Before you do," said the earl. "May I ask you one more question?"

"Of course."

"How do you expect Athena and Zeus to rise to their godlike potential if you keep them confined in a stall?"

It was a fair question and probably one that Lucy should have asked herself before now. She suddenly felt shamed by her neglectful treatment of the horses, though they had never lacked for food or warmth. In exchange for two dozen of Georgina's fresh scones, a local farmer's son would clean out the stalls every morning and see that fresh hay and water were fed to the animals. But that was the extent of it. The only exercise the animals received was a jaunt into town now and then, pulling the cart for her mother.

Lucy glanced down at her hands, not knowing how to explain or even correct such negligence.

The truth is always best, her father's voice came to mind. But when the truth was bookended in lies, was it still best? Or did it not matter at that point?

"I . . ." Her voice sounded small and pathetic, so she cleared her throat and tried again. "I am afraid of horses, Collins."

He did not respond right away, but a slight smile touched his lips as he carefully wrapped the lead rope around his hand, keeping Athena securely at his side—another perplexing kindness. "You, who has dug up worms, gutted your own fish, and once captured a toad to keep as a pet, are afraid of horses? Please explain. I am extremely intrigued."

Is the answer not obvious? she thought. All one had to do was compare the differences between a toad and a horse to understand. "A horse is vastly larger than a toad," she said finally, hoping he would leave it at that.

Lord Drayson's lips twitched ever so slightly. "Yes, but a toad is also slimy and unpredictable. There is no trust or loyalty to be earned from a friendship with an amphibian. A horse, on the other hand, can offer wisdom and protection and even"—he smiled—"cheerful weather."

"I am not so certain about that," said Lucy, refusing to let him tease her so. "I trusted my toad and he trusted me."

"He shouldn't have," said the earl. "Was it not you who buried the poor creature alive with a toad-eating reptile?"

Apparently some stories should be left untold, thought Lucy crossly. "I can see your memory is quite sharp since your accident."

His eyes twinkled at her through the dimness in the stables. "Are you wishing another accident to befall me, Miss Beresford, so as to swipe my more recent memories?"

"No, Collins. But I do see that these animals require more care than I have been giving them. Perhaps I could . . ." Her voice trailed off. Would little Tommy be willing to exercise the horses if she increased her payment by a loaf of bread as well? Could Tommy even ride? He would look so small sitting atop Zeus. And what if he took a fall? She could never live with herself if something happened to a mere child because she, an adult, lacked the courage to ride.

"Have you never ridden?" said Lord Drayson.

Lucy really ought to chastise him for his impertinence and enforce at least a modicum of propriety, but she found that she wanted him to understand her reasons.

"My father attempted to teach me to ride when I was young, but I never could quite get the hang of it. I took a spill and broke my arm. My mother lost a close friend to a riding accident and refused to let me back on an animal, much to my relief. I had never been more afraid in my life than sitting atop that horse."

"What about driving?"

Lucy sighed. "I prefer to let my mother handle the ribbons."

He fiddled with the lead rope again, unwinding it from his fingers. "What if the day comes that your mother can no longer do the driving?"

75

Lucy had thought about that before and immediately dismissed it because she had preferred not to think on it further. "As I told you before, I am very good at walking."

"Lucy . . ." he said.

Her eyes snapped to his in a stern look of reproof. Earl or servant, she had not given him leave to call her by her Christian name, nor did she appreciate being made to feel like a silly coward. It was too much.

"Forgive me, Miss Beresford," he said, having the good sense to appear remorseful.

Too bad for him that Lucy was not in a forgiving mood. "How many times do you plan on asking my forgiveness, Collins? I should think more than once a day is too much." Lucy picked up her skirts and whisked away, leaving him to exercise the horses alone.

COLLINS TOSSED A DUSTY SADDLE onto Athena's back and tightened the strap with quick movements. This came easily to him—brushing a horse, saddling a horse, riding a horse. He realized he knew a great deal about horses and breeding and what constituted good blood. These hacks, for example, were good for pulling a wagon or cart, but not necessarily the best riding horses. Collins frowned. Perhaps he had been an insolent coachman in his former life. It made sense like nothing else had since his accident, and yet it didn't at the same time. His cultured speech, his natural air of command, the fact that he knew more about Arabians and thorough-breds than trotters or hackneys—he couldn't have been in service.

More and more the question of his true identity bothered him, especially when it came to Miss Beresford. He had acted the perfect cad earlier, attempting to use whatever powers of persuasion he possessed to lure her on the back of an animal that she had made clear frightened her. And then he had called her Lucy.

Collins hadn't meant to speak her Christian name. He had not said it to tease or even try her. The name had slid out of its own accord, the way an old friend's name would roll off one's tongue. Yet Miss Beresford was not an old friend. Those expressive eyes of hers had reflected hurt at his slip of the tongue, and Collins despised himself for being the cause of it.

He quickly hoisted himself onto Athena's back and clicked his tongue, urging the horse forward. It responded slowly, the way an old rusty carriage might respond after sitting unused for years and years.

"Come now, girl. Surely you can do better than this." Collins teased her belly with the heels of his boots, encouraging the horse to pick up the pace. It responded slightly, bouncing Collins along at barely a trot. Good grief. How long had it been since this horse had done more than trot? After further coercion, the animal finally broke into a canter, but it wasn't long before Athena's breathing became labored and her coat glistened with perspiration.

The damp chill in the air went straight through Collins's thin shirt, but he did not care. He felt free in a way he had not since he'd awakened without a memory. He luxuriated in the feel of it. Even on rusty Athena, the wind whipped at his hair and recharged his soul. How could Miss Beresford live without this euphoria? Did she have any idea the freedom that awaited her if she could overcome her fears?

Collins leaned forward over the horse as they crossed the meadow, and at the top of a small rise on the other side, he finally slowed the animal to a stop, allowing it to catch its breath. Looking around from this vantage point afforded him a glimpse of the manor house. Tangle-something-or-other, Miss Beresford had called it. There was a halo of familiarity surrounding the stone walls and the overgrowth, but no matter how much he tried to place where he had seen the structure before, the memory eluded him.

What if the doctor was wrong and Collins's memory did not return? Would he remain here indefinitely, struggling to understand his place, or would Lucy—er, Miss Beresford, finally lose all patience with him and send him packing?

The more Collins thought on it, the more questions surfaced, to the point that he began to think that he ought to pay the good doctor a visit himself. Perhaps if he found a reason to venture into town, someone might recognize him or at least shed some new light on his current predicament. At the very least, he could meet with the doctor and, with any luck, discover a few of the answers to his many questions.

For the next two days, Collins attempted various strategies to find a way to town.

"Do you need supplies? I am happy to drive the cart to town and collect them for you," he said one morning.

"That is good of you to offer, Collins," answered Miss Beresford, "but my mother made sure we had sufficient for our needs before she left so that we would not have to make such a trip while she was away."

"What about fresh milk and cheese?" he had asked.

"Georgina collects them from a nearby farm when we have a need."

"Do you have any social calls you would care to make? Now that you have a coachman, I would be happy to take you any direction you choose."

"Thank you, Collins, but I shall wait for Mother's return to call on our friends. She enjoys a good visit as much as I and would be saddened if I went without her."

When no other excuses came to mind, Collins finally asked which afternoon he would be free from his duties and reconciled himself to walking to town on that day. If Miss Beresford could make the trip on foot, so could he.

"Sunday," Miss Beresford had replied. "You will have the entire afternoon to yourself on Sunday."

But Sunday was still three days away.

ON FRIDAY MORNING, THE CLOUDS parted, revealing the full magnificence of the sun. Lucy found the sight of it breathtaking. She tipped her face to its warmth and leaned close to her window, allowing the feeling to radiate through her body. *Blessed sun,* she thought as she washed and dressed in her one of her older day dresses. She quickly pinned up her hair and burst from her bedroom, nearly knocking down poor Georgina holding a breakfast tray.

"Thank you, Georgy," said Lucy, stealing a piece of toast and eating it as she trotted down the stairs. "Isn't it a beautiful day?"

"It is, Miss," agreed Georgina, following quickly behind. "Yer up and about earlier than usual."

"How could I sleep with such wonderful light gleaming through the windows?" Lucy answered as she entered the kitchen. "Good morning, Collins."

"It is," he agreed, munching on a light fare of scones and a poached egg. "A very good morning. What would you like me to do with such a day?" he asked.

Lucy leaned toward the kitchen window, smiling. The outdoors beckoned to her in the most alluring and delightful way. She spun around and faced Collins and Georgina.

"I think we should spend some time in the gardens."

Georgina bustled around the kitchen, and Collins arched an eyebrow. "We?" he asked.

"Yes, we," said Lucy, turning to face the window once again. "We can trim and prune and rid the beds of those vile weeds and perhaps even take a jaunt through the woods to collect some firewood."

Collins cleared his throat and flicked a look of confusion at Georgina before returning his attention to Lucy. "Georgina's schedule is quite full already. Surely you don't mean—"

"Of course not," said Lucy, slightly piqued by his question. She didn't appreciate his assumption that she would further burden Georgy, nor did she like that he always used Georgina's full Christian name and yet continued to slip up with her own. More and more often, Collins was heard to say, "Lu—I mean, Miss Beresford." For whatever reason, it poked at Lucy's nerves the way one might poke at a fire to stoke it. He had no problem showing Georgina respect, whereas with Lucy, it felt forced, as though he was merely trying to keep up the pretense of respect and didn't actually feel it.

"When I said 'we' I was referring to you and me, Collins," said Lucy. "Georgy has far too many other duties to attend to this day, and her mother is ill so she has requested the evening off to see to the needs of her family."

Georgy gave Lucy a grateful smile. "Thank you ever so much, Miss. Ma will be so grateful ter you as well."

"It is no problem at all, Georgy. The health of your mother and family should always come first."

"Where is your family home, Georgina?" asked the earl.

"The ovver side of town," answered Georgy.

"If Miss Beresford will allow it, I should be glad to take you in the cart when you are ready," he offered.

"Thank you, Collins, but Mr. Crandall is goin' that way and 'as already offered me a ride."

"I see."

Did the earl look a little downcast at that news? Lucy's smile wilted a little. Could it be that the earl was developing a fondness for her maid? Surely not. That would never do. He was an earl and she a maid and . . . no, that wasn't it. The truth of the matter had nothing to do with proprieties and everything to do with an emotion Lucy did not enjoy experiencing in the least—envy. It was beyond silly for her to feel such a thing. She wasn't even sure she liked the man, and even if she did, what chance did she have of gaining his affections? Some day he would discover the truth of her deception and would likely never want to speak to the likes of Lucy Beresford again. She needed to remember that and push aside the nagging sense of loss that accompanied it.

"Do not you worry," said Georgina to Lord Drayson. "You will not be laborin' alone. Miss Beresford likes noffin' more than ter roll up 'er sleeves and dig in the dirt. There is nah stoppin' her from tendin' ter 'er roses. Believe you me, I've tried." The indulgent smile on Georgina's face unwilted Lucy's smile.

"'Tis true," Lucy agreed. "I do love my roses."

"As does the rest of the town," Georgina added. "They'll sell like mad come summer."

Lucy wished Georgina had not been quite so open with the fate of the roses, especially when she saw Lord Drayson's brow wrinkle in confusion. "Sell?" he questioned.

Georgina was quick to amend her slip of the tongue. "Wot I meant ter say was . . ." Her voice trailed off, probably because no other explanation came to mind. Obviously, she wasn't nearly as good at story-telling as Lucy, who sighed and came to her rescue.

"What she meant to say was that I sell flowers in the summer. Or rather, Georgy sells my flowers for me." She lifted her chin, challenging the earl to find fault with her for being involved in the business of trade.

He surprised her. "Is it a very profitable business?"

"Not *very* profitable," answered Lucy hesitantly, because it was far from that. "Just . . . profitable." Enough to hopefully enable her to splurge on a new gown for her mother and a new pair of shoes for Georgina and herself. It had been too long since they had splurged on anything.

Lord Drayson nodded slowly, apparently mulling it over. Whatever conclusion he drew was unbeknownst to Lucy for he said nothing more. He merely gulped down the last of his ale and stood. "Where might I find pruning shears and a shovel?"

"Our gardening equipment is housed in a little shed off the back of the house," said Lucy. "If you'll follow me, I'll take you there now."

"What of your breakfast?" asked the earl.

"I had a bite of toast earlier," said Lucy, tying on her straw bonnet. "It's too glorious a day to remain inside a moment longer."

The earl's lips lifted into a slight smile as he held the door for her. She breezed past with a "Thank you, Collins," and he followed her to the shed.

In no time at all, Lucy had them both outfitted with work gloves and began handing tools to Lord Drayson. They would need a scythe, a dibble, a—

"What is this?" Collins asked when she handed him a long-handled tool that ended in an angled pick.

"A daisy grubber," she said. "It is used to rid the lawn of unwanted wildflowers."

"I would think you, of all people, would want to keep every flower, regardless of where it grows."

"Not when they have the tendency to overtake the lawn. As much as I love wildflowers in the wilderness area, when it comes to the more formal gardens, flowers should grow only where flowers ought to grow."

"I see," said Lord Drayson with another hint of a smile. "Obviously, I was not a gardener in my former life. Is there anything else you would like me to carry? As you can see, my head is still free and possibly my boots. I am sure I can balance something on top of them. A bucket, perhaps?"

Lucy stopped her pillaging of the shed to look at Collins. As he'd implied, his arms held a precarious looking heap of tools. It was a wonder he hadn't dropped any as of yet.

"Oh dear," she said, wondering which she could take from him without sending the rest toppling to the ground. "I've quite loaded you up, haven't I?"

"I'm glad we are in agreement on that. Will you be so kind as to tell me where I might put down my burden?"

She went to reach for the grubber, thought better of it, and pointed to the closest rose garden instead. "If you can manage to drop them near those roses, I shall be most impressed."

The earl had to crane his neck to see around the pile of wood and metal in his arms, but he managed to make it to the spot Lucy had shown him without incident and immediately relinquished his hold, allowing the tools to crash to the ground in a disorganized heap.

Lucy snickered. "When I said 'drop' I didn't exactly mean 'drop,'" she said, hoping nothing had broken in the fall.

"Perhaps you should clarify that next time," said Lord Drayson, brushing his gloved hands together to rid them of some dust. "What now?"

Lucy grabbed the shears and walked over to where the

earl stood. She bent down next to the heap and picked up the scythe, shaking it loose from the rest of the mass. "Why don't you begin taming the grass while I tend to my roses?"

He took the scythe and studied it a moment. "I am definitely not a gardener for I haven't the faintest notion what to do with this contraption. Am I to sweep it across the ground like so?" he said, his movements a little awkward and not quite right.

Lucy held out her hand for the tool, demonstrating how to grip it and move it across the ground in a smooth side to side motion. "You sweep it both directions," she explained. "One way cuts the grass, and the other way lifts it back up to make the cutting easier for the next swipe."

"Do not say you have operated this before," said the earl, not bothering to hide his surprise and perhaps displeasure. "Surely the manor house employs grounds-keepers, who should also take care of your grounds."

Lucy studied the earl, wondering about the extent of his knowledge of Tanglewood before the accident. Had he known how minimal a staff had been retained for the manor? Could he not see that the grounds around the dower house were in a much better state than the grounds surrounding the manor house?

"The owner employs one groundskeeper," she said carefully. "His name is Jeb and he is a dear man, but one man cannot maintain the entire estate on his own. He does what he can for the manor house and helps us now and again, but mostly we do the work ourselves. So in answer to your question, yes, I have operated a scythe before."

"Why the devil does the owner maintain only one gardener?"

Lucy made a valiant effort to keep her laughter at bay. If only he knew he had just condemned himself. "I haven't the faintest notion, Collins. Perhaps his attics are to let." She couldn't resist smiling at her joke.

"Then he ought to sell his estate to someone who will do a proper job at managing it."

Lucy's smile immediately diminished for she did not like that answer in the slightest. "If he should sell," said Lucy, choosing her words carefully, "my mother and I would be out of a home. Surely you would not wish that on us."

He continued to stare across the expansive meadow to where the manor house sat. "No, I would not. But I can only assume the inside staff is as paltry, which means something must be done soon or the only valuable part of the estate will be the dower house."

This conversation was doing nothing for Lucy's desire to maintain a happy disposition. She preferred to not think about the other end of the equation in her plan to gain the earl's sympathies. What would happen to Tanglewood if things continued as they were? Would it truly become of little worth? Would it become a drain on the family's finances? Before the earl had arrived, it had never occurred to Lucy to think about the property from a business perspective, but now that he had brought it up as Collins, the impartial servant, she could help but think about it. This entire charade hinged on the hope that she could somehow convince him not to sell for the sake of her and her mother. But what if there was far more at stake than she realized? The discouraging thought weighed on her the way a large peony weighed down its stem.

Lucy glanced at the earl only to find that he was now watching her with a curious expression. She cleared her throat and pointed at the lawn. "You may start trimming the grass there, next to the wilderness. If left to its own devices too much longer, that area will soon become part of the wilderness."

The earl lifted the scythe and rested it against his shoulder. "Very well. But only if you revise my job description to butler, footman, coachman, *and* grounds-keeper."

"*Temporary* groundskeeper," she bargained.

"I do like the sound of that better," he answered with a smile before making his way to the area of the lawn she'd indicated. Lucy watched him go, unable to keep from staring at the wide line of his shoulders, his tapered waist, and strong legs. It took him a few attempts to figure out the best motion of the scythe, but once he did, his strokes became quick and efficient, with the muscles in his arms rippling against the fabric of his shirt. Lucy couldn't help but wonder how he came by his strength. Did he enjoy a bout of fisticuffs with his friends? Did he like to hunt? Or was he, like her, not afraid of hard labor?

At times, Lucy wished the earl's memory would return so that she could ask him such questions and learn more about the various sides of him. The trouble was, once his memory did return, rather than answer her questions, he would likely wish her to the devil.

COLLINS STOPPED SCYTHING FOR A moment to give his weary arms and shoulders a rest. As he did, he glanced at Lucy, who was still hard at work, trimming and yanking weeds from the ground near her still-dormant rose bushes. In their current state, they appeared tangled, untamed, and gnarly, and yet she treated them with a light touch, trimming a stem back here, overturning the dirt there, and humming all the while. She always hummed, and he was becoming quite fond of the sound.

A rosy hue ripened her cheeks, and even in an old muslin dress, with her hair pulling free from the pins beneath her drab bonnet, she looked lovely. Her movements were graceful, her smile delightful, and the lines of her body beautiful. As she bent and stretched, crouched and snipped, Collins noticed every curve. He found himself unaccountably drawn to her. Lucy had a way of making him feel renewed and invigorated, as though he had just returned from a fast-paced ride through the country on an animal built for speed.

Collins frowned at his thoughts, wondering where the comparison had come from. Though he could not remember ever taking such a ride—Athena was most certainly not built for speed—he knew he had, just as he knew riding was his favorite sport and that he enjoyed a good hunt every once in a while. Yet he couldn't place a setting, a horse, or even a face. His memories felt lodged in the back of his mind, unable to break loose.

With each passing day, Collins's discontent increased. He wanted to know who he really was, where he had come from, and what had brought him to Askern in the first place. What had brought him here—to Lucy, service, and scything?

Drawing in a frustrated breath, he clenched his fingers around the handle of the scythe and began whacking away at the unruly blades of grass, slashing them with each and every sweep of the blade. Perhaps if he worked his muscles to the bone it would somehow loosen all those memories.

"I must say that you are quicker than the gardener," Lucy said from behind, pulling him from his thoughts. He glanced over his shoulder to find her standing not far away, staring at his upper body. "I can't help but wonder what has made you so . . ." The rest of her words withered, and her cheeks turned a bright shade of pink.

Collins lowered the scythe and finished her sentence. "Strong?" he asked with a grin. "Masculine? Devilishly handsome?"

The escaped strands of her dark hair blew into her face. His fingers itched to sweep them away and feel the softness of her cheek, but she brushed them aside herself and tilted her face into the breeze to keep them away.

Without looking at him, she said, "There is much I wonder about you."

Collins let the blade of the scythe drop to the ground and rested his palms on the top of the handle. "I believe I must have been a boxer at some point. It would explain my crooked nose, along with a few scars I've discovered on other regions of my body."

She frowned at that, peeking back at him. "Are they dreadful scars?"

"Only small ones. A nick here, a scuff there. Apparently I must have been a very good boxer."

"A humble one too, I gather."

"Undoubtedly."

Her lips twitched, and she quickly turned her back on him to look over the house and the surrounding property. After a moment, she pointed to a circular area near the far corner of the house that was currently infested with weeds. "See that small spot of garden over yonder?"

"You mean the bed of weeds?"

"Precisely. I have tried a number of times to grow roses there, but they will not take, and I have no idea as to why. Can you venture a guess?"

"Afraid not," he said. "If there is one thing I am certain of, it's that I am no gardener. I take it you wish to make your business more profitable by growing additional flowers, is that it?" She already had so many beds filled with rose bushes. Did she really want another?

"Yes and no," she answered. "There is no real need for more roses, and yet I hate to leave such a happy spot as that barren. Not even Jeb, the gardener, can understand why roses refuse to grow there."

Collins leaned the scythe against a nearby tree and sauntered over to the spot to get a better look. Lucy stepped beside him, her hands clasped behind her back, apparently waiting for whatever conclusion he was supposed to have drawn.

"Weeds seem to thrive here," he said, stating the obvious. "Perhaps you should let them be. You could use them as the filler for your bouquets."

"You're teasing me, I hope," said Lucy. "But you are

correct in that those dreadful plants have no problem growing here. So why not my roses?"

"Perhaps you should hum while planting them," Collins suggested, liking the way her lips twitched when she tried her best not to smile. But she could not keep her eyes from smiling. They twinkled and glowed with mirth.

"As a matter of fact I did hum to them," said Lucy. "I didn't exactly mean to, but I always find myself humming while working so that is obviously not the answer."

"Have you tried singing instead?" said Collins, wishing she would.

"Heavens no," said Lucy with a laugh. "That would do far more harm than good, I'm afraid, for I most definitely am not a singer."

"I don't believe you."

"Three years ago, I accompanied my parents to an assembly. I had always thought myself a decent sort of singer, so when asked to perform, I readily agreed and sang my heart out. The applause that followed was tepid at best, and only my parents met my gaze with smiles. Everyone else looked vastly uncomfortable. One woman even patted me on the arm afterward, and said, 'I'm sure you have many other talents, my dear.' I was never asked to sing again, so I took up humming instead. But only in my gardens and in my own home."

She looked down at the bed of weeds and pursed her lips in thought. "Perhaps that is why the roses never took. The sorry sound of my humming likely shriveled their tender roots."

Collins chuckled. "If that is the case, I think you should sing your heart out to these weeds. It would be far easier to kill them off that way rather than plucking each from the ground. What do you think?"

"I think that is another story I should not have told you," she said, making him laugh again. "Really, Collins, if you refuse to be of actual help, you should return to your scything."

He squelched his laugh immediately and strove to maintain a straight face. "If those are my only options, then I will do my best to be of actual help." He studied the weeds again and nudged a few with the toe of his boot. "Have you considered planting something other than roses here?"

Her expression became quizzical. "Such as?"

Collins shrugged. "Another kind of flower, perhaps? Or, better yet, a . . ." He glanced around. "Do you have a vegetable garden?"

She shook her head. "Georgy grows some berries on the other side of the house, but that is the only food grown here. I know nothing of growing vegetables."

"Why not try that?" Collins suggested. "You could plant some cabbage, potatoes, and turnips, or whatever else Georgina prefers to cook with. And, should you produce more than you need, you could always sell the extras in town with your flowers."

"Or use them for trade," said Lucy. Her gloved finger tapped against her chin as she stared at the plot of ground. "Do you think vegetable plants would grow here when roses will not?"

"Only one way to find out," he said, examining the small plot. "It is not a large area, so I propose we cut away some of the grass and create a larger rectangle. We will need a plow, of course."

"A plow?" Lucy repeated, biting on her lower lip. "We do not have a plow."

"One of neighboring farms might," he suggested.

"But . . . I have never used a plow before," said Lucy.

"And I daresay neither have you, considering you had no idea how to use a scythe."

"I am certain we can figure it out," said Collins. "What do you say?"

"What if we were to cut away the lawn, plow the dirt, invest in seeds, and still nothing grows?"

"I guarantee the weeds, at least, will make a home of it," teased Collins. "Come now, Lu—I mean Miss Beresford. I would have thought you, of all people, would be more optimistic."

"I do believe in optimism, but . . ." She sighed, then faced him with an expression he couldn't quite decipher. Worry, perhaps? Anxiety? "What if Mother and I should need to leave Tanglewood before our crop arrives?"

Collins blinked, wondering where such a worry stemmed from. "Why should you need to leave?"

Lucy cleared her throat and looked away. "If you must know, the ownership of Tanglewood has recently changed hands, and . . . well, there are no guarantees in life, are there?"

"No," agreed Collins, feeling a bit sad at the thought of Lucy moving away. Hopefully the new owner would take better care of the estate. But would he also care about roses as Lucy did? Would the dower house be filled with warmth and laughter as it was now? Or would it lay dormant and forgotten, like the manor had become?

Collins quickly shook off the depressing feeling, reminding himself it was of no concern to him what happened to the house or its current occupants.

"Suppose you do leave," said Collins. "All you would be out is some wasted effort and a few packages of seeds, correct?"

Lucy nodded slowly, her brow wrinkled in thought.

After a moment, a spark of determination appeared in her eyes, and she lifted her chin. "You're right, Collins. I have very little to lose. A vegetable garden it shall be."

"That's my girl," said Collins without thinking. He quickly cleared his throat and amended, "What I meant to say was—"

"That we should not waste any more time," Lucy finished for him. "Let us hitch the cart to the horse, purchase some seeds in town, and stop at the Coopers' on our way home. I am certain Mr. Cooper will lend us his plow for the day." Lucy paused, rethinking the plan. "And by 'us' hitching the cart to the horse, I mean you."

"Considering I am the coachman, I gathered as much," he said, thrilled at the prospect of finally having a reason to drive into town. "But I feel the need to point out that if you would like to bring the plow home with us, we will need something larger than a cart."

She frowned and pursed her lips in thought. After a moment, she brightened and nodded in the direction of the manor house. "Perhaps we might find a wagon in one of those outbuildings."

"Will they not be locked? Or has the new owner taken up residency already?"

"I don't believe he ever will," said Lucy as she tugged a pin from her hair. "But that is of little consequence."

Collins watched her in confusion. "I am almost afraid to inquire as to what is going through that pretty head of yours."

She blushed slightly but grinned, holding up the hairpin for his inspection. "Do you recall my youthful friend, Ben? The one who convinced me to bury my toad with a snake?"

"Yes," he said the word slowly.

"He also instructed me on how to pick locks with a hairpin."

Collins blinked, staring at her. Good gads, the woman was serious. She could pick a lock, or at least believed she could, and she was contemplating breaking into the outbuilding.

"That is a highly unusual skill set for a vicar's daughter," Collins said.

Merriment filled her expression, and she linked her arm through his and began pulling him toward the manor house. "Not to worry, Collins. We are only borrowing the wagon, not stealing it."

"Why do I find no comfort in that?"

She gave his arm a pat. "Take comfort in this then. If you are anxious about borrowing a wagon from an absentee owner, it is highly unlikely you were a thief in your former life."

"Just in my new life, it seems," he muttered, pulling her to a stop. "Before you drag me across the overgrown meadow, might I ask a question?"

"Certainly."

"How do you propose we remove the wagon from the building without the aid of a horse or two?"

She bit down on her lower lip and glanced back toward the stables. "Drat, you are right. We will need Zeus and Athena, won't we?"

"Unless you are planning to add 'horse' to my list of responsibilities and hitch *me* to the wagon, then yes."

Her lips twitched before settling back in a straight line, and she nodded. "Perhaps you can fetch the horses while I pick the lock?"

Was she that frightened of horses that she would not even lead one across a meadow? How a woman as adventurous as she did not wish to learn to ride completely baffled him. Somehow, someway, Collins vowed, he would find a way to get Miss Lucy Beresford on the back of a horse and show her exactly how glorious it felt to ride with the wind.

Collins released her arm and gestured toward the outbuilding. "Very well, Miss Beresford, go ahead and pick your lock. But should we get caught, I ought to warn you that I can play deaf, dumb, and incredibly thick. The constable will have no one to point the finger at but you."

"Ah," she said. "So you are an actor then. Tell me, does the name Drury Lane sound familiar? What about Haymarket or Covent Garden? Do you sing, perchance? Opera? I think you should try a few notes so that we might see."

The girl was incorrigible and, though he hated to admit it, irresistible. He could not help but play along. "I am not an actor nor an opera singer, though apparently I can play the part of a hero rather well."

"To which heroic acts are you referring?" she asked as her hair whipped about her face.

"Rescuing a damsel in distress, of course."

"What damsel?"

"You, of course."

Her eyes narrowed. "I am no damsel in distress."

"Are you quite certain?" he said, challenging her with his eyes. "Because I believe you only just asked me to save you from having to lead a horse across a meadow to that outbuilding."

LUCY'S FINGERS CLUTCHED THE LEAD rope, as though a tight grip would somehow keep the horse from nearing her. She soon learned that she had nothing to fear. Athena did not intend to chase Lucy down and trample her underfoot because Athena, as it turned out, did not intend to do anything. The horse merely sniffed the ground and occasionally flipped her tail.

Lucy tentatively pulled on the rope. When the horse did not budge, she pulled harder. Still, no movement.

"What is wrong with her?" Lucy asked the earl, annoyed at how easily he had swung onto Zeus's bare back and was now guiding the horse around.

"You simply need to show Athena who is in charge," he said. "I think you would find it an easier thing to do if you mounted the animal. I can toss a saddle on her, if you'd like."

"No, I would not like." Lucy frowned at the horse, wondering how one went about showing an animal who was in charge and who wasn't. She cleared her throat. "Athena, we are going to steal—I mean *borrow*—a wagon from that building across the meadow, and I'm afraid I need your help."

Athena raised her head for a moment only to drop it back down and continue sniffing.

"Apparently this horse does not wish to break into the building any more than you do, Collins."

He chuckled. "Perhaps I was a bit hasty in suggesting a vegetable garden."

"Perhaps you were," Lucy agreed. "But it is too late to retract the suggestion now. It has already taken root in my mind and will not budge. We will plow that spot of ground, we will plant seeds, and we will watch vegetables grow." Although the idea of a garden did excite Lucy, her desire to proceed with the plan wasn't necessarily fueled by her desire to see vegetables grow. Rather, the garden gave her conscience something to think about that did not weigh her down with guilt.

"We could begin smaller, you know," Lord Drayson said. "We can remove the weeds in the existing area and plant only a few things. If all goes well, then perhaps next year . . ." His words trailed off quickly, for they both knew that next year would be very different from this year.

"No," said Lucy firmly. "If we are going to do this, we are going to do it right. We will get these stubborn animals to the shed, hitch them to the wagon, and collect that plow."

"You left out the part about picking the lock," he said.

"If you continue to be impertinent," said Lucy, "I shall send you to collect the plow without a wagon or horses and make you drag the thing back on your own."

"It might be the faster option," he said, his lips twitching at her continued struggle to coerce Athena into moving.

"Oh, do be quiet," said Lucy crossly.

Lord Drayson laughed, and Lucy glared at him. The man could irritate her as no else had ever been able to do. He seemed to take great delight in teasing her, and why she continued to allow him to bait her, she couldn't say.

"Stay there." He directed Zeus over to her and chuckled when Lucy dropped the rope and skittered away.

"He is not going to eat you." The earl used that commanding voice he often used which irritated her almost as much as his teasing.

"I know," Lucy spoke without conviction. She watched the horse's rather large mouth, thinking it could easily take a chunk out of her shoulder if he chose to give it a try. The closer the horse came, the more Lucy's body trembled. Goodness, what was wrong with her?

Collins pulled Zeus's head to the left, turning the animal until the earl's leg brushed against Lucy. Her body still trembled, but not because of fear.

Lord Drayson leaned down and held out his hand. "Ride with me," he said, his voice gentle. "I give you my word that nothing bad will happen to you."

"But—"

"Lucy." This time his use of her Christian name did not irritate her. The way he spoke it in a soft, hushed tone made it sound more like an endearment. It softened her heart and ignited it at the same time.

"Trust me," he said, holding out his hand.

Lucy found that she did trust him, this man who had gone from being an odious evictor to her friend in a matter of days. She trusted him enough to place her hand in his and allow him to swing her up on the horse in front of him as though she weighed nothing more than a kitten. Her legs dangled off to the side, and the horse felt uncomfortable beneath her, but as soon as the earl tucked her body tight against his, Lucy felt safe. Actually, she felt more than safe. A delightful sensation began in her chest and radiated through the rest of her body, warming her in a way that the sun or a blazing fire never could.

Lord Drayson maneuvered Zeus around so that he could retrieve Athena's lead rope. Once he had it firmly in his hand all it took was a click of his tongue to get both horses moving slowly toward the outbuilding.

"I told you it helps to be on top." Lord Drayson's breath tickled Lucy's neck, sending shivers down her back. Aside from her father, Lucy had never been this close to a man before, at least not like this. After the earl's fall, she and Georgy had to wrap their arms around his chest to get him on the bed, but that had been different. Lord Drayson had been the despised enemy then. Now, however . . . well, Lucy wasn't quite sure what to think anymore.

She no longer felt animosity toward him, except when he teased her, but even then it wasn't true animosity. Lucy couldn't deny that he continually surprised her, either. She had expected him to complain about all the chores, or at the very least, complete them in a sluggish, half-hearted manner. But Lord Drayson had cleaned the chimney flue, scoured the yellow salon, worked wonders in the stables and the yard, and had tackled every other job given him with alacrity. Now he was even willing to aid her in breaking into an outbuilding and plowing a new plot of ground for a vegetable garden. *Her* vegetable garden.

Not even the gardener would have agreed to such a scheme.

Lucy had once thought Lord Drayson cold and selfish, the type of person who couldn't possibly be missed by anyone. But now she couldn't help but wonder if someone was missing him and who that someone, or someones, might be. His family, certainly. Friends, possibly. Was there a woman in his life? Lucy's entire body stiffened at the thought. Could the earl possibly be married or have an understanding with someone?

"Relax, Lucy," the earl said and immediately muttered a curse under his breath. "Blast it all, I can't seem to stop calling you that. It comes out so naturally. Why is that?"

"I do not know, Collins," Lucy answered, speaking the truth. "Perhaps it is because you do not hold me in very high esteem."

"On the contrary," he answered. "I hold you in too high esteem, which is likely my problem."

He said it so casually, as though he was working through his thoughts aloud and didn't mean for anyone else to hear them. But Lucy had heard his words loud and clear. They filled her soul and made her body stiffen even more. They caused her heart to race and her mind to whirl. With his arms around her waist, his solid chest against her back, and his breath on her neck, Lucy's emotions had never been more muddled. She needed to slide off Zeus and put a stop to this. Wife or no wife, he should not be holding her this way, saying such things to her, or making her feel so . . . confused. Her plan had not included developing a partiality for one another. Such feelings would only cause additional complications when the truth finally came out.

"You're tensing again," said the earl in her ear. "You must learn to relax and ride *with* the horse, not against it."

Lucy willed her body to relax, refocusing her thoughts on the movements of Zeus rather than the man seated behind her.

"That's better," he said. "Now take the reins."

"Me?" Lucy gasped, shrinking against him. "Have you lost your senses?"

He chuckled, and she felt the reverberations down her spine. Lucy wanted to melt against him and leap from the animal at the same time. If only the ground wasn't so far away.

"This animal is the most docile creature I have ever ridden," he said. "You ought to take the reins and see for yourself."

Lucy felt shaky and weak, though she wasn't sure if it was the horse or Lord Drayson that caused it. Probably a combination of the two. Yet she found herself allowing the earl to thread the reins through her fingers and hold them captive beneath his.

"That's it," he said quietly, showing her how to guide the horse one way and then another. "That's not so bad, is it?"

On the contrary. Lucy's mind had never been filled with more upheaval. Everything about this was wrong, wrong, wrong. If Lord Drayson knew who he really was—who she was—he would not consider touching her this way, whispering in her ear, or holding her on any level of esteem.

When at last they reached the outbuilding, Lord Drayson gave her hand a squeeze and said, "Hold Zeus steady a moment." Before Lucy realized what was happening, he had slid off the horse and had raised his hands with the intent to help her down. The top of the horse suddenly felt a great deal safer.

But Zeus took a step forward and Lucy panicked, lunging for the earl's arms. He caught her with a laugh and held her tight against him for a moment before releasing her waist and holding her shoulders captive instead.

"So tell me," he teased. "How does it feel to survive a barebacked horse ride?"

"It feels . . ." Lucy looked into his striking blue eyes and lost all coherent thought as feelings and emotions crashed and collided about inside her. Wonder, fear, confusion, desire, guilt . . . they were all there, skirmishing it out like a group of unruly farm boys.

"I couldn't agree more," said the earl quietly, as though Lucy had finished the sentence.

Ever so slowly, he ran the knuckles of his fingers along her cheekbone, igniting sensations Lucy had never felt before. "You are so beautiful," he murmured.

With a gasp, she drew away from his touch, taking a quick step back. "What if you are married?" she blurted. "Or have an understanding with someone? Or . . . ?"

His jaw tensed, and his hand dropped to his side. "You think me the sort of man who would run away from a wife or fiancée? You did say I appeared on your doorstep like a coward, fleeing something in my past."

"Yes," Lucy murmured, for that is precisely what she had said even though it was not even close to the truth.

"I would never leave a loved one to fend for themselves," said the earl firmly. "That, I know."

"Of course not," Lucy said, berating herself for devising such a wicked lie in the first place. This was exactly the reason impressionable young ladies should not read novels. They placed silly ideas in one's head that would pop out at the most untimely moments. She should have told Lord Drayson the truth as soon as he'd opened his eyes.

"You are right to shrink away from me though," he said with a sigh, raking his fingers through his wavy hair. "You do not know me and I do not know myself." He paused, staring off into the distance at nothing in particular. "There was a time when I was so certain you knew more about my past than you let on, but I don't believe that anymore. You are not the sort of person who would intentionally deceive another. I know that now, and my sincerest apologies for ever thinking otherwise."

Lucy had never felt the need to utter a curse more than now. In the skirmish of her emotions, guilt planted the others a solid facer and now stood triumphant, lording over the rest of them. Guilt, shame, remorse. What had she become? The earl had been right about one thing. He *did* hold her in too high esteem. Lucy dreaded the day when she would come crashing down in his eyes.

She looked away from his handsome face, wishing she had the courage to blurt out the truth. Instead, she swallowed the words, needing time to think, to prepare, to figure out exactly how to tell him she was a worse person than he could imagine.

Why the devil had she ever broken her promise?

Lucy glanced up to see Lord Drayson watching her. Before he could verbalize his thoughts, her fingers fished the hairpin from her pocket, and she strode forward with purpose.

"Ready to learn how to pick a lock, Collins?"

"Ready as I'll ever be, Miss Beresford."

Lucy hesitated only a moment before shoving the pin into the old and rusty lock. She wanted to tell him she was not deserving of any sort of respect and that he ought to call her Lucille, for that is the name her mother used whenever she found it necessary to bring Lucy to task.

How very sad that one could exert a great deal of effort over one's entire life and climb so far only to tumble all the way back down in a matter of days.

MUCH TO COLLINS'S SATISFACTION, he and Miss Beresford discovered not only a wagon in the outbuilding, but a plow as well. It was quite ancient. The wood was dry and brittle and the metal rusted, but it seemed solid enough to do the job, so Collins hefted it into the back of the wagon, hitched up both horses, and assisted Lucy onto the seat before jumping in next to her. His arm brushed against hers, and she quickly scooted away, leaving enough space for a small child to fit between them. It was a far cry from the cozy horseback ride they'd shared earlier, but it was probably for the best. Although Collins had assured Lucy that he would never leave anyone behind, he really had no idea what—or who—laid in his past.

Was he capable of running away from a family, or simply running from life in general? Collins prayed not. He craved the return of his memory, but there were moments, like now, when he couldn't help but wonder if he might be better off not knowing the events that had brought him to this point. But life could not continue as it was forever. Like it or not, he needed to know.

With Lucy quiet and stiff at his side, they rode back to the dower house in relative silence, each lost to their own thoughts. Once they arrived, Lucy quickly made her excuses—something about helping with luncheon—and disappeared inside. Collins watched her go, berating himself for his earlier actions. Who was he to take liberties with the daughter of a respectable vicar? Lucy had been right to remind him of his place and keep him firmly in it.

With a sigh, he jumped from the wagon and squinted into the sun. It was now high overhead, promising more than enough daylight to plow the area and return the borrowed equipment to its rightful place before dark. If he hurried, perhaps there would also be enough time for that jaunt into town, so Lucy could purchase her seeds and Collins could track down the doctor.

Unfortunately, the work didn't go as quickly as he had hoped. It took some time to learn how to use the plow effectively, and when he was finally beginning to make progress, Georgina brought him some freshly baked bread, along with ham, cheese, and a pitcher of ale. He gratefully took a break and enjoyed the food before returning to the rigorous work.

Hours later, Collins paused to rub his sore and blistered hands. As he did so, he spied Lucy walking quickly away from the house in the opposite direction from him. He pulled Zeus to a stop and watched her rapid movements. She was heading down the carriage path, presumably in the direction of town. He frowned and glanced at the sky. Was she so determined to purchase seeds that she would travel on foot at this late hour? He could think of no other reason for her hasty departure.

Collins worked quickly to unhitch Zeus from the plow and returned the worn horse to the stables. Then he hitched Athena to the small cart and jumped in, giving the reins a quick flip. Not ten minutes later, he turned from the carriage path onto the road in a very slow pursuit of Lucy. He could only hope he was traveling in the right direction.

"Come now, girl. I know you can do better this," encouraged Collins, whipping the reins yet again. At the rate Athena meandered along, they would not overtake Lucy until her journey home from town.

After a bit more encouragement, Athena finally broke into a canter, though it was still several bends in the road later before he finally caught sight of Lucy. She certainly had a quick stride.

As Collins neared, Lucy glanced back once, then again before stopping and spinning around to await his approach.

"What are you doing?" she spluttered as he pulled the cart alongside her.

"Accompanying you to town," he answered, holding his hand out to help her onto the seat beside him. She looked beautiful in a fresh pink day dress and a matching straw bonnet.

"I did not ask you to accompany me, Collins," she said, refraining from taking his hand.

"You did not have to ask," he said calmly. "I know my duty as coachman."

"I would prefer that you do your duty as gardener and finish plowing the garden."

"I am nearly finished, and Zeus was in need of a break." Both of which were true. It would take Collins an hour at best to finish the plowing now that he knew what he was doing. "Had you bothered to come and have a look, you would have seen for yourself."

She glanced behind at the road from whence they'd come. "But—"

"Surely you did not intend to walk to town unaccompanied at this hour," said Collins. "What would your mother say?"

"She would give me a kiss and say, 'hurry back,' for I do it all the time. This part of the country is more lenient about silly proprieties."

"Or perhaps it is the Beresfords who are lenient," teased Collins.

Her beautiful brown eyes flashed at him in anger, reminding him of the conversation they'd shared when he'd first awoken, along with another distant memory that he couldn't quite place. How many times had she been angry with him in the past?

Collins cleared his throat. "I beg your pardon, Miss Beresford. It seems that I must call upon your forgiveness yet again. But if I may be so bold, would your mother really condone a trip to town this late in the afternoon? It will likely grow dark before your return."

Lucy opened her mouth to argue before snapping it closed and looking away. When she finally spoke, it was to quietly say, "No, Collins, she would not. I suppose I should have waited until tomorrow."

"So this part of the country is not as lax as all that," said Collins with a hint of a smile. "Is not Georgina coming this way to visit her family soon? Why did you not beg a ride with her and . . . Mr. Crandall, was it?"

"They are not to go until after dinner, and the mercantile will be closed by then," explained Lucy.

"Well then," said Collins, holding his hand out to her once again. "Might I offer you a ride, Miss Beresford, so that you may purchase your seeds and return home before the sun retires for the day?"

Still she hesitated, biting down on her lower lip. "The townspeople," she said finally. "There might be talk."

Collins lifted a brow. "A great many people employ a coachman, Miss Beresford."

"Yes, but—" she quickly cut herself off. "Oh, never mind. I suppose it is a silly concern anyway. Yes, Collins. I shall be glad of the ride." She accepted his hand only until she was up in the cart, then quickly let go, sitting as far from him as possible.

Collins whipped the reins and they were off, trotting toward town at a leisurely pace. This time he did not mind the slowness of the journey. He let the horse go as it pleased.

"Have you decided on which seed packets you will purchase?" Collins asked in an effort to make conversation. He'd missed Lucy's company these past few hours and refused to spend what remained of the ride in silence.

"It will depend on what is available, I suppose," said Lucy. "I am sure the owner of the mercantile will be able to offer suggestions."

"I'm sure he will," agreed Collins, and the conversation ended. Something told him that he had never been one for small talk. It felt much too trying and not at all his style. Perhaps silence was preferable, for he absolutely refused to comment on the weather.

"It's a lovely day, isn't it?" said Lucy. When Collins chuckled, she cocked her head at him. "What was so amusing in that?"

"I do not think small talk suits us very well, do you?"

She laughed softly. "Not at all. I'm quite dreadful at it, actually. You already know how fond I am of lovely days."

"You did make that very clear this morning."

She lapsed into silence. Another bend in the road later, she said, "You are very good with the ribbons. Who taught you how—" She immediately stopped and blushed. "How silly of me to ask a question you cannot answer."

"My absent memory does make conversation difficult," he said, trying not to be annoyed by the large void in his past.

He cast a quick glance Lucy's way, noticing her pensive expression, and pulled on the reins, bringing Athena and the cart to a stop.

"What are you doing?" Lucy glanced behind them. "Is something the matter with the cart?"

"The cart is fine."

"Why have you stopped?"

"I was merely thinking that you cannot answer that question either."

She frowned in confusion. "What question?"

"Tell me, Miss Beresford. Who taught you how to drive?" he asked, quirking an eyebrow at her. "Isn't it interesting that neither of us can provide an answer to that question but for completely different reasons?"

Her body stiffened, and she clasped her fingers in her lap, eyeing him warily. "Your point, Collins?"

"Only that it would be a great feather in my cap if you could one day say that your butler/footman/coachman/gardener taught you to drive.'"

"And what if I do not wish you to add that particular feather to your cap?"

Ignoring the question, Collins shifted to face her and propped an elbow on his knee. "Perhaps we can make it a competition."

"Make what a competition?" she said a bit testily. "You already know how to drive."

"Yes, but I do not know who taught me how to drive. It could have been my father, a friend, a cousin, a sibling, or perhaps I taught myself. Someday, I hope to recall the answer, but for now, it is a mystery. So what I propose is this: The first to provide an answer to the question wins."

Her gaze moved from his face to the reins and back to him. "Wins what, exactly? A feather in one's cap? Because I don't care a farthing for boasting privileges."

Collins studied her with interest. Was the lovely vicar's daughter proposing an actual wager? It caught him off guard a bit, only because Collins had been expecting her to dismiss the challenge completely. Yet here she was, not only considering it, but desiring to set terms.

He ran his finger across his chin as he gave the matter some thought. "I have it," he said after a moment. "The other day I was doing the unthinkable and poking around below stairs when I stumbled across something that one might call a hat. It is tall and black, with a wide brim that is stitched up on one side. I believe it is made of felted wool and has the most intriguing matted red feather sweeping up the side of it."

"I know the one," said Lucy. "It was left there by the previous occupants, and as I wasn't sure what to do with the thing, I left it alone. It is quite ghastly, is it not?"

"And therefore perfect for our wager."

Her eyebrow lifted in an intriguing way. "Go on," she said.

"I propose that the loser must wear that hat for an entire day. A mandatory visit to town might also be required."

"But it is a man's hat!" Lucy protested.

"I am certain you can pull it off smashingly, if it comes to that," said Collins. "You are not afraid of losing, are you? Only think how perfectly ridiculous I'd look wearing it."

Based on the way she drew her lower lip into her mouth, she was considering it. Collins could almost hear her mind clinking away as she glanced at Athena, the reins, and back at him.

"Do you swear to be the very best driving instructor you can be?" she asked.

"Certainly," he said.

"What will it take to prove I am a competent driver?"

He gave it some thought before saying, "You must drive all the way to town and back without assistance."

She frowned. "Alone?"

"Of course not. I shall be at your side, but I cannot help with the ribbons or instruct you in any way."

She sighed, chewed on her lower lip once more, and finally nodded. "Very well, Collins. I accept your challenge, so prepare yourself to wear that ridiculous hat." She scooted closer to him and held out her hands. "The ribbons, if you please."

THE DRIVE TO TOWN WAS nothing short of a fiasco. Lucy was a deplorable pupil with too-soft hands and an even softer heart. She did not want to pull on the reins or whip them against Athena's back or even guide the horse in the proper direction. She merely wanted to carry the ribbons and allow the horse to go wherever it may. And what the animal wished to do most was to munch on the fresh grass alongside the road.

"Athena, you are behaving very badly," Lucy said in frustration. "You may eat later. Right now, you need to move."

"You must show her who is in charge," Collins tried to explain.

"How do I do that, exactly?" Lucy snipped.

Collins gently took the reins from her hand, flicked them twice, and pulled hard on the left one, saying, "Heave and ho, girl. Come now. Off we go."

Athena responded, and as soon as they were back on the road, Collins handed the reins over once again.

Now that the horse was moving, Lucy could not seem to relax. She jerked the ribbons to the left, and when Athena trotted dangerously close to that side of the road, she yanked them to the right, then left again, causing Athena to move in a criss-cross pattern across the road. Collins attempted to coach Lucy, but it was to no avail. She turned out to be the most abominable driver Collins had ever known. No wonder her mother insisted on doing the driving.

When they had finally reached town, thankfully with the horse and cart still intact, Collins had no choice but to take the ribbons from Lucy for fear she would drive them into another rig, or worse, a pedestrian. No passerby was safe with her at the head.

"I think, Miss Beresford," Collins said as he pulled the cart to a stop in front of the mercantile, "that you had better purchase some extra fripperies to make the ghastly hat a little more fashionable. I strongly believe that you shall be the one wearing it."

"Oh, do be quiet," she said crossly, refusing his help as she climbed from the cart.

"Do you require my assistance in the mercantile?" he asked, hoping she would send him away, giving him the time to finally search out the doctor.

Her frustration with him worked in his favor. "No," she said, striding toward the door. "You may return for me in an hour."

"Very good, Miss," he said with a cockney accent, unable to refrain from grinning as she disappeared inside.

At last, Collins was able to do as he wished, and he had an entire hour at his disposal to boot. He cast a quick glance up and down the street, wondering where to begin. One might call the village of Askern charming, but it lacked any sort of familiarity to him. From the milliner to the inn to the cobblestone streets, everything looked as foreign as it felt. People milled about, going in, coming out, or driving by—many of whom cast curious glances his way.

This is not my home, he thought. Not one person exhibited even a spark of recognition.

Collins sighed and hailed a passerby. "Excuse me, sir. Could you possibly tell me where I might find the doctor at this time of day?"

He nodded down the road. "The leech 'as an office at the norf end of the village, but you'll be lucky ter find 'im there. 'E's a 'ard one ter track down. Always samplin' the waters and scribblin' in 'is book."

Collins nodded his thanks and headed north, but as the man had warned, the good doctor was nowhere to be found, and the proprietor of the tavern next door had not seen him for hours.

"Check by the lake," he grumbled. "Says 'e's writin' a book about the waters or sum such fin'. Spends more time doin' that than tendin' ter the people, I'd say. Fool leech."

On that recommendation, Collins left the tavern, his optimism not quite as high as before. Still he tried the lake, where he learned the doctor ate often at the inn and might be found there, so off he went to the inn, only to discover he'd missed the man by a good hour.

Devil take it, thought Collins as he strode from the inn, unsure where to try next. Not one single occupant in the room could give him a clue as to where the doctor could be. Perhaps back at his so-called office?

Leaving Athena and the cart at the inn, Collins once again strode toward the doctor's office. The sun was beginning to sink low over the horizon, threatening darkening skies. He didn't have much longer before he would need to collect Miss Beresford.

Not far away, a horse whinnied, and Collins glanced its way, then stopped and looked harder. Held captive behind a rickety fence, the black Arabian appeared out of place and even . . . familiar. Collins walked toward the animal as a memory began to surface, caught somewhere between the unknown and known. A man and his son filled a trough nearby, eyeing Collins with distrust as he approached.

"Is there somethin' you needed?" the man asked, holding his son tightly by the hand.

"This horse," said Collins. "Where did you get it?"

"He's a beaut, ain't he?" said the man. "I found 'im roamin' the 'ills not far from 'ere. He 'ad on a fancy saddle but lost a shoe, so I calmed 'im down and brought 'im ter me blacksmif's shop ter fix the shoe. Been tryin' ter figure out 'oo he belongs ter ever since. Recognize 'im?"

The memory was so close Collins could almost see it. He did recognize the horse but he didn't know how. He couldn't even remember its name. "I . . ."

"Lil' darlin', it's time for supper." A woman stood at the back door of a small, but tidy house, wiggling her fingers at the small boy. She cast a curious look at Collins but didn't say anything. When the boy ran to her, she swooped him into her arms and carried him inside.

But the endearment . . . *Darling*. It meant something. Collins could feel it, almost see it, but like a fly buzzing around, he couldn't snatch it.

"Are you new ter Askern?" asked the man, eyeing Collins skeptically.

"I believe so," he answered. "The Beresfords have recently employed me as their . . . coachman, among other things."

"You don't sound like a coachman."

"I find that rather odd myself." Collins stroked the nose of the Arabian, scouring his memory for something more than a hazy familiarity. It was there, so close and yet still out of reach, making him feel as though he would go mad at any moment.

118

"Me cousin, Georgy, works for the Beresfords. Do you know 'er?"

"I do," said Collins. "She's a sweet girl and a hard worker. Miss Lucy is quite fond of her."

"And Georgy be quite fond of Miss Lucy. They've been good ter 'er." He continued to watch Collins closely, his expression more confused than anything else. "Things must be lookin' up for the Beresfords if they 'ave taken you on. 'Appy ter 'ear it. It's about time somethin' good 'appen ter them for a change."

Collins looked away from the horse and at the man, who couldn't be much older than him. Wearing tattered trousers and a dingy shirt, he had obviously spent the day laboring in some way.

"What do you mean 'for a change?'" asked Collins. "Are you referring to the passing of Miss Lucy's father?"

"That, and 'e left 'is family wif noffin'. They would be 'omeless if not for Lord Drayson."

Lord Drayson.

The name screeched through Collins's mind, stirring, colliding, and opening memories. Like interlinking cogs, scenes from his past began to emerge and come together. His home in Danbury. His family. His father, now gone. His nieces. Darling. Tanglewood. Dark, flashing eyes. Everything came back in an overwhelming rush of facts, images, details—right down to the moment he had raced away from the dower house in the freezing rain. Everything made sense now. Why he wanted to give orders instead of be ordered, why he knew horses but had no idea how to clean a flue or plant a garden or polish silver. Why he detested that ghastly pink shirt.

"Mister?" asked the blacksmith. "You feelin' alright?"

Collins blinked at him a few times before he could

answer. "I am perfectly well, thanks to you. And I do know this horse. He is called Darling and has a small round scar on the back of his right hind leg."

The blacksmith immediately inspected the spot and lifted an impressed brow. "That he does."

"If you would be so kind as to keep the horse for another few days, I can provide further proof and see that you are handsomely paid for your kindness on behalf of this animal."

The blacksmith ran a hand along Darling's sleek coat. "Might I ask 'oo he belongs ter?"

"Yes. He belongs to Colin Cavendish, the fifth Earl of Drayson," answered the earl. *And Lucy Beresford, the late vicar's daughter, knows exactly who I am.*

Colin strode down the road, his jaw clenched and his hands fisted. He had been played for an utter fool, and for what reason? Had Miss Beresford wanted revenge? Had she hoped his memory would never return so that she could remain in the dower house for as long as she wished? Had she purposefully placed him in a compromising position with the hopes he would do the honorable thing and propose?

What the deuce had inspired such deceit—such disregard for integrity, propriety, and common decency? Colin had been due in London last week. His sister and valet were likely besides themselves with worry, wondering what had become of him. Had word reached his mother? Were people out searching for him?

Had Miss Beresford bothered to consider any of that?

Fury burned through Colin like a hearty swig of brandy—something he could certainly use at the moment.

He turned toward the inn and quickened his pace, striding into the establishment moments later. The demand for a strong drink died on his lips when he realized he had no way of paying for it. He uttered a curse under his breath.

Where had she stashed his purse? His clothes? His boots?

Colin sat in the nearest chair and glared out the window. It was past time for him to retrieve Miss Beresford, but he did not care. She could wait on him for a change or even make the journey home on foot—not that it would be her home much longer. He would see to that straightaway.

A twinge of conscience pestered him at such thoughts, but Colin shoved it aside. Miss Beresford had seemed so genuine and kind. What reason could she possibly have for doing such a despicable thing? Colin could not understand it. Had Georgina known as well? Of course she had. The two were as thick as thieves.

A burly-looking man pulled out a chair across from Colin and plopped down with a drink in hand. His red beard appeared as though it had not been washed or combed in weeks.

The earl glanced at him, wanting—no *needing*—answers. "Do you happen to know Miss Lucy Beresford?" he asked.

The man studied Colin for a moment before grunting. "Everyone knows Miss Lucy."

"What sort of person is she?"

The man set down his drink, and Colin watched the dark liquid in the man's glass sway back and forth until it settled.

"'Oo's askin'?" he asked, his expression distrustful.

The earl returned his gaze to the window, where tiny droplets slapped against the pane and trickled down. When had it begun raining? "No one of consequence," he finally muttered. "Forget I asked."

The man took another long drink. When he set the glass down again, he said, "Miss Lucy's the sort of person ter bring soup, flowers, and fresh bread ter me and me wife and offer ter 'old our lil' one so that we could 'ave a bite to eat. She always 'as a kind word ter say. People look out for 'er 'round 'ere."

"Have you known her long?" asked Colin.

"Most of me life," he answered. "Miss Lucy and me brother, Ben, used ter get in all sorts of scrapes. Pickin' locks, racin' grass'oppers, buryin' snakes, and the like."

The earl nodded. So she hadn't lied about everything. The rain continued to trickle down the window, and he felt some of his anger trickle away. He had come to know Miss Lucy as well—her quick wit, frank speaking, soft curves, and flashes of anger. Goodness seemed to emanate from her soul, which was why he could not understand the lies. What would she say if he demanded answers? Would she continue to lie, or would Colin finally hear the truth—the whole truth?

Lightning flashed in the skies, and a rumble of thunder followed moments later. The sound awakened Colin from his self-centered thoughts and caused his brow to furrow in concern. Where was Lucy now? Had she taken refuge in a shop, or had she ignored the graying skies and set out on foot? Despite her deception, she did not deserve to be out alone in this weather.

Colin immediately drew himself up, nodded his thanks to the man, and finally went in search of Lucy.

LUCY HAD WALKED NEARLY HALFWAY home by the time Collins pulled the cart alongside her. After waiting in front of the mercantile for twenty minutes, she had run out of patience and begun the trek home. Not ten minutes later, she regretted the decision. The gray clouds had opened up, dropping down rain that quickly soaked through her thin muslin dress and wilted her straw bonnet. Each gust of wind made her cringe and shiver, and beneath her thin gloves, Lucy's fingers became numb. It was amazing how quickly the temperature dropped when the sun was no longer around to share its warmth.

"You're late, C-Collins." Lucy's voice quivered from the cold. She probably sounded vexed, but her frustration wasn't entirely aimed at him. The chilly walk had given her time to ponder on her problem, and the person she was mostly vexed with was herself.

The earl offered his hand to her, which she accepted gratefully and climbed into the cart. The sooner they returned home, the sooner she could wrap herself into a warm blanket in front of a blazing fire.

"My apologies for being late," said Collins in a

distracted sort of way. "I ran into a bit of trouble that needed sorting out."

Lucy set her bundle on her lap and hugged her arms to her chest in an effort to bring some warmth back into her body. "What s-sort of trouble? Is everything all r-right?"

"It was nothing I couldn't sort out on my own." He peered closer at her and frowned. "You appear to be quite sodden. And frozen. Are *you* all right?"

"I'm not s-sure why you would th-think that," she said, unable to keep from stuttering the words. "I am as t-toasty as a log on the f-fire." Perhaps if she thought it, she would feel it. If only Athena would pick up the pace.

Lord Drayson shot her a look of concern. "I shall be sure to add a great many logs to the fire once I return you to your home. Perhaps I could toss you in as well, if you enjoy being that toasty."

"That sounds q-quite heavenly, actually," she said as another gust of wind whipped around her.

The earl removed one of his driving gloves and lifted his bare palm to her cheek. "Good gads, woman, you *are* cold." He slid closer and swept his arm around her back, pulling her snug against him. He began rubbing her upper arm to warm her. It was a strange sensation to be so cold and yet on fire at the same time.

Lucy tried to move away because she ought to, but it was a feeble attempt at best. So she tried words instead. "Collins, I appreciate what you're t-trying to do, but this isn't s-seemly. You must r-remove your arm from about my p-person."

"I will do no such thing," he countered. "Not when it feels as though I am holding a block of ice."

"I would p-prefer to speak of fire," she said, deciding she'd rather snuggle closer than move away. He felt so good and smelled so masculine, like earth, hard work, and sandalwood. It reminded her of her father. A gust of wind swept past, going straight through her thin dress, and she huddled nearer to him.

"How is it you are s-so warm?" she asked. "The wind is so c-cold and you are damp as well."

"Only damp—not soaked to the bone like you." The earl continued to rub her arm with greater intensity and simultaneously flicked the reins repeatedly, encouraging Athena to move faster.

"I would suggest that you drive and not me," he said, "but you'd likely run us off the road, and I'm certain you'd prefer to get home."

Lucy knew he was attempting to distract her from the cold, and she was grateful for his efforts. "I'll w-wait until tomorrow," she said. "I must l-learn as quickly as p-possible so I do not have to w-wear that ghastly hat. R-red is not my color."

"I beg to differ," he said. "I've seen a rosy hue on your cheeks rather often, and it is quite fetching."

"F-fetch is what a dog does with a s-stick," said Lucy, not comfortable talking about her appearance, or the fact that he seemed to notice how frequently she blushed around him.

"Or what a servant does with a cup of tea?" he countered.

"Tea . . . that sounds h-heavenly too," she murmured.

"Perhaps I will fetch you a cup when we get back."

The lighthearted banter only served to increase Lucy's guilt. Lord Drayson would not treat her with such kindness if he knew of her deceit. She didn't deserve it any more than he deserved to fetch her a cup of tea. It was past time to tell him the truth and accept the consequences of her rash stupidity.

But how? When? She didn't know how to begin such a conversation.

Lucy felt trapped in the middle of a large, self-made muddle, and she had no one to blame but herself. Perhaps she should blurt it all out right now and be done with it. After he'd left her to freeze in the drizzle, he might go a bit easier on her. More likely, though, he'd dump her on the side of the road and leave her for dead, just as she had once contemplated doing to him.

Perhaps today was the day she would reap what she'd sown.

Lucy drew in a deep, shuddering breath. "Col—" she cut herself off, realizing she could no longer call him by that name. How she could have ever done so was another testament that she was not nearly as good as he seemed to think her. So she cleared her throat and began again. "There is s-something I need to tell y-you."

A long pause followed, and his hand stopped rubbing warmth into her arm. He cast a quick glance her way but said nothing to encourage further conversation, so she forged on. "I have b-behaved very badly. Y-you see, I—"

"Purchased your seeds?" He nodded toward her bundle. "I noticed the parcel on your lap. What did you get?"

"Carrots, s-spinach, cauliflower, and p-peas," she answered. "But that is not what I w-wish to tell you."

"Whatever it is can wait until you are cozy and warm," he said, his hand rubbing her arm once more. "I see the house now. We are almost there."

Even through the murky gray skies, the dower house had never looked more beautiful or inviting. It beckoned Lucy the way the clear skies and warm sun had done to her this morning, only now she could not wait to be back indoors.

"Perhaps I w-will allow you to fetch that cup of t-tea after all," Lucy's voice came out as a whisper. "But only this last t-time."

The earl said nothing. He merely pulled her body tighter against his and cracked the reins a few more times. Then he called out "Whoa!" and the cart came to an abrupt stop. If it wasn't for the earl's arm about her, Lucy would have flown off her seat.

Once he had steadied her, Lord Drayson jumped from the cart and swept Lucy into his arms. He left Athena and the cart where it was and carried her straight into the house.

"Georgina!" he called upon entry. "Georgina, where are you?"

"She likes being c-called Georgy," said Lucy. "And she isn't h-here, remember? Her mother is ill and needed her."

"And now you're going to be ill if we don't get you warm soon." He deposited Lucy on the sofa and tucked a rug around her before moving to the fireplace to start a fire. Several minutes later, it began to snap and pop, and Lucy felt some of its wonderful warmth. She curled into a ball and rested her head on the arm of the sofa.

"We need to get you into dry clothes."

"We?" Lucy pulled the blanket tighter around her shoulders. Her body might be numb but her brain was still very much intact, and there would be no "we" when it came to changing her clothes.

The earl rolled his eyes. "Tell me where I might find some dry clothes for *you* to dress yourself."

She was too tired and cold to argue. "Top of the s-stairs. Second door on your right. And do t-try to stop commanding me."

He hustled up the stairs and returned a moment later, tossing a shift and a blue day dress beside her on the sofa.

She would have blushed that he had gone through her unmentionables if they didn't appear so inviting at the moment. She would save her blushes for another day and simply be grateful.

"Th-thank you."

"I will attend to Athena while you change, then I will try to figure out how to put the kettle on." He was gone before she could thank him again.

The moment Lucy relinquished the rug around her, the cold air seemed to blast her. She didn't waste any time tugging the curtain closed and slipping out of her favorite pink dress. Her damp shift soon followed, and she worked quickly to put on the dry clothes, all the while standing directly in front of the fire. Then she grabbed the quilt and dropped down on the floor, greedily soaking up the warmth.

As her body began to slow its shivering, Lucy's thoughts strayed to the earl and how chilled he must be out in the cold stables, tending to her horse when he should be back home in Danbury enjoying his family.

With great reluctance, Lucy pulled herself away from the fire. Keeping the quilt tight around her body, she walked to the kitchen. Fifteen minutes later, she returned to the parlor holding two steaming mugs of tea when a knock sounded on the door. It opened a crack, and the earl's voice called, "Are you decent?"

"Quite," answered Lucy. "Do come in and warm yourself up with a cup of tea." She handed him a mug as he entered the house then returned to her spot on the rug in front of the fire, where she sipped the steaming liquid. It burned as it ran down her throat, but the soothing, warming effects made her sigh.

"Would you prefer to sit on the sofa?" asked the earl, leaning a shoulder against the doorway as he took a sip of his tea. His hair was damp, his face was beginning to show a day's worth of growth, and his eyes were a murky blue that sent her heart to racing.

"I wish to remain exactly where I am," said Lucy. "You may take the sofa if you'd like."

"I am damp and smell of the stables."

"That is of no consequence, but perhaps you ought to change as well," said Lucy. "Dry clothes have made all the difference. I am feeling much better already."

The earl took another sip before setting the mug on a side table and excusing himself to presumably do just that. Through the quiet house, Lucy heard his footsteps descend below stairs, and she felt another bout of that dratted guilt. He should not be going down to where the air was even damper and chillier. He should be going up to warmth, coziness, and a valet ready to assist him.

What was more, Lucy became keenly aware that she should not be alone in the house with him. What had she been thinking giving Georgina the evening off? Yes, her maid had been needed elsewhere, but she was also needed here at this moment. Lucy's mother would be shocked if she could see her daughter now, huddled in front of the fire, all alone in the house with only the esteemed Earl of Drayson as company.

Sometimes Lucy wondered if she would ever acquire the wisdom that was supposed to come with age.

18

COLIN STARED AT HIS REFLECTION in the small mirror above the dresser. Now that he had donned a fresh change of clothes and scrubbed away the grime, he didn't look any different than he had that morning. But he felt different. Older, much more knowledgeable, and confused by the emotions plaguing him.

After he'd left the inn, Colin had been ready to demand an explanation the moment he laid eyes on Lucy again. But once he'd helped her into the cart and she began shivering and stuttering in such a pitiful way, his heart had softened, and he found himself unable to demand anything from her.

She had shivered against his side, fitting perfectly in the crook of his arm and wreaking all sorts of havoc on his emotions. He wanted to kiss and shake her at the same time. Nothing made sense. *She* didn't make sense. His intense desire to believe the best in her, even though he knew the worst, didn't make sense.

It was at that point that Lucy had said she wished to tell him something. He'd felt the tension in her body, noticed the guilt and worry in her expression, saw the fear in her eyes, and Colin knew exactly what she wanted to say. It was what Colin had thought he wanted from her—what he'd been so ready to demand—but when the time came for confessions, he had panicked and changed the direction of the conversation, putting her off for another time.

Why?

The rest of the ride home, the answer had eluded him. It wasn't until Lucy had handed him the steaming mug of tea and settled herself charmingly in front of the fire, looking up at him with those mesmerizing eyes, that he had finally understood. The moment she confessed or he admitted to knowing his true identity was the moment everything would end. There would be no more riding lessons, no more talks, no more chores to complete together, and no more glances, teasing remarks, or touches. She would stay, he would leave, and nothing would ever be the same.

Why did that bother him so? Colin had a vast estate in Danbury, several other holdings scattered about, a town-home in London, a wonderful family awaiting his return, and all the comforts a wealthy lord of the realm enjoyed. Yet he wanted to remain here, in this small dower house, sleeping below the ground in a damp and cramped, airless room.

Perhaps he was going mad. Perhaps he wanted his own chance at revenge. Or perhaps he wanted to continue to hear Lucy's laughter, tease a smile from her lips, lure a blush to her cheeks, listen to her stories, watch her pick a lock with a hairpin, or allow her to land them in a ditch with her ineptitude at driving.

Colin did not understand fully what Lucy Beresford had become to him, but he knew it was something more than he had ever felt toward another woman. He simply needed more time to figure everything out.

Slowly, he walked up the stairs, through the kitchen, and down the hall to where Lucy awaited him in the parlor.

She'd finished her tea, and the mug now rested on the wood floor not far from where she sat. The blanket hung loosely around her shoulders like a shawl, and in her hands was a book. With a few locks of hair falling across her forehead and face, she had never looked more endearing.

Alone. We are all alone.

The thought clung to Colin's mind like a warning, telling him to walk back down those stairs and stay away. But he stepped into the room regardless, unable to resist the pull she had on him.

"Are you certain you would not be more comfortable on the sofa?" he asked.

She lifted her face to his and smiled. It was a radiant smile, filled with teasing, joy, and perhaps something more. She tilted her head in the most beguiling way. "Would it shock you to learn that this is my favorite place to read?"

Colin needed to focus on something besides her lips and how kissable they looked at the moment, so he crouched down in front of her and stole the book from her hands.

"*Robinson Crusoe,*" he read aloud, balancing on his haunches. "An interesting choice."

"Have you read it?" She took the book from him and flipped through some of its pages.

"Yes."

"Did you enjoy it?"

"No," he answered honestly. "You?"

She laughed lightly and set the book aside. Then she pulled her knees to her chest, arranged her skirts to keep her ankles covered, and wrapped her arms around her legs. "It was one of my father's favorite reads. I have always enjoyed a good novel, and I adored him, so I have tried my absolute hardest to finish that book without success. What my father saw in that story I will never understand."

"Crusoe found God while stranded on an island. Perhaps that is the reason?"

"Perhaps." She nodded. "Still, I wish Crusoe would encounter a lion or make friends with a chimpanzee or something more exciting than drying grapes to make raisins. He is just so . . . dull."

The earl laughed and twisted around to sit next to her on the rug, draping an arm across one knee. "One could never accuse you of being dull, Miss Beresford."

"I shall take that as a compliment," she said.

"As you should."

Their gazes locked, and Colin noticed gold flecks embedded in the dark browns. They made her eyes look richer, deeper, more mesmerizing. Before Colin could question his motives or remember the events that had brought them to this point, his hand lifted to lightly stroke her cheek. Her smile froze in its place, and her body went rigid. But she did not pull away.

"You're no longer cold," he said.

"No," she whispered. "I'm quite warm now. Maybe even a bit too warm. Perhaps I should move to the sofa."

"Perhaps you should," he said, though she stayed exactly where she was. With the exception of the rapid rise and fall of her chest, she sat still, her eyes round with uncertainty, fear, and even desire.

Colin shifted positions and lifted his other hand to her face. She trembled beneath his touch but remained on the rug next to him. It wasn't until he whispered, "I think I might kiss you," that she blinked and tore her face from his hand, turning away.

Colin wanted to groan in frustration but at the same time felt a certain relief. Any woman trying to trap him into marriage would have never pulled away. It gave him hope that her reasons for lying to him were not as nefarious as he'd feared.

She wrung her hands for a few moments before looking up at him. "Do you think there is ever a good enough reason to tell a lie?" she asked softly, surprising him from his thoughts.

Before today, Colin would have answered "no" immediately, for he had no respect for a liar. But wasn't he living a lie now? His memory had finally returned and he had made a conscious decision to keep it from her.

The world, he realized, was not simply truth or lies, right or wrong. There was a precarious in-between area where one could teeter back and forth, not exactly right and not exactly wrong. It reminded him of the rope he and his brother used to stretch between two trees and try to walk across without falling, though more often than not, they would fall to one side or the other. Where would he and Lucy fall when this was all over?

Rather than answer her question, Colin turned it back to her. "Do you?"

She sighed and closed her eyes for a moment before dragging them to meet his. "No. No, I do not. There is something I *must* tell you."

Colin lifted her hand and ran his thumb across the tips of her fingers. "Will it change things between us?"

"Yes," she breathed, closing her eyes.

He touched her chin, gently turning her face to his. "I do not wish for things to change," he murmured.

"Nor I," she whispered. "But—"

Before she could say anything more, Colin leaned in and kissed her. A small gasp escaped her lips and her body went rigid, but his mouth remained on hers, moving gently but with purpose, teaching her what it felt like to be kissed.

Gradually, she began to respond, first with her lips and then with her hands sliding up his arms and around his neck. Colin's skin ignited with every touch. Kissing Lucy was like racing the wind on the back of Darling or leaping from the tallest tree to dive beneath the surface of a cool lake on a hot summer's day. It felt exhilarating, refreshing, and incredible.

With great strength of will, Colin finally released her. Lucy was as innocent as she was refreshing, and he should not be taking advantage of her in this way. She stared at him wide-eyed, her faced flushed and her hair half undone. Colin had to pry his eyes away or come undone himself.

What the devil had gotten into him? "I forget myself yet again, Miss Beresford."

She said nothing for a moment, and then murmured, "At least you have an excuse for forgetting yourself. What is mine?"

She sounded lost and anxious, as though not sure what to make of it all. Colin understood, for he felt the same. Slowly, he pushed himself to his feet, offering his hand to her, along with an excuse. "You were rudely left in the rain and became thoroughly frozen. It obviously numbed your mind."

"Yes." She placed her fingers in his and offered him a timid smile. "That is an excellent excuse. I'll take it."

He helped her to her feet, wanting to pull her against him and carry her off to the nearest bedchamber. But he forced his hand to relinquish hers and cleared his throat instead.

"What would you say to scavenging the kitchen for something to eat? Perhaps some food will satisfy our . . . hunger."

A deep blush appeared on her cheeks, and Lucy nodded. "Yes, we should definitely eat." They went to the kitchen, where she made a ruckus with the teapot, rummaged through the pantry, and avoided looking at him the entire time. They sat across the table from one another and ate some bread and cheese, drank more tea, and tried to pretend that nothing at all had changed.

Lucy's fingers tapped out an irregular beat on the table in the dark kitchen while she waited anxiously for her maid. The midnight hour was approaching when Georgina finally came through the door. Lucy practically bounded up from the stool she'd been sitting on and grabbed her maid's hand.

"Come with me," Lucy hissed. "Quietly please."

"Miss Lucy, wot 're you about?"

"Hush, Georgy." Lucy dragged her poor maid up the stairs and into her bedchamber, where she closed the door quickly behind them. She stared wide-eyed at her maid and blurted, "He kissed me."

"Wot?"

"Lord Drayson," continued Lucy. "He kissed me. And I may have kissed him back and—" The full weight of the situation slammed into her, and she dropped down on her bed and covered her face with her hands. "Oh, Georgy, how could I have let this happen? Sir Walter Scott knew what he was talking about when he wrote that bit about tangled webs. Every time I open my mouth or don't open my mouth, the lies twist tighter around the truth, and I'm not sure I'll ever be able to untwist them now. It's all such a muddle, and I have no idea what to do. Why did you have to leave today of all days? How is your mother, by the way? I do hope she's feeling more the thing."

Georgina sat on the bed next to Lucy, looking tired and

more frail than usual. "Me ma will be fine, don't you worry about that, and I'm sorry for leavin'." She paused before breathing out a weary sigh. "You ought not ter 'ave kissed 'im, Miss."

"I know, I know, I know," Lucy groaned, jumping up to pace the floor. "Did I not just say that? But the thing's been done, Georgy, and I cannot undo it. What am I to do now?"

Georgina covered a yawn with the back of her hand before answering. "It seems ter me that you 'ave but two choices, Miss Lucy. You can tell 'im the truf or keep twistin' yourself into knots."

Lucy had already known what she needed to do, but hearing Georgina spell it out so clearly made it seem less complicated somehow. "You're right. That's exactly what I shall do, even if he doesn't want to hear the truth just yet."

Georgina furrowed her forehead in confusion.

"Never mind," said Lucy with a wave of her hand. "He'll surely despise me, rage about, possibly even evict us immediately, but at least my conscience will be clear—or, as clear as it can ever be."

Georgina rose and patted Lucy's shoulder. "It's for the best, Miss. Perhaps 'e will not rage about as much as you fin'. 'E obviously 'as feelin's for you."

"Feelings that will come to an abrupt end the moment he realizes that he's far above me in height, station, and integrity. Collins, the servant, may have developed a partiality for me, but the Earl of Drayson would never countenance any sort of relationship with a deceiving daughter of a seamstress, I can assure you."

Georgina clasped Lucy's hands in hers, forcing her mistress to look her in the eye. "Your ma is Mrs. Beresford, the kind-'earted wife of the late Mr. Beresford, and yer their daughter. Don't you forget that."

Lucy threw her arms around her maid and hugged her tight. "And you are my dearest friend, Georgy. Don't you ever forget *that*."

Although Georgina smiled, it was a weary smile, so Lucy quickly shooed her away. "I'm sorry, Georgy. I've kept you awake too late as it is. You must sleep now, for tomorrow we might have a great deal of packing to do."

Georgina gave her a look of sympathy before disappearing into the dark hallway and closing the door behind her. Lucy stared at the wall for a moment, feeling suddenly alone. Though she had embraced the independence that came with her mother's absence, Lucy missed her dreadfully now. She ached for her mother's comforting arms, her wisdom, and the way she could take a weighty problem and make it lighter somehow.

Trouble was, Lucy was fairly certain that even her mother could not make everything right this time.

19

Lucy set off for Mr. Shepherd's house as soon as she'd eaten some toast. The skies were a dull gray and the air a bit nippy, so she tugged her shawl tighter around her chest. Thankfully, the earl had already awakened and was out plowing the remainder of her garden. In an effort to avoid him, Lucy crept out the front door and stayed out of sight, following the slightly overgrown path through the wilderness that separated Tanglewood from Knotting Tree, where Mr. Shepherd had resided for most of his adult life. Having lost his wife not long after they were married, he had moved to Askern to start anew and had become a bit of a recluse over the years. The Beresfords had befriended him and introduced him into local society, but although he attended a dinner party or soirée now and again, mostly he preferred the comforts of home, surrounded by his massive library containing every book imaginable.

Lucy had always enjoyed visiting Mr. Shepherd—he was incredibly knowledgeable on every subject—and she and her mother made an effort to stop by Knotting Tree most Wednesdays and Saturdays. Since she had been otherwise engaged last Wednesday and wasn't quite ready to face Lord

Drayson just yet, Lucy opted to visit Mr. Shepherd instead. It was Saturday, after all, and he would be expecting her.

She lifted her lavender skirts a bit higher to step over a fallen log that blocked the path and continued another hundred yards before breaking through the copse of trees to see Knotting Tree. It was a large and majestic house—one that Mr. Shepherd had said was far too cavernous for his tastes. But the moment he'd laid eyes on the expansive library, he couldn't see himself anywhere else. "Books feed my soul," he'd always said. "Without them, I'd be nothing but a shell."

Lucy had always found it sad he thought that. If only he could realize that people could feed one's soul too, he might not be as lonely. For he was lonely. His eyes lit up every time she and her mother came around and always dimmed when the time came for them to leave.

She held up her skirts once more to walk up the front steps, then raised the knocker and gave it a few quick raps. A moment or so later, the door opened, revealing Mr. Shepherd's rather stodgy butler.

"Hello, Geoffries," said Lucy with a bright smile. "How are you this morning?"

What was left of his dark hair stayed in exactly the same place when he bowed, as though it had been glued to his head. "I am well, Miss Beresford, thank you."

Sometimes Lucy wondered if Geoffries ever felt unwell. He was never anything but "well" and it sometimes annoyed Lucy that the man didn't seem to have any other moods, or perhaps he thought servants weren't allowed to have moods.

"I'm here to see Mr. Shepherd. Is he at home?" It was a silly question, for they both knew he was. Mr. Shepherd awoke with the sun and spent every morning ensconced in his library surrounded by the things he loved most in the world.

"Yes, Miss. He is expecting you. If you will follow me, I shall show you into the library."

"Thank you, Geoffries." Their footsteps echoed through the large foyer, and Lucy couldn't help but wonder if anyone could feel at home in such a house.

Geoffries opened one of the meticulously carved wooden doors leading into the library and announced, "Miss Beresford is here to see you, Mr. Shepherd."

Mr. Shepherd immediately set down the book he was reading and stood, removing his glasses. Though the man spent most of his days seated in his favorite winged chair or at his desk, his body still looked healthy and robust. He must pace a lot, Lucy decided. That, or he had a secret, adventurous life that she knew nothing about. Anything was a possibility with Mr. Shepherd. He was nearly a decade older than Lucy's mother, yet he still had a head full of thick, graying hair.

"Lucy, it is wonderful to see you today." He moved forward and clasped her fingers in his. "With your mother gone, I wasn't sure if I should expect a visit from you or not."

"I apologize for not coming on Wednesday."

He waved aside her words. "Never apologize for having a full and busy life. I am happy you are here now, and that is all that matters." He gestured to a nearby settee. "Have a seat, my dear, and tell me how you have fared in your mother's absence."

Lucy sank down and gave Mr. Shepherd a glowing smile. "I have decided to plant my very own vegetable garden, if you can believe it."

Mr. Shepherd took a seat next to her and lifted her hand, inspecting her fingernails and the small amount of dirt he found beneath them. "Fingernails never lie," he said.

Lucy laughed. "I did try to remove all the dirt, but it

collects in the smallest of cracks and refuses to budge. I shall have to try harder before Mother returns or she will take it upon herself to scrub them raw. I am her greatest trial, I'm afraid."

Mr. Shepherd pointed a finger at her. "Her greatest joy too, make no mistake about that."

"How very right you are, Mr. Shepherd. If I weren't such a trial to her most days, then she would never fully appreciate my rare, angelic moments, would she?"

He threw back his head and laughed, as though "angelic" was an absurd way to describe her. If Lucy wasn't so fond of Mr. Shepherd she might have taken offense.

"How you do make me laugh sometimes," he finally said. "I have always thought you should write a book about your life. It would be the most delightful of comedies."

A comedy of errors, Lucy thought, especially if she included this past week's escapades. With the way she was fumbling her life as of late, it would likely become a tragedy. A comedic tragedy. Were such tales ever written?

"Perhaps one day I shall," she answered. "But it would be for your eyes only. And Mama's, I suppose. The rest of the polite world would think me a hoydenish rustic not fit to breathe the same air as they."

"How silly they would be if they did," he said gallantly.

"You are always too kind, Mr. Shepherd. Mama and I missed you at the Bidding's house party a fortnight ago. Why did you not come?"

"A new book about herbs arrived in the post, and I made the mistake of opening it. Once I began reading, I could not put it down."

Lucy arched an eyebrow. "Admit it, Mr. Shepherd. You did not wish to put the book down because you did not wish to mingle and socialize or come up with yet another way to dissuade the attentions of a certain Mrs. Wallace. She has set her cap at you, hasn't she?"

"Yes, I'm afraid. She has made her desires quite obvious," he said with a pained expression. "I'm afraid she sees it as her duty to reform me from a recluse to a socialite."

"By becoming your wife, no doubt," said Lucy dryly.

"She hasn't said as much, but judging by the way she hangs on my arm and laughs at any comment I utter, even when it isn't remotely humorous, I would say she might be angling for something that I never intend to grant her."

Lucy watched Mr. Shepherd closely, realizing how dear he'd become to her and her family. "Do you never mean to marry again?" she asked quietly. It had been a question she had wanted to voice many times in the past but had always lacked the courage. Today though, she couldn't keep it from slipping out. She only hoped he wouldn't think her impertinent. While some opinions didn't matter at all to Lucy, his did.

Mr. Shepherd opened his mouth to respond when the door to the library opened and a footman walked in carrying a tea tray and some biscuits. Mr. Shepherd thanked the man, allowed Lucy to pour them both a cup of tea, and sipped it slowly until the footman disappeared and they were alone once more.

Lucy wondered if Mr. Shepherd would use the interruption as an excuse to talk about other things, but he didn't. He merely said, "If I do marry again, it will be for love. Not for companionship, not for social distinction, and not for money. Only for love."

"Do you never get lonely?"

He set down his tea and considered the question. "At times, I suppose, for I do look forward to your and Mrs. Beresford's visits, but my books give me ample companionship. I rarely feel alone in my library."

"Truly?" Lucy asked, for she couldn't quite believe it. She, too, enjoyed a good book, but they could not replace human connection. The feelings she had experienced when Lord Drayson had kissed her could never be mimicked in a book, no matter how good the writer. The goose bumps on her arms, the shivers down her back, the warmth that began in her belly and spread through her entire body, warming her in a way fire never could.

"You're blushing." Mr. Shepherd smiled over the rim of his teacup. "I would love to see inside that lovely head of yours right now."

Lucy set down her cup with a bit of a clatter and snatched a biscuit to nibble on. Mr. Shepherd was altogether too perceptive. She looked everywhere but at her host.

"Lucy?" he finally said. "Has something happened?"

"No," she said a little too vehemently, especially considering she still could not meet his eyes.

He chuckled and set down his cup as well, leaning against the back of the settee with his arms behind his head. "When the cat is away the mice will play, hmm?"

Lucy could feel her cheeks grow even warmer. Yes, Mr. Shepherd was far too perceptive. Did she dare confide in him? Was that the real reason she didn't want to miss their usual visit today—because she knew he would be a close second to her mother?

Lucy bit down on her lip for a moment before finally dragging her eyes to his. "I wouldn't exactly call it play."

"What would you call it then?" he questioned, watching her closely. "When the cat is away, the mice will . . . what, Lucy?"

She fiddled with the biscuit in her lap until it became a heap of crumbs. When there was nothing left to crumble, she finally blurted, "Contemplate murder, lie, steal—well, I

146

should say borrow—and, er . . . cavort with a servant, though he's not really a servant, he just believes he is."

Other than his eyes widening slightly, Mr. Shepherd's expression remained impassive. He seemed to be waiting for her to continue, and when she did not, he brushed what appeared to be a nonexistent crumb from his breeches before leaning forward and resting both elbows on his knees and fixing his gaze on her. "I couldn't help but notice that you did not include cheating among your list of sins."

Lucy blinked in surprise, not knowing what he meant by that. "I have not cheated, sir. At least not in the usual sense of the word."

"Ah," he said. "There you have it then. You are not as gone as all that. And you did say you only *contemplated* murder, correct? You didn't actually do the deed?"

"No, sir," said Lucy, feeling her spirits lift with his teasing. He wasn't shocked or appalled and didn't seem to think less of her. If only her mother would react the same way.

"Well then," said Mr. Shepherd, rubbing his hands together. "Now that you have summarized all your sins—"

"You mean confessed," interrupted Lucy.

"No, I mean summarized," he said. "I am a scholar, not a vicar, and have no use for confessions. Summaries, on the other hand, are a wonderful place to begin."

"Begin?" she asked.

"Indeed." He nodded. "You have hooked me like a fish on a line. Now please indulge this lonely old man, for I really must hear the unabridged version of the story."

Lucy set her crumb-filled plate on the table and clasped her fingers together. "Very well, Mr. Shepherd. I will tell you my story in its entirety on one condition. Once I am finished, you must promise not to call the authorities or send me off to Bedlam."

His lips twitched as he replied, "You have my word."

And so Lucy began her tale, introducing Mr. Shepherd to the dreadful man who had appeared on her doorstep only a week ago. She embellished here, exaggerated a bit there, omitted a few less important details—like a passionate kiss—and finally finished with, "So the fact of the matter is, Mr. Shepherd, that we may not be neighbors for much longer. I am fairly certain that Mother and I will need to make other living arrangements much sooner than we would like."

Lucy couldn't say when Mr. Shepherd's amused expression had dwindled into something more akin to shock, but it had. Mr. Shepherd, a man of many words, seemed quite bereft at the moment. When he finally did speak, it was to say, "Good gads, Lucy. You really ought to write a book."

"Perhaps I should," she said, feeling a return of her earlier melancholy. A heaviness settled on her shoulders, making her slouch. Everything was going to change. There was no tidily packaged outcome leaving all involved happy and content.

"When is your mother due to return?" asked Mr. Shepherd.

"Friday next," she said.

He heaved a long, drawn out sigh. "All things considered, I think Lord Drayson needs to find other accommodations as soon as possible. Georgina is not a sufficient chaperone, and if word were to ever get out . . ."

He appeared so serious—more so than Lucy had ever seen him. It frightened her. For if the usually sanguine Mr. Shepherd thought Lucy's predicament so precarious, then she really had gone too far this time. It hurt that she had so thoroughly botched her first and probably only chance to assert her independence. When would she finally learn to be wise like her mother or Mr. Shepherd? When would she ever really grow up?

"I know," Lucy managed to say. She felt like she'd regressed back to the day when she had lied about the grasshopper race to her parents and felt their disappointment in her heart. Only this time it was Mr. Shepherd who appeared disappointed. There was nothing worse than losing the respect of someone you cared about.

As if reading her thoughts, Mr. Shepherd gently picked up her hands, giving them a squeeze. "I shall come with you to explain everything to Lord Drayson if you'd like."

"Please allow me to do it," Lucy was quick to say. "I'm sure he would not appreciate an audience for such a conversation, and well . . . I should do this on my own."

"Very well," he agreed. "But you may tell him he is welcome to stay at Knotting Tree for as long as he wishes. I am here to assist you in any way I possibly can."

"Thank you." Lucy stood slowly, wishing she could return to the day she had opened the door to Lord Drayson. This time, she would not yell at him or condemn him or close the door on him. She would accept her fate as a grown woman, send a note to her mother with the distressing news, and thank the earl for what he and his father had done for the Beresfords thus far. Perhaps then he wouldn't have sped off so recklessly and taken that fateful tumble from his horse.

As Lucy walked away from Knotting Tree, she drew in a breath of nearly spring air and lifted her face to the lightest part of the sky, knowing the sun lurked behind the blanket of clouds. Despite all her regrets, she was most definitely wiser today than she had been yesterday, and that knowledge bolstered her spirits a little. Perhaps there was hope for her yet.

20

Lucy found the earl in the stables, leading Athena from her stall. He looked fresh and handsome, and the memory of the kiss they'd shared came back with a jolt. Her pulse quickened her heartbeat, and Lucy felt the sudden urge to run away. Only moments before, as she'd walked through the wilderness that separated Tanglewood from Knotting Tree, she had felt so courageous, so ready to blurt out the truth and accept the consequences of her actions. But a mere sighting of Lord Drayson sent all that courage skittering away like dozens of mice on the run.

"Yellow suits you, Miss Beresford," said the earl when he spotted her. Admiration gleamed in his eyes, and his lips quirked up in a smile. "You look like sunshine itself this morning."

"Thank you," she said, too distracted to think much of the compliment. She wished he would return to ordering her about and making demands in that high-handed way she'd once so despised. It would make confessing much easier. "I think we have moved beyond Miss Beresford, don't you? I give you leave to call me Lucy. And where are you taking Athena?"

"Your timing couldn't be more impeccable, Miss Beresford. I am about to hitch her to the cart for your next lesson. And I have been wrong to call you by your Christian name. While I am still your coachman, I'm afraid that Miss Beresford it must be."

He led the horse toward her, and although a little less intimidated by its size, Lucy still stepped back, giving Lord Drayson and Athena plenty of space. She followed at a safe distance, determined to say what needed saying and be done with it.

"That's just it, sir." She settled on calling him "sir" for the time being because she could no longer call him Collins, nor could she blurt out his title yet either. "The truth of the matter is that you are not my coachman. In actuality, you are—"

"Anxious to see you wear that ghastly hat?" he interrupted, glancing over his shoulder at her. "Of course I am. But I also promised to do my best to instruct you how to drive, and a promise is a promise, is it not? Do you also wish to learn how to hitch a horse to the cart, or will that be a lesson for another day?"

If only there would be another day to look forward to, Lucy thought sadly as she followed him toward the cart. "Before you proceed, there is something of great importance that I absolutely must say to you, and it cannot wait another moment."

He continued to harness the horse as though he hadn't heard a word she'd said, or perhaps he didn't want to hear it, which was strange. If Lucy were in his position, she would be all ears, her curiosity such that it was.

Lord Drayson finished with the horse and patted its side. "Whatever you have to say can wait until after our drive."

"No, it cannot." She folded her arms to emphasize her point, but as before, he didn't seem to care.

"Yes, it can," he said a little more firmly as held his hand out to Lucy. His mouth lifted into a smile that sent her heart racing again. "Today is not so beautiful as yesterday, but it is somewhat warm and we mustn't waste it. I propose an exhilarating drive before we plant your precious seeds."

It didn't escape Lucy's notice that a much-needed talk had not factored into his plans for the day, and she refused to allow that to happen. "And I propose we talk *now*."

He let out a sigh, but his hand remained extended toward her. "After our drive. Please, Lucy? One more drive is all I ask." It was both a plea and a compromise, and along with the use of her Christian name, Lucy felt her resistance begin to crumble. Why was he so unwilling to listen?

"Besides," he added with a smirk. "I already know what you are planning to say, and I don't wish to hear it."

"And what is it you believe I'm planning to say?" asked Lucy, suddenly anxious. Had his memory returned? No. He would be yelling at her or demanding answers. He certainly wouldn't be trying to convince her to take a ride with him. Or perhaps the reason he wanted to drive with her was because he planned to strangle her without anyone hearing and leave her body for the crickets and grasshoppers.

Lord Drayson stepped close to her, and Lucy suddenly found it very difficult to breath. Goodness, he was heavenly to look at.

He spoke slowly. "You are planning to say that you are incapable of learning the art of driving and wish to be released from our wager."

Lucy blinked at him in confusion. Surely he didn't really think such a ridiculous thing. She might be afraid of horses, but she would not stoop to the cowardly act of crying off from their wager. "I would never—"

"Prove it," he said. "Allow me to assist you into the cart and show me that you can do better than yesterday."

"I can," she blurted, for she certainly could not do any worse. "But not until—"

"No buts." He tapped his finger against her lips, causing Lucy's heart to drop to her slippers.

Her mind lost all coherent thought, and the only thing she could manage to say was a repeat of his words. "No buts."

His lips lifted into a wide smile as he took her hand in his and led her toward the cart. This time, he did not meet much resistance. She climbed slowly into the cart, feeling like she'd lost the first battle in a war she was fated to lose as well.

As soon as the earl had joined her in the cart, Lucy gathered the ribbons in her hands and immediately whipped them the way Lord Drayson had done. Much to her surprise, Athena began walking.

Her mouth parted as she glanced at the earl, first with awe and then in triumph. "Did I not tell you I would do better than yesterday?"

His hands grabbed hers and yanked them to the left to keep the cart's wheel from smashing into a fence pole. "Do not put the cart before the horse, Lu—Miss Beresford—or it will surely be your downfall."

Lucy glared at the earl before taking control of the ribbons again, this time directing her focus on Athena and where she wanted the horse to go. It went much better, and she even found herself enjoying the ride.

"Tell me, Miss Beresford," said the earl as they traveled along. "What would you do if a highwayman burst from the trees and pointed a gun at you?"

Lucy pretended not to be surprised by the question and kept her expression impassive. "I would stop Athena like this." She tugged on the reins and felt a moment's thrill when the horse ceased walking. "And then I would say to the man, 'What is it you wish to steal from me, sir? My cart? My horse? My dress? Because I'm afraid that is all I can offer, unless you would care to hear a sermon about the merits of living a life devoid of thievery. I am a vicar's daughter, you know, so I do have a great many things to say on the subject.'"

The earl laughed, and his shoulder brushed against hers, causing her arm to erupt in gooseflesh. "I almost feel sorry for the poor fellow."

"Poor fellow, indeed. He is attempting to rob me."

"Yes, and is about to receive a lecture on the importance of integrity as a result."

Integrity. Who was Lucy to offer up a sermon on that particular subject? She frowned as an oft-quoted verse from the bible came to her mind. *He that is without sin among you, let him first cast a stone.*

Lucy shouldn't be allowed to cast *that* stone.

"What if a carriage came racing toward us on the opposite side of the road?" asked Lord Drayson. "How would you respond to that?"

Perfectly content to dismiss her guilt-ridden thoughts, Lucy coaxed Athena to the side of the road. The earl only had to grab her hands once to keep the cart from falling into a ditch.

The lesson continued, and two hours later, Lucy drove up the path with far more confidence in her driving skills. After coming away from Mr. Shepherd's feeling like a silly and reckless schoolgirl, it bolstered her to finally do something right. And not just anything—Lucy could now drive a cart.

Ever since the death of her father, she had worried what

would happen to her if the same fate befell her mother. Lucy had led such a sheltered existence that she had never felt ready to be on her own. It was one of the reasons she had begged and pleaded to remain behind with Georgina. She wanted to prove to herself, and her mother, that she could manage perfectly well on her own should she wind up an orphan or a spinster. That, and Lucy did not wish to accompany her mother in the slightest. She had little desire to be trapped inside the small hovel her cousins called home. The last time she had made the journey, Lucy had vowed never to return. It had been filthy and overrun with children, two of which Lucy had to share a bed with.

In the end, Mrs. Beresford had relented, only because she knew how miserable her daughter would be if she came along. And so Lucy had stayed. Now here she was, driving a cart and getting ready to plant seeds for a vegetable garden—all due to Lord Drayson's encouragement. How very sad it was that while she had been occupied with pulling the wool over his eyes, he had, in many ways, opened hers.

The guilt gnawed at her insides as she drove the cart back to the stables and pulled Athena to an efficient stop.

The earl clapped. "Bravo, Miss Beresford. Bravo. Perhaps there is hope for you yet."

Lucy couldn't help but glow a little with the praise. As he lifted her down from the cart, she even went so far as to inquire, "Does this make me the victor of our wager? Am I free to gloat now and go fetch that hat for you to wear?"

He sat her on the ground and smiled, keeping his hands on her waist. "Gloat away, Miss Beresford. You have earned it."

"I owe it all to you." She attempted to keep her tone light, but the words sounded far more somber than playful. Lucy swallowed, knowing the time had come for their talk.

He had asked that she wait until after their drive, and she had. But before Lucy angered him with the truth, she wanted him to know how indebted she was to him. So with her hands still on his shoulders, she said, "Thank you, Col—sir, for not only teaching me to drive but for helping me with my garden and making me a little less afraid of the horses."

"I shall be glad to help you conquer your fear of the beasts completely if you'll let me," he said.

Lucy fingers fiddled with the collar of his shirt. Her next words would have him withdrawing that offer, along with his hands from around her waist. If only she could live in this fairy tale a while longer.

If only . . .

"When we first met," Lucy began, "I did not hold you in the highest of regard, and as a result, I did something—*said* something, really—that I—"

"Do you hold me in high regard now, Lucy?" He drew her nearer, and she came willingly.

"I thought you mustn't call me that," she whispered.

"It seems I cannot help it."

Lucy was fully in his arms now, her body pressed against his and more than happy to remain there. But she shouldn't. She needed to tell him the truth—now—before he did something he would undoubtedly regret.

"I'll say it again," he said, searching her face. "Do you hold me in high regard now?"

Lucy closed her eyes, not wanting to see the warmth in his eyes dwindle into anger. "The highest," she said. "But—"

She gasped as his warm lips landed on hers, silencing the words that were proving very difficult to say. This would be the last time she would ever kiss the Earl of Drayson, and so Lucy threw caution to the wind and wound her arms around his neck, returning his kiss with a fervor that would shock her mama. She wanted to remember this moment forever—remember him—so she slid her fingers through his hair, feeling each bump and curve of his head. He tasted like peach preserves and smelled of the outdoors, with that familiar hint of sandalwood.

It was a kiss of remembrance and goodbye, and Lucy held nothing back, wishing it could be a kiss of new beginnings instead.

"Lucy Beresford, get away from that man this moment!" shrilled a voice that made Lucy's stomach twist into knots. She sprang away from the earl and glanced at him only briefly before closing her eyes in shame. Of all the people who could have happened upon them now, why did it have to be Mrs. Bidding?

The woman was standing not far away with her hands on her hips, her lips puckered tightly, and her face redder than Lucy had ever seen. The shade looked dreadful against the orange ribbon tied under her chin.

"Explain yourself, sir!" she commanded the earl. "How dare you take advantage of this young woman in the absence of her mother."

Lucy peeked at Lord Drayson, surprised that he didn't appear the least embarrassed or shamefaced. How was he not trembling in fear as she was? Obviously he had never known the displeasure of Mrs. Bidding.

He cleared his throat. "You are quite right to find me at fault, Mrs. . . ."

"Bidding," the woman supplied.

"Mrs. Bidding," he repeated. "I am very much in the wrong and apologize profusely for taking advantage of such an innocent as Miss Beresford. I have no excuse other than to say that her loveliness overcame my good sense."

"You have compromised her," Mrs. Bidding said, not

one to mince words. "In her mother's stead, I must demand that you do the honorable thing by her."

Lucy's eyes widened, and she gaped at Mrs. Bidding. Surely she was not suggesting the earl make an offer of marriage for her. Good gracious! Lucy could not expose Lord Drayson now or Mrs. Bidding would surely insist on a wedding.

Feeling an urgent need to protect Lord Drayson, Lucy forced her tone to remain calm. "Would you have my coachman propose, Mrs. Bidding? As much as I appreciate you for looking after me in Mother's absence, I don't believe she would be in favor of such an alliance."

"I am your butler first, not coachman," the earl inserted, as though that should help matters, which he knew perfectly well it wouldn't.

"Your butler!" Mrs. Bidding had never looked so appalled. Her face became quite purple, which, oddly enough, had a relaxing effect on Lucy's nerves. That, or the sight of the earl's twitching lips. A serious situation suddenly became quite humorous, and Lucy had to battle the urge to laugh.

"You are a much better coachman than butler," Lucy said to the earl, "so I think that is what you shall be from here on out."

"Your mother hired a coachman?" Mrs. Bidding was obviously trying to make sense of the situation. "Why have I heard nothing of this until now?"

"I hired him," said Lucy. "Or, to be more specific, Georgy and I found him injured in the road, so we took him in as any good Christian would do. When he awoke, he could not recall his name, so I made him our coachman while we waited for his memory to return. I could see no reason for all those fine muscles to go to waste." Lucy quickly clamped her mouth shut, knowing she'd gone a trifle too far. It didn't help that the earl's shoulders were shaking with suppressed laughter.

Mrs. Bidding's eyes grew very round indeed. "Lucy, I want you to go inside and pack your trunk this instant. I am taking you home with me and posting a letter to your mother directly. As for you . . ." She glared at the earl, waiting for him to supply his name.

"Collins," he answered, meeting Mrs. Bidding's gaze unflinchingly.

"Collins," she spat his name as though he were nothing more than a chimney sweep. "You shall leave this house immediately. I never want to see your person anywhere near Miss Beresford—or Askern—again. Have I made myself clear?"

The earl's expression lost all of its humor. "Quite," he said. Then, bowing to Lucy, he added, "It's been a pleasure, Miss Beresford. I do hope we shall meet again one day."

"Not if I have anything to do with it," seethed Mrs. Bidding, taking Lucy by the arm and dragging her away.

Lucy panicked. The earl could not leave without knowing the truth. Where would he go? What would he do? When would his memory return? Lucy could not allow him to go away with no explanation, but what else could she do?

Lucy dug in her heels and attempted one last plea on the earl's behalf. "Mrs. Bidding, if I am to go with you, surely Collins can be allowed to stay—at least until his memory or my mother returns. You cannot, in good conscience, turn him away when he is still in need of our help."

"I can and I will," she answered firmly. "He has helped himself to a great deal too much from you and has brought disgrace upon you and your family. If word of this gets out you will be ruined. Do you not see that? I can only hope my coachman has more honor than this man. He should be grateful I haven't sent for the constable yet."

"But—" Lucy thought frantically, not knowing what more she could do. Mrs. Bidding was dragging her toward the house again, lengthening the distance between Lucy and Lord Drayson. All too soon, she was pulled inside.

Georgina came out of the kitchen, her brows furrowed in concern. "Is summit the matter, Miss Lucy?" she asked.

Lucy snatched her arm from Mrs. Bidding's, cast the woman a warning glance, and drew in a deep breath before facing her maid. "Will you help me pack my things, Georgy? It seems I am to go with Mrs. Bidding until Mama returns."

Georgina nodded and followed her mistress up the stairs. Mrs. Bidding brought up the rear, standing on the threshold of Lucy's bedchamber like a rigid sentinel while the two women packed. Lucy had hoped for a few minutes alone with her maid, but it was not to be.

With the help of Mrs. Bidding's groom, the trunk was carried downstairs and mounted on the back of the waiting carriage. Lucy glanced at the stables, but the earl was no longer there. Before she climbed into the carriage and sacrificed her freedom, she threw her arms around Georgina in a dramatic show of goodbye and whispered in her ear, "Lord Drayson's clothes and personal effects can be found in the bottom drawer of my wardrobe. Please see that he gets them and show him the way to Mr. Shepherd's, would you? He can explain everything." Georgina could explain as well, but Lucy did not wish to put that weighty responsibility on her sweet maid, not when Mr. Shepherd could do the job with greater ease and eloquence.

Georgina nodded, appearing relieved and yet worried as well. Lucy climbed into the carriage with heavy steps, praying everything would turn out all right. As the horses pulled Mrs. Bidding's coach down the path, Lucy peered back at an empty stable yard with far too many regrets.

If only Lord Drayson hadn't fallen from his horse. If only she hadn't told that lie. If only her heart had remained locked tight.

21

THE DAY FOLLOWING LUCY'S FORCED removal from her home, Mr. Shepherd sent a note to Lucy that read:

You may cease your fretting. All is well.
—Mr. Shepherd

Lucy frowned at the note. What did it mean, exactly? That Lord Drayson had finally been made aware of his true identity or that the Beresfords could remain in the dower house for the time being? Was Georgina busy packing while Lucy remained confined in this room?

For a scholar who loved to read lengthy works, Mr. Shepherd apparently didn't enjoy writing detailed missives. It was no wonder he had never written a book of his own.

Lucy asked Mrs. Bidding if they could call on Mr. Shepherd so that she might question him further, but Mrs. Bidding would not allow it. Nor would she allow Lucy to write a letter in return.

"You are not to have any communications with anyone outside this home until your mother returns and can oversee them," was the final word.

So Lucy had tossed Mr. Shepherd's note into the fire

and flopped down on her bed, feeling like a prisoner. Although the room Mrs. Bidding had deposited her in was grander than her own, Lucy despised the way it enshrouded her, cutting her off from the rest of the world.

Lucy was allowed to eat meals with the family and spend time in the drawing room with Mrs. Bidding, listening to lectures on proper etiquette while bettering her needlepoint and calligraphy skills, but Lucy preferred the silence of her bedchamber and remained there much of the time.

Three days into her imprisonment, Lucy was ready to escape out her window and scale down the stone wall. She had been studying the bumps and ridges beneath her window and had determined it would be possible, if not a tad dangerous, to do exactly that. So it was with great relief that she was summoned to the drawing room the morning of her fourth day. Her mother had finally arrived, and Lucy had never been so glad to see anyone.

The dark circles around Mrs. Beresford's eyes showed her weariness, but her traveling dress and bonnet looked as though she'd only just put them on. Other than a few strands of mahogany hair escaping her neat bun, she was as put-together as always.

Apparently Mrs. Bidding had taken it upon herself to enlighten Mrs. Beresford about the deplorable behavior of her only daughter, for her expression was quite grim. Lucy tried not to be annoyed that she had not been allowed to do her own confessing. Mrs. Bidding did not know the half of it, and Lucy could only imagine the embellished—and undoubtedly disparaging—rendition her mother had been made to listen to.

Mrs. Beresford sat stiffly in an armchair looking thinner than she had when she left. She eyed her daughter sternly.

"We shall talk when we get home, Lucille. Please thank Mrs. Bidding for looking after you and collect your things."

Lucy obediently curtsied to her hostess. "Thank you, Mrs. Bidding. I shall be forever in your debt." She hoped it sounded more sincere than it felt. Then she picked up her skirts and practically ran from the room. Her mother would undoubtedly impart many lectures of her own, but Lucy couldn't deny that she was thrilled to go home.

Once they were seated in the carriage and moving in the direction of home, Lucy asked, "How is Aunt Beth and the new baby?"

Her mother sighed. "She finally gave birth to the boy they have desperately wanted and is healing nicely."

"That's happy news," said Lucy, mustering her most cheerful tone.

"If only I could have arrived home to equally happy news." Her mother eyed her with a look that said, *I had better like your version of events more than Mrs. Bidding's, or you will find yourself locked in another tower.*

Lucy swallowed and stared out the window, knowing her mother would not find much to like in Lucy's version either. She felt every rut and bump during the long ride home. Georgina greeted them on the doorstep, helped to lug in Lucy's trunk, and said she had some tea and scones ready if they would like some refreshment.

With her hand on the banister, Mrs. Beresford drew in a deep breath. "I should like to clean up first, Georgy. I need to cleanse my body and my mind before I partake of your wonderful tea with my daughter."

Her daughter. Mrs. Beresford couldn't even bring herself to use Lucy's name.

"I'll keep it warm for you, Mrs. Beresford," said Georgy. "Do you need any assistance?"

"I can manage on my own, thank you." Without even glancing at *her daughter*, Mrs. Beresford walked upstairs, her movements slow and heavy. Lucy felt immediately penitent. Her mother had spent nearly two weeks helping a sister in need, only to be greeted with worse troubles at home, and all because Mrs. Beresford had made the mistake of trusting her fully-grown daughter.

Lucy looked at Georgina in a solemn way. "Well, Georgy, it seems my plan to save us was an utter failure in every way. I should have listened to you."

Georgina offered a look of sympathy, then nodded her head in the direction of the kitchen. "I baked a cake to celebrate your and Mrs. Beresford's return. It's been awful quiet 'round 'ere. Want a slice?"

Lucy answered with a forced smile of her own. "Is it lemon?"

"Is there any ovver kind?"

"If there is, there should not be." Lucy's smile felt more genuine now. "I would love a slice, Georgy. A big one."

Georgina led the way, cutting Lucy a large slice and herself a small one when Lucy insisted she join her.

"Tell me what happened with Lord Drayson," said Lucy, savoring the rich flavor of Georgina's wonderful lemon cake while trying not to appear too anxious for news of the man.

Georgina frowned. "I don't know much. I gave 'im 'is things and showed 'im the path through the woods ter Mr. Shepherd's. I 'aven't seen 'im since. Is there any news from Knottin' Tree?"

"Only a short note saying, 'All is well.'"

"All is well?" Georgina asked. "Wot does 'e mean by that?"

"I haven't the slightest notion," said Lucy. "It is perplexing, is it not?"

Georgina nodded, appearing disappointed as well, and no wonder. Lord Drayson had become a friend to both of them, and Georgina had probably been as anxious for news as Lucy.

"As soon as I am able, I will pay a visit to Mr. Shepherd," Lucy promised. "I take it you've received no notice of eviction as of yet?"

"Eviction?" said a voice from behind. "What on earth are you talking about, Lucy?"

Lucy's body froze, and Georgina hopped up and began to clear away the dishes. "Would you like some cake wif your tea, Mrs. Beresford?" she asked, giving Lucy a few moments to compose herself.

Lucy's mother ignored Georgina, directing a hard look at her daughter instead. "Lucy, it is time for you to explain yourself. I must know what has occurred in my absence."

Lucy blew out a breath and nodded before slowly pushing herself to her feet. The positive effects of the lemon cake faded in an instant. The time for reckoning had come. "Let's adjourn to the yellow room, Mother. Georgy can bring us some tea, and we can . . . talk."

And talk they did. Seated in the room that had once been covered in ash and soot, Lucy told her mother all, beginning with the moment the earl had arrived on her doorstep and ending with the high-handed way Mrs. Bidding had carted her off, treating her like a misbehaving child. As with her rendition to Mr. Shepherd, the only elements Lucy kept to herself were the two kisses. One did not speak of such things to one's mother, especially if one's mother was the widow of a vicar.

"I know you will likely never trust me again, Mother, and I do not blame you, but . . . well, there are no buts, really. I simply appreciate that you listened to the full account. Mrs.

Bidding did not ask, not that I would have told her if she had."

Throughout it all, she had shown no sign of emotion, not even when Lucy had mentioned the fact that they would be without a home soon. Her mother had merely sat erect and sipped her tea. Her biscuits and slice of cake remained untouched on her plate.

"Was that the full accounting?" Mrs. Beresford asked, her eyebrow lifted in question.

Lucy looked down at her lap, knowing what her mother hinted at. Unfortunately, Mrs. Bidding had been party to one of the scenes Lucy would have kept a secret forever.

"Not quite," she grudgingly admitted, feeling her face burn as though it had been touched by the sun. "The earl, er . . ."

"Kissed you?" her mother said, far more bluntly than Lucy had ever heard her speak.

Lucy's eyes flew to hers. She was surprised to see a hint of humor in them. "Yes."

Mrs. Beresford nodded, immediately masking her feelings once again. "Mrs. Bidding implied that it was quite a passionate embrace."

Curse Mrs. Bidding and her prying eyes and wagging tongue! Lucy thought crossly, feeling her face grow even warmer.

"Perhaps it was," Lucy admitted, quieter this time. She offered no excuses for her behavior because she had none to offer. She had surrendered to a strong temptation, and though she was sorry for behaving so unseemly, she wasn't sorry about the kiss. She had enjoyed the earl's affections immensely and would hold onto those memories until the day she departed this earth.

What is to be my punishment, Mother? she wanted to

blurt out. *Please get on with it so that we can be done with this awkwardness.*

Once again, her mother surprised her. "Mrs. Bidding said you kissed a coachman, not an earl," she said.

"Mrs. Bidding knows only what little she saw. I did not think it wise to enlighten her further."

Her mother cocked her head and gazed at her daughter. "Even though she would have insisted that he do the honorable thing by you?"

Lucy set her jaw and lifted her chin. "You don't intend to ask such a thing of the earl, do you Mama? That is not the way I wish to enter into matrimony."

For a brief moment, Lucy thought she saw a spark of pride in her mother's eyes, but Mrs. Beresford set her teacup on the table and when she looked up again, it was gone.

"Lucy, there is something I haven't told you before, something I hadn't planned on telling you at all. But I believe I will now." Mrs. Beresford smoothed the folds of her skirt with her palms. "Your father and I didn't have what you'd call a regular courtship. One afternoon, he accompanied his sister into a shop where I worked, and it was I who helped his sister choose a design and fabrics. Not two days later he returned on his own, saying he wished to commission a new pair of gloves for his mother and would like to speak to Miss Julia Jenkins about the purchase. He actually called me 'Miss' if you can believe it, and that became the first of many purchases."

The glow in her mother's eyes faded into a sadness that intrigued Lucy. "Rumors soon began. Talk. Whispers. People believed that your father and I . . . well, I couldn't blame them, really. No one of his standing would ever consider taking a mere seamstress to wife, so what else was there to think?"

As comprehension came, Lucy's mouth parted and righteous indignation took its ugly hold. "That you were just as respectable, if not more so, than any woman of the gentry. How dare they!"

Mrs. Beresford leaned forward and took her daughter's hand in hers. "Lucy, there are expectations in this world. Rules of decorum. If you do not heed them, there are consequences to pay. You may think Mrs. Bidding did you a disservice by carrying you away and keeping you confined until I returned, but in reality she did you a great service. She kept your reputation safe. It was I who did you a disservice by leaving you here alone with only Georgina as a chaperone, and for that, I hold only myself to blame."

Lucy felt any hope at future independence float away, like a dandelion on the breeze, sailing above her head and out of reach.

"As soon as I learned of the gossip about your father and I," her mother continued, "I asked him to cease his attentions towards me. But he wouldn't hear of it, and I, young and inexperienced as I was, didn't insist. So we began to see each other in secret. For a time it was exciting and thrilling, and I fancied myself quite in love with your father. But one horrible night, we were discovered embracing, much like Mrs. Bidding discovered you and the earl. Only in my situation, word spread, and what little reputation I had left became tattered beyond repair. I was considered a fallen woman. I lost my job and my dignity, and when my parents allowed me to remain under their roof, they were shunned as well. Your father felt dreadful and insisted on doing the honorable thing to save me from ruin, and so we were married."

"He would not have offered for you if he hadn't loved you, Mama," inserted Lucy, feeling fiercely protective of her parents all of a sudden. She had always supposed they had married for love and did not care what others said about their differences in station. It was a sad blow to discover that the reason her parents had married was because they *had* cared.

No, Lucy refused to believe that. Her parents would have married in time. They had loved each other too much to ever walk away.

"Oh, he did love me in a way, I suppose," continued her mother. "And that love grew stronger and deeper as the years passed. But he lost so much in marrying me. Your papa had great dreams of fighting for his country and proving himself a hero. Your grandfather was prepared to purchase his colors for him, but when your father offered for me, his family cut him off, and all of his dreams went away. The only reason we are in this house now is because the current Earl of Drayson's grandfather was an old family friend. He took pity on us and offered us a living in Askern. It was truly good of him, and we were most grateful, but it also served to sever the friendship the old earl once shared with your father's family." A small smile lifted the corners of her mouth. "The old earl once said that he may have lost a friend in the bargain, but he gained another son. And better a son than a friend."

Lucy sat back in her chair, shocked and speechless. She had no idea her parents had such a distressing past. They'd always seemed so blissfully happy, so perfectly suited to the life that, as it turned out, had been forced on them.

"Your father told me he had no regrets and that he would have offered for me eventually," said Mrs. Beresford softly. "But I always wondered if that was the truth of it. He would have gone off to war, fought a valiant battle, and lived the life he was meant to live. Whether or not that would have included me, I do not know. Yes, we grew to love each other dearly and had a wonderful life together—you brought us both so much joy—but I would not wish the same beginning on you. So in answer to your question, no, I would never attempt to force the earl's hand. I would, however, like to ring a peal over his head and turn him over my knee."

Lucy's lips lifted slightly. "He is a good man, Mama. It was I who behaved unpardonably."

"Obviously I cannot rake you over the coals either, considering your papa and I shared several kisses before we were discovered, but I am grateful it was Mrs. Bidding who happened upon you and not someone else. She may be a bit stern and domineering at times, but a more loyal friend I cannot claim."

Lucy appreciated her mother's perspective of the events. It gave her a grudging respect for Mrs. Bidding, and Lucy was determined to send the woman a note of thanks as soon as she could. But she still had one more matter of business to discuss with her mother.

"Mama, are you not at all concerned about losing this house? I am certain the earl was quite upset when he learned of my deception, and at any moment we could—" Lucy stopped talking when she saw the dismissive wave of her mother's hand.

"We will come out all right, my dear," assured her mother.

"How can you be so certain?" Lucy asked. "You do not know the earl as I."

"No, but I do know Mr. Shepherd," she said with a hint of hesitancy in her voice.

Lucy frowned, not understanding what Mr. Shepherd had to do with anything.

Mrs. Beresford began hesitantly. "Do you recall when

we last visited Mr. Shepherd together and he asked to have a private word with me?"

Lucy nodded. "Are you referring to the ball he wished to host for me?"

Her mother blushed. "That was a falsehood, I'm afraid, because I did not wish to tell you the true nature of our conversation."

"Mother." Lucy tried to sound properly appalled, though deep inside, her heart warmed. All these revelations made Lucy feel less like a troublesome daughter and more like a confidant and friend. She had never felt closer to her mother.

"Mr. Shepherd did not offer to throw you a ball," her mother said carefully. "Rather, he made an offer for my hand. Apparently, he's been harboring a tendré for me for quite some time, and . . . needless to say I was rather shocked."

"You are to marry Mr. Shepherd?" Lucy gasped, feeling overcome. She tried to picture Mr. Shepherd and her mother locked in a passionate embrace and immediately wished she hadn't.

"I merely told him that I needed some time to think about it and that I would give him my answer after I returned from my sister's, once I had a chance to speak with you."

"And what have you determined?" Lucy asked, not knowing how she should feel about this latest revelation.

Her mother sighed. "To be honest, not much. I have only ever thought of Mr. Shepherd as a kind neighbor, not a prospective husband. I had planned to explain that I needed more time to see if I could come to think of him in a romantic way. He is so different than your father. But now . . . well, it seems I am destined to enter into another marriage out of necessity rather than desire." She smiled as she said the words, but Lucy's heart broke for her only remaining parent. Her mother had been down such a road before. It wasn't fair she be required to go that way again.

"Surely there is something else we can—"

"It will be all right, Lucy," said her mother, giving her hand a squeeze. "Mr. Shepherd is a good man and a lively conversationalist. I am confident that, in time, I will develop tender feelings for him as well. He has been so good to us."

Lucy suddenly felt more grown up than she had the day her mother had left her alone with Georgina. She realized then that maturity had little to do with independence and more to do with discovering that life wasn't all roses and lilies. It included thistles and thorns and complexities that a grown person faced head-on, with poise and courage, like her mother was doing now.

Still, Lucy wasn't ready to allow her mother to take on this latest complexity—at least not yet. "I think you should hold off giving Mr. Shepherd your answer for now," said Lucy. "Let us first wait to see how Lord Drayson retaliates."

"Is that fair to Mr. Shepherd, do you think?" Mrs. Beresford asked quietly.

"Is it fair to marry him when your reasons for doing so are different than his?" Lucy countered.

"No," came her mother's answer, her mouth drawn down in a frown.

"Then let us wait and hope and pray," said Lucy. "I have come to learn that Lord Drayson does, indeed, have a heart. Perhaps, once his rage has cooled, he will allow his heart to rule his head and will let us remain in the dower house." Although Lucy's voice sounded confident, deep down she felt like she was standing in an open field during a thunderstorm waiting for the lightning to strike.

THE FOLLOWING MORNING, LUCY awoke early and made her way to Mr. Shepherd's, anxious to interrogate him about his encounter with the earl and what he had meant by "All is well." Unfortunately, all was not well in Knotting Tree. Mr. Shepherd had come down with a dreadful cold and had confined himself to his bedchamber.

"I hope he recovers soon," Lucy told the butler, trying to persuade herself that she was distressed by the news because she was concerned for Mr. Shepherd's welfare and not because it meant waylaying a conversation she very much wanted to have. But the sad truth of the matter was that she was as much concerned with her own welfare as Mr. Shepherd's. What a sorry excuse for a vicar's daughter she made.

Guilt-ridden, Lucy walked back to her home and, with Georgina's help, made Mr. Shepherd some apricot cakes— one of his favorite snacks. It gave her mind something to think about, her hands something to do, and served to lessen her guilt somewhat. As she stacked them carefully in a basket, her mother walked into the kitchen.

"My goodness, I slept late, didn't I?" said Mrs.

Beresford, stealing a treat and popping it into her mouth. "You must think me a complete lazybones."

Lucy kissed her mother's cheek. "Perfectly understandable after the trying few weeks you've had. Mr. Shepherd is ill, so Georgy and I have made him some cakes, which I shall deliver to his butler straightaway. We left a few extra for you because we know they're a favorite of yours as well."

Mrs. Beresford's forehead puckered. "Is he very ill?"

"No. I believe he's just a bit under the weather is all. Geoffries thinks he should feel up to receiving visitors the first part of next week."

"Very well. Take those treats to him, and let Geoffries know I will stop in to see him on Monday. Have we received any correspondence today?"

Lucy draped a napkin over the plate and said, "Not from Lord Drayson if that is what you mean. But there is a stack of letters in the study that came while you were away."

Her mother sank down on a stool and sampled yet another cake. "Those can wait a few minutes. I find myself quite famished this morning, and I intend to enjoy these delicious treats. Georgy, you are a wonder in the kitchen."

Georgina blushed with pleasure. "Thank you, ma'am. Me ma says I could be a cook in a great kitchen, and I tell 'er I wouldn't get treated nearly so good elsewhere."

Mrs. Beresford covered the maid's hand with her own. "You're a dear, Georgy. I am certain you're as concerned about having to leave the dower house as we, but I want you to know that you will always have a place with us if that is your wish."

A look of relief and joy lit Georgina's face. "Thank you, Mrs. Beresford. That is 'appy news for sure."

Lucy realized that she could have put Georgina's

worries to rest hours ago, but she had been too caught up with her own concerns to spare a thought for her maid. Mrs. Beresford, on the other hand, always put the troubles of others ahead of her own, and someday, Lucy vowed, she would learn to be more like her mother.

Basket in hand, Lucy slipped out the door and tilted her face toward the sun. It peeked through the clouds, teasing and taunting her as she traveled once more to Knotting Tree. When she broke through the trees and spotted the large stone house, she felt a renewed sense of peace that quieted the more selfish side of her. She could wait to speak with Mr. Shepherd until he had fully recovered. And when she saw him again, it would be as a caring friend and not an anxious neighbor ready to pounce.

After she had delivered the cakes, Lucy planted the seeds in her new garden. She took her time, sowing them in neat rows and even went so far as to carve the name of the vegetables into wooden stakes so that she could remember where she had planted which seeds. Then she watered each row with a rusty watering can and tried her best not to think of Lord Drayson as she hummed.

The weekend was a gloomy one, filled with thick gray skies, chilly temperatures, and rain—all of which kept Lucy confined indoors. The inner peace she had clung to with such relief began to fade as more days passed with no word from Lord Drayson. Even her mother seemed on edge, unable to sit for long periods of time and in a constant state of distraction. Lucy had tried to engage her in a conversation or two, but after repeating herself for the third time, she gave up.

The rain finally let up Tuesday morning, and Lucy stopped on the threshold of the yellow room to behold a glimpse of blue sky out the window. In the fireplace, the logs snapped and crackled, and the memory of the earl covered in soot and ash assailed her. Lucy's face became warm as she thought of another moment they'd shared on the rug. From the garden and stables to the kitchen and this room, every spot held a memory that Lucy could not shake no matter how hard she tried.

In the beginning, it had been about not losing this wonderful house that she and her mother called home. But as she glanced around and allowed the memories to flow, Lucy realized that it had become about a great deal more. It wasn't just her home she stood to lose. She had also lost someone who had become very dear to her, and that hurt worst of all.

Footsteps sounded on the stairs, and Lucy turned to see her mother coming down, tugging on a pair of worn kid gloves.

"Going somewhere?" asked Lucy.

"Knotting Tree. Now that the rain has let up, I would like to see how Mr. Shepherd is getting on. Would you care to accompany me? I asked Georgy to hitch Athena to the cart after breakfast, so it should be ready for us."

"Er . . ." Despite Lucy's resolve to care more about Mr. Shepherd's physical health than her own emotional well being, she desperately wished to speak to him. But her mother needed to speak with him as well about other, more personal, matters—matters that could not be discussed with Lucy in the room.

"I would very much love your company, my dear," said her mother, as though she could read her daughter's mind.

"Are you certain?" Lucy asked.

"Very certain. Perhaps we can learn what we are to expect from Lord Drayson when we finally do receive word from him."

Lucy nodded. "I would be happy to accompany you, Mama. But should you need a few moments alone with Mr. Shepherd, simply say the word and I shall take the footpath home."

"You will do no such thing. It will be a mucky mess after all that rain. Besides, whatever I have to say to Mr. Shepherd can wait another day or two. In fact, it probably ought to wait as I do not yet have an answer for him."

Mrs. Beresford remained in the foyer while Lucy ran to retrieve her gloves and shawl. Together they walked down the front steps to where Georgina stood holding tightly to Athena's halter.

"May I drive, Mama?" Lucy asked, anxious to display her recently acquired skills with the ribbons.

Her mother shot her a look of surprise. "You want to drive?"

"Yes. I may not be so proficient as you, but thanks to Lord Drayson, I am confident I can get us to Knotting Tree without incident. He challenged me to learn to drive, and I have." More memories came. The wager she'd made with Lord Drayson. Riding bareback with his arms about her. His smile, his laugh, his warm breath on her neck.

Mrs. Beresford cleared her throat, and Lucy glanced up to see her mother already on the seat. She gestured to the ribbons. "Very well then. Let us see how accomplished you've become."

Lucy quickly climbed into the cart and lifted the reins, saying to Georgina, "Hopefully we shall be back with some news."

"I cannot wait to 'ear it, Miss." Georgina gave a quick curtsy, and Lucy encouraged Athena into a slow saunter. It probably took longer to drive to Knotting Tree than it had ever taken to walk the path through the trees, but the road was a little dryer.

"I must say, I'm impressed," said Mrs. Beresford when they arrived. "Well done, my dear. Did Lord Drayson teach you anything else?"

Lucy immediately thought of his kisses and heat rushed to her face. "Only that I should not give up on a plot of garden, that I should never show fear to an animal, and that I should always tell the truth."

A humorous gleam appeared in her mother's eyes. "And did you teach him anything?"

Lucy cast her mother a mischievous look. "Yes, as a matter of fact. I taught him how to pick a lock with a hairpin."

Mrs. Beresford chuckled softly. "I should very much like to meet this Earl of Drayson someday. He has me most intrigued." A familiar stable boy materialized from somewhere, and Mrs. Beresford accepted his help as she stepped down from the cart. Beneath a mop of sandy curls, the boy was small and thin and couldn't be much more than twelve or thirteen.

"Thank you, Roddy," Mrs. Beresford said to the boy. How she knew his name, Lucy had no idea, but it was yet another thing that made her proud of her Mama.

The boy blushed and dipped his head, saying, "Mr. Shepherd says we's ter treat the Beresfords like royal folk."

A gentle smile touched her lips. "Did he now?"

"Aye, Mrs. Beresford. That 'e did."

The ladies were ushered inside by Geoffries and shown into the morning room. Mr. Shepherd sat in a large armchair by a blazing fire holding a book, which he set down the moment he spied them.

He shifted forward as though to rise, but Mrs. Beresford quickly lifted her hand. "Please do not stand on our account, Mr. Shepherd. You are still recovering from your illness and ought to conserve your strength."

He ignored her and rose, albeit a mite slower than usual, then arched an eyebrow at Mrs. Beresford. "What is this, Juliet? I make you an offer of marriage and suddenly you think you can order me about, is that it? If you must know, I will always stand for you, my dear."

"Honestly, Mr. Shepherd." Lucy's mother blushed rosily, whether from the compliment or the frank way Mr. Shepherd spoke of his offer, Lucy did not know. She held back a smile.

"I thought we agreed that you would call me Stephen," said Mr. Shepherd.

"And I thought we agreed that you would say nothing more on the subject of marriage until I was ready to speak of it," Mrs. Beresford shot back.

"Ah, but you broke our agreement first by calling me Mr. Shepherd, thus allowing me to bring up my offer, which you have yet to accept, I might add. Perhaps I will apply to Lucy for help in persuading you. We would make the perfect match, would we not, Lucy? The reclusive scholar and the beautiful, kind, and vivacious widow. I must say I am quite sold on the idea."

"I'm beginning to think I am as well." Lucy laughed. It was beyond delightful to see her mother color and squirm under such attention. When was the last time any man had publicly noticed her?

"Stephen, you must stop, or my answer will be an emphatic no."

He grinned. "And if I do stop?"

"Then I will finally be able to inquire about your health."

His eyes still sparkling with humor, he settled back in his seat and steepled his fingers against his chin. "No need to inquire, Juliet. As you can see, I am perfectly well."

"You look a mite pale and weak," said Mrs. Beresford. "Perhaps you should lie down. We can return tomorrow or the next day."

"No," blurted Lucy at the same time Mr. Shepherd said, "I'd rather you stay."

Lucy clamped her mouth shut while Mr. Shepherd turned his appraising eye on her. "I know why *I* do not wish to lie down, but why do you not wish me to, Lucy?"

It was Lucy's turn to squirm. If only she could be as selfless and patient as her mother. "It's just that . . . well, sir, you look perfectly robust to me. I think it would be a shame for you to sleep away such a beautiful morning." There, Lucy congratulated herself. That sounded much better than *Because I refuse to leave this house until you explain to me exactly what transpired between you and Lord Drayson.*

"Yes," Mr. Shepherd said, a slow smile appearing on his face. "My thoughts exactly. Now then, shall I ring for some tea?"

"I would love some," said Lucy, clasping her fingers together and wondering how she could delicately bring up the subject of Lord Drayson. She waited as he put the request to Geoffries, but the moment the butler left the room, Lucy inquired, "Have you had any visitors lately, Mr. Shepherd?" She attempted a nonchalant tone and purposefully kept her gaze away from her mother's. Fishing for information was not very ladylike.

"I do not know," came Mr. Shepherd's reply. "Until this morning, I've been ensconced in my bedchamber for days, though it felt more like weeks. If I did receive visitors, Geoffries no doubt turned them away."

"What about before you fell ill?" prodded Lucy, quickly adding, "It seems an age since I've last spoken with you. Surely something exciting has happened to you between then and now."

A gleam appeared in Mr. Shepherd's eyes as though he knew exactly to what she was referring and planned to tease her about it. "Not that I can recall at the moment."

Lucy tried again. "Have you been introduced to any new acquaintances of late?"

Mr. Shepherd chuckled and finally nodded. "Now that I think on it, the Earl of Drayson did stop by for a chat some days ago."

Lucy had reached the end of her patience. "Mr. Shepherd, for heaven's sake please stop this nonsense and tell me what it is you said to Lord Drayson."

"Lucy has been most anxious over the matter, Stephen," added Mrs. Beresford.

Maybe it was Lucy's pleading tone or the fact that Mrs. Beresford had made the request, but Mr. Shepherd finally ceased his teasing. "I am afraid I don't have much to tell you. Our conversation was quite brief."

"You did tell him his name, did you not?" Lucy pressed, hoping the earl was not wandering about somewhere, oblivious to his true identity.

"There was no need," said Mr. Shepherd. "The gentleman already knew his name. Geoffries announced him as Colin Cavendish, the Earl of Drayson."

"What?" Lucy's eyes widened. How could that be? Georgina had not said anything; she would have told Lucy as much. Perhaps he had found a calling card in his purse with his name written on it. Yes, that must be it.

"What is it you spoke to him about?" Mrs. Beresford asked, interrupting Lucy's thoughts.

"As I said, not much. He merely wished for me to know that he had regained his full memory and that he needed to return to Danbury."

Lucy's brow furrowed at this news. His full memory had

returned? When? Perhaps when he had spied his name on his calling card—if, indeed, he had? How long, exactly, had Colin Cavendish known he was Lord Drayson? Her brow furrowed as she thought about her last days with him. The way he had continually put her off told Lucy it had likely been longer than she thought.

"What about the house?" pressed Lucy. "And my deception and . . ." *me?* she thought, unable to voice her last concern out loud. Her frown deepened as she realized the ridiculousness of such a thought. Had she honestly believed Lord Drayson had grown to care for her as she had him? Not only did he not wish to remain in Askern, but he was a lord and she the poor daughter of a vicar.

"As to the house, I do not know," Mr. Shepherd continued. "Lord Drayson did not confide his plans to me. The only thing I can tell you is that he did not seem angry or upset, merely guarded."

So much for getting answers, Lucy thought dismally. The waiting was not over, nor the fretting either. How long did Lord Drayson plan to wait before he showed his hand? Hopefully not too long. Lucy could not continue to live life normally when so much could be taken away at a moment's notice. Perhaps she and her mother should begin preparations to leave the dower house as soon as possible. But where would they go?

Mr. Shepherd leaned forward and, in a rare moment of earnestness, said, "I hope you both know that should you find yourself without a home, I will help you in any way that I can, whether or not you agree to marry me, Juliet."

Lucy's heart warmed at his words. Yes, Mr. Shepherd was a good man. Lucy had always known as much, but now she hoped her mother would come to see him in a romantic light—not because he could provide for them better than they could themselves but because Lucy sincerely believed he could make her mother happy.

"Thank you, Stephen," said Mrs. Beresford quietly, obviously touched by his kindness as well.

The door opened, and the jolly and slightly plump housekeeper entered, carrying a large tray filled with all sorts of pastries and tea. Mr. Shepherd brightened. "Excellent timing, Mrs. Holmes. You have saved us from becoming far too sentimental. Tea will be just the thing to restore liveliness, will it not, Mrs. Beresford?"

"Indeed it will, sir—"

"Stephen," he interrupted.

"Stephen," she said. "Thank you so much, Mrs. Holmes. This looks wonderful."

The housekeeper clasped her hands together. "Will there be anything else?"

"No, thank you," said Mrs. Beresford before realizing her mistake. "I mean . . ." Her face reddened in embarrassment.

Mr. Shepherd had never looked so pleased in all his life. The grin he wore was almost too large for his face. "Mrs. Beresford is quite right, Mrs. Holmes. We will never expire from hunger with you around."

The housekeeper bobbed a curtsy and quit the room.

Only after the door shut behind Mrs. Holmes did Mr. Shepherd give voice to the thoughts that made his eyes dance in merriment. "Trying on the role of matron, are you, Juliet? How does it feel?"

"Quite uncomfortable if you must know," she quipped.

Lucy laughed, wondering why she had never thought of Mr. Shepherd and her mother in this way. It seemed so obvious now, like a blurry scene made suddenly clear. She only hoped that her mother would soon see clarity as well.

23

MARCH BLENDED INTO APRIL and April into May. The weather changed almost daily, teasing Lucy with sunshine one day and rain the next and changing her mood as well. She felt like she was walking over uneven stepping stones—up, down, and up again.

Tiny leaves began to emerge from the dirt, much to Lucy's delight, but only until she remembered that the garden may not be hers for much longer, and down she went again. The days stretched on almost painfully as the Beresfords attempted to live life normally, accepting dinner invitations, attending musicales, and entertaining visitors, all the while not knowing what their future held. It was most vexing and tiresome, and Lucy was ready to write the earl herself and ask the question that continued to plague her mind. *Are we to be out of the house or have you had a change of heart?*

No news meant what, exactly?

Meanwhile, Mr. Shepherd had taken up his suit of Mrs. Beresford in earnest. He visited the dower house almost daily, sent flowers or a plate of Mrs. Beresford's favorite pastries, and even began making regular appearances at social gatherings. He went from being a reclusive scholar to a dashing suitor, and the entire town was buzzing and speculating about his increased attentions toward Mrs. Beresford.

One particular evening in early May, Lucy and her mother traveled home from a small dinner party hosted by none other than Mr. Shepherd. He'd been all that was engaging and charming, even arranging transportation for the Beresfords to and from the event in his comfortable coach.

As the coach rumbled along, carrying the two women back home, Lucy noticed the joy and contentment written across her mother's face. "You're becoming more and more partial to Mr. Shepherd, are you not, Mama? I can see it in your eyes."

Mrs. Beresford shook her head slowly as though still uncertain of her feelings. She peered out the darkened window, her voice pensive. "What sort of man makes an offer of marriage first and courts second?"

"The sort who wants to make his desires known from the very beginning, then reinforce them while patiently waiting for the lady to come around. How long do you plan to keep him in suspense, Mama?"

Her mother dropped her gaze to her hands and fiddled with the straps of her reticule. "I must admit, I have grown quite fond of the man. It is wonderful to be publicly sought after by someone who seems so certain of what he wants."

"He is certain, mama. What he wants is you."

"He has made that quite clear, hasn't he?" She chuckled lightly. But her smile soon wilted as she met her daughter's eyes. "Your father once sought me out as well, only in secret, and what he wanted most was to go off to battle. In many ways, I feel as though I'm experiencing the opposite of what I have lived through in the past."

"And the problem is?"

Mrs. Beresford lifted her head, and the piercing look in her eyes went straight to Lucy's heart. "We were lucky, you know. Your father and I grew to love each other deeply. What if the opposite holds true for Mr. Shepherd and me?" Her voice was so quiet, Lucy could barely hear the words above the noise of the carriage wheels and horse hooves.

"What if it doesn't?" countered Lucy. "What if this is simply a better start to another chapter of a wonderful life?"

"If I knew that for certain, I would accept his proposal tomorrow."

Lucy sat back and glanced out the window, watching the shadows of the trees dance in the moonlight. "Can you ever be certain of anything?"

Silence met her question, along with a gentle sigh. "I suppose not," Mrs. Beresford finally said. "Goodness, I'm beginning to wonder who is the mother and who is the daughter."

"Oh, Mama." Lucy leaned forward and clasped her mother's hands. "You will always be my mother, I will always be your daughter, and we will always help each other. That is the way of things, is it not?"

Mrs. Beresford gave Lucy's fingers a hearty squeeze. "These past few months as I have watched you, I feel as though I've witnessed a rose grow from a delicate bud into something so much more. What an exquisite flower you are turning out to be, my dear."

Unexpected tears came to Lucy's eyes. She had to blink quickly to keep them at bay. "A mother should not make her daughter cry," she teased.

Mrs. Beresford smiled and sat back. Despite the darkness that surrounded them, her eyes shone with light that Lucy hadn't seen since her father first became ill. "Do you recall the lie I once told you about Mr. Shepherd offering to throw you a ball?"

"Yes," said Lucy hesitantly.

"Well, tonight he has made me an honest woman. He informed me that he would like to host a ball in your honor."

"What?" Lucy gasped, feeling a knot tighten her stomach. A ball? Perhaps if there was a man she would like to stand up with, Lucy might be excited about the prospect, but there were not a plethora of dashing young men in Askern. Lucy would prefer a picnic or a dinner party any day.

"He says it is past time for you to have a ball of your own and wanted to know if it would be improper for him to host one on your behalf."

"What did you say?" Lucy asked, all the while thinking, *Please say you told him no.*

"I said that it was good of him to think of you, but an arrangement like that would be most improper as I am not his wife and he is not your relative."

Lucy sighed in relief. At least until her mother added, "But I believe I spoke too hastily."

"What?"

"I have made my decision," pronounced Mrs. Beresford. "Tomorrow, I shall accept Mr. Shepherd's suit and marry him as soon as he would like."

Ball forgotten, Lucy flew from her seat and threw her arms around her mother. "Oh, how wonderful! You know he will likely go straightaway to procure a special license, if he does not already have one."

"Then so be it," said her mother, patting Lucy's knee once she'd settled on the seat beside her. "We have been living for too many weeks with a cloud hovering over our heads. It is time for that to end. As soon as we have settled on a date for the wedding, I would like you to write Lord

Drayson and inform him that we will be removed from the dower house by that day. Stephen has offered us his heart, his protection, and his home, and I find that I am quite thrilled to accept it now."

"I'm thrilled as well," said Lucy, her heart soaring high. "This has turned out to be a happy night, indeed."

"Yes. And once Stephen and I are married," inserted her mother, "we can throw you a ball together, as husband and wife. What do you think of that? "

And down went Lucy yet again.

24

DEAR LORD DRAYSON,

I hope this missive finds you well. I would like to inform you that my mother is to be married in two weeks' time, on the ninth day of June. I understand that you wished for us to be out of the dower house by the first part of May, but I am hopeful that you will be so kind as to allow us to stay until my mother becomes Mrs. Shepherd, at which point we will remove ourselves from your house and take up residence at the neighboring estate of Knotting Tree.

> *Yours sincerely,*
> *Miss Lucy Beresford*

Lucy signed her name with a flourish, reread the note, and immediately crushed it into a ball and tossed it in the fireplace, adding it to the dozen smoldering balls already there. They were all the same. Brief, curt, and without feeling, as though she and the earl were mere business acquaintances. Lucy didn't want to be brief or curt, yet so much uncertainty dangled between them that she didn't know how else she could be. If he had bothered to communicate with her, would his letter have been brief and curt or would he have been more personal, which is how she would very much want it to be?

Lucy sighed, knowing one fact for certain. She was the poor daughter of a vicar who had no right sending a letter of a personal nature to an earl. So she pulled out a clean piece of paper and began anew. Once again, she signed her name, this time without a flourish, and sealed it without rereading anything.

Georgina rushed into the room, pulling Lucy from her uneasy thoughts. "Oh, Miss, you must come and see. There's a great to-do at the manor 'ouse."

Lucy left the note on the table and followed Georgina out the door and around to the side of the house, where her mother already stood, shading her eyes. Across the meadow and through a thicket of trees, Lucy could make out several coaches coming up the path toward Tanglewood Manor.

"What is going on?" Lucy asked.

"That is what we would like to know," said her mother. "Georgina said she has noticed more bustle about the place during the past couple of weeks—workers arriving and such—but she assumed they came to ready the place to sell. Now, however, from the amount of luggage strapped onto those coaches, it appears as though someone is coming to stay for a while."

"You mean lots of someones," added Georgina with a reverent quality to her voice. "Do you fin' they've sold it already?"

"Surely not," said Lucy. "Not with us living here."

"Unless Lord Drayson made arrangements for the new owners to allow us to stay," said Mrs. Beresford. "Has he responded to your note, Lucy?"

Lucy frowned. The date had been set a few weeks ago, which meant Lucy should have sent a missive a few weeks ago as well. "I, er . . . have not sent the letter yet."

"What? Why not?" asked her mother.

"Because I only wrote it this morning," Lucy admitted. "And by that I mean I wrote my final draft of the letter this morning."

"I see," said Mrs. Beresford in that rather stern, *I am disappointed in you* way she sometimes used. Then she sighed. "I suppose we can only hope that the occupants of those coaches are not expecting this house to be empty, and if they are, pray that they will be kind enough to allow us to remain for another fortnight. I will ask Mr. Shepherd to call on them soon so that we may discover who they are and what they expect from us."

"Do you fin' it could be 'im?" Georgina asked.

"You mean Lord Drayson?" Lucy studied the coaches, wondering the same thing, before she immediately dismissed the notion. "I don't believe it could be, Georgy. Lord Drayson said his family was happily settled in Danbury and had no plans to make Tanglewood even a temporary home. That is why they wished to sell."

"But that was before 'e got ter know you, Miss. 'Appen—"

"Georgy," Lucy was quick to interrupt. The last thing she needed was to hope for something which would not be. After being deceived and foisted into the role of a servant by an inexperienced and silly girl, Lord Drayson would never return to a place he did not wish to live. Unless . . .

"If that *is* him," Lucy finally said. "The only possible reason he would be here now is to settle the score in some way. So let us all pray that one of the occupants of those carriages is not the Earl of Drayson."

MR. SHEPHERD AGREED TO PAY a call at Tanglewood the day after the coaches arrived. He would have given them a few more days to get settled had not Mrs. Beresford said, "We must know what is going on, Stephen, or poor Lucy will wear a hole in our carpet from all her pacing."

"But it will not be your carpet much longer," Mr. Shepherd said logically, earning a warning look from his intended.

"No, Stephen. But Lucy will be your step-daughter *always*, so . . ."

"I shall go straightaway tomorrow morning," he said, earning a peck on his cheek from his soon-to-be wife and a hug from his soon-to-be step-daughter.

That had been yesterday—a gloomy, miserable day that had kept Lucy cooped up indoors because of the rain. She now sat at the breakfast table picking at her food and wondering who Mr. Shepherd would discover at Tanglewood Manor. Would it be the earl or a new owner? She wasn't sure what to hope for. All she knew was that her stomach would not tolerate even a bite of toast.

A thick layer of clouds still coated the sky, but the rain had subsided, so Lucy left her breakfast uneaten and grabbed a pair of work gloves instead. She donned her boots and her straw bonnet and went outside. Weeds were beginning to encroach on her vegetable plants, so she decided to tackle them first. Her mother had often reminded Lucy that they would not be her plants much longer, but Lucy didn't care. While she lived under this roof she would tend to this garden. And once she had removed to Knotting Tree, she would still tend to this garden. It had become more than just a plot of neatly lined vegetables. It was something that she still shared with Lord Drayson, and she wasn't ready to let it go just yet.

One by one Lucy yanked the weeds, easily pulling them free from the damp soil. She breathed in the smell of earth and vegetation, feeling the invigorating, cleansing effects almost immediately. Her skirts and gloves soon became muddy but she did not care. She continued to extract the weeds, determined not to stop until they were all gone.

The faint sound of hooves pounding into soft earth met her ears, and Lucy stiffened, listening more intently. The sound grew louder until she knew with absolute certainty that a horse was coming toward the dower house from the direction of the manor house. Slowly her gaze rose, followed by the rest of her body. In the distance she spotted a man wearing a beaver hat and riding a beautiful black horse.

"Colin," she whispered, unable to move. Her heart pounded in cadence with the horse's hooves, thrumming loudly in her ears. Her breathing became short and irregular, as though she'd just raced across the meadow and could no longer catch her breath. All she could do was stand still and watch his handsome form grow closer and closer until the details became clear. A dark blue jacket that fit him far better than any of her father's shirts had. Tan buckskins and dark riding gloves. A freshly shaven face, side whiskers, and those incredible eyes that she knew to be blue but appeared dark and mysterious under the brim of his beaver.

Lucy had never felt more ill-prepared for any moment.

He slowed his horse and gracefully slid from the saddle before it stopped completely. With deft movements, he tied the reins around a post and gave the horse a pat before turning to Lucy. Hands behind his back, one step at a time, he approached, and all Lucy could do was attempt to swallow a lump that refused to be swallowed.

Colin removed his hat and looked her up and down, finally quirking an eyebrow. "Do you normally receive visitors covered in dirt, Miss Beresford?" he finally said.

Lucy opened her mouth to respond, then immediately clamped it shut. She wasn't sure what she had expected him to say, but it certainly wasn't that. She glanced down at her muddy skirt and hands and immediately tore the gloves from her fingers. "Do you normally visit people unannounced, Lord Drayson?"

His smile widened, and he dropped his gaze to his feet, shaking his head. Then he took a few steps closer, lifted his eyes to hers, and reached out to wipe something from her cheek. "There," he said. "Now you are not completely covered."

He wore gloves, but the thrilling sensation of his touch tickled her cheek even after his hand dropped back to his side.

"Are you here to ring a peal over my head, my lord?" she blurted, unable to keep the question at bay any longer. "If so, would you mind doing so at once and be done with it?"

He watched her a moment before cocking his head. "Are you under the impression that I am displeased with you?"

Lucy stared at him in confusion. He didn't seem angry

or perturbed that she and her mother were still living at the dower house. Nor did he comment about the fact that she was now calling him Lord Drayson.

"That seemed the most likely conclusion to draw, considering the way I so shamefully deceived you," she said slowly. "But if you are not angry with me, why have you come?"

"To the dower house?" he asked. "Truth be told, I needed a break. We have had nonstop visitors since we arrived. First it was Mr. Gilbert. Then Mr. and Mrs. Hudson, along with a few others."

"Have you seen Mr. Shepherd?" Lucy asked.

"I would have welcomed a visit from Mr. Shepherd," said the earl. "But as of a few moments ago, he had not arrived. As soon as Mr. Bidding left, I did as well. I suppose I could no longer take the inquisitions. If one more person asks me why I have removed here and how long I plan to remain, I will go mad."

Lucy frowned. This seemed like such an odd sort of conversation to have after all they had experienced together, not to mention the distance and time they had been apart. Lord Drayson carried on as though nothing amiss lay between them, and Lucy didn't trust it. How could he possibly make amends so easily? What was his true purpose here? Surely not to ingratiate himself in the neighborhood, when he was only planning to—

Her eyes snapped to his. "Did you say Mr. Bidding came?"

"Yes. Do you know him?"

"Quite well," she answered carefully. "But not as well as I know Mrs. Bidding. She's an acquaintance of yours too, I'm afraid."

He seemed to consider the words before replying in a

nonchalant way. "The name did sound familiar. I take it you have received an invitation to the soirée they are having on Friday as well?"

Lucy felt her throat begin to tighten. Her next words came out as a hoarse whisper. "Yes, we have already accepted it."

"Wonderful. I shall look forward to seeing a familiar face in the crowd then."

She made to grab his arm but stopped herself. "Lord Drayson, you must not go."

A dark eyebrow lifted as he studied her. "Why is that?"

"Because Mrs. Bidding knows you only as my former coachman, and because . . ." Good heavens. Why did she have to explain this? A fifth generation earl should be well-versed enough in the ways of society to know what would happen if Lucy's former coachman turned out to be the Earl of Drayson.

"I take it that your reputation is safe then." He phrased it like a statement, but there was an underlying question in his eyes.

"Yes," she answered. Was that why he had come back? No, of course not. Why would he care about the reputation of a liar? "Mrs. Bidding is not a gossip, as it turns out."

"I'm relieved to hear it."

"But she is many other things," Lucy added quickly. "She's domineering, opinionated, stands on high moral ground, and has a very sharp memory. Which is the reason you cannot go to the soirée or ever encounter Mrs. Bidding again. It will only bring you problems."

"Do you care so much about my welfare?" he asked, attempting to sound flippant, but there was a slight edge to his voice.

Lucy looked away from his piercing eyes and drew in a deep breath. It was finally here. The moment she could bare

Rachael Anderson

her soul, assuage her guilt, and with any luck, set things to rights—or, at least as right as they could be after what she'd done to him.

"I don't know why you are here," she began, "but I can only assume it has to do with justice and perhaps closure. What I did to you was abominable and unpardonable. I was angry and distressed by the news you delivered and the impersonal way you delivered it. I reacted badly and have regretted my rash actions almost every day since. For that, I must beg your forgiveness."

His lips twitched slightly. "*Most* every day?"

"Yes," she replied honestly. "There were a few days where I very much wished you to the devil, my lord."

He threw back his head and laughed. The sound echoed in her ears and penetrated her soul, reminding her of the good times they'd shared and how much she had come to care for him. His smile, his laugh, his touch, his wit, his kindness . . . why had he returned? If he stayed for too long it could very well be her undoing.

"Were those days at the beginning or end?" he asked.

"Beginning," she admitted. "Only the beginning. When, exactly, did your memory return?"

He stuffed his beaver under his arm and shrugged. "I can't quite recall."

"You're shamming me."

He lifted an eyebrow. "I believe this is a case of the pot calling the kettle black."

"And I believe you are attempting to divert the conversation."

"Right you are." He stepped around her to examine their garden. "Tell me, Lucy, Lucy, quite contrary," he glanced her way and quirked an eyebrow, "how does your garden grow?"

She smiled, finishing the song with a twist of her own. "With silver bells and cockle shells, and Lord Drayson's help to sow. Not that you helped with the sowing," she added. "But plow doesn't rhyme with grow, so that's the best I could do. Now stop trying to distract me. When did your memory return, my lord?"

He knelt to examine the plants closest to him, gently touching the crudely carved wooden sign labeling the leafy greens as "Carrots." "I liked it better when you called me Collins. I would like it even more if you would call me Colin."

Lucy shook her head. "It wouldn't be proper."

Lord Drayson stood and brushed the dirt from his gloves. "It wasn't proper for you to make me your servant either," he pointed out.

"I have since mended my ways, *my lord*," she said, emphasizing his title.

He sighed. "I suppose that means I cannot call you Lucy then."

"No."

"What about Lucille?"

Her lips twitched at that. "Definitely not. My full name is only to be used when I am in the gravest of trouble."

He cocked his head and studied her with the most perplexing look in his eyes. "How do you know that you are not in trouble now?"

Lucy couldn't fathom the meaning behind his words. This entire conversation was beginning to feel most surreal, and she still had no answers to the dozens of questions swirling around in her head.

"Lord Drayson, why have you returned to Askern? If it is to personally see that we are removed from the dower house, rest assured that we will be out by the ninth of June."

His eyes widened slightly at the news. "That is not why I have come. You and your mother are—"

"My mother is to be married to Mr. Shepherd, and we shall make our home with him in a few weeks' time. I am sorry we were not removed by now, but we will be soon. You are now free to sell Tanglewood to the highest bidder."

Lord Drayson did not look at all pleased with this news. In fact, he appeared more disconcerted than anything. "Is your mother making this match out of necessity or does she wish to marry Mr. Shepherd?"

"She wishes to marry him," answered Lucy. "She has grown very fond of him, as have I."

"I am glad to hear it." Lord Drayson nodded, then took a few steps away, removed his beaver from under his arm and set it back on his head. "I'm afraid I must take my leave for now, but I shall see you on Friday evening at the soirée."

Lucy opened her mouth to respond, but he was already swinging up on his horse. He tipped the brim of his hat in a gesture of farewell and was off, leaving Lucy in a greater state of confusion than she had been in before his arrival.

LUCY GAPED AT THE LINE of carriages ahead of them. The Biddings were known for throwing rather dull parties and had likely never seen this sort of turnout. The only reason the Beresfords accepted invitations from Mrs. Bidding was because Mrs. Beresford had the softest of hearts and could never say no to a friend.

"What on earth?" Lucy turned to her mother and Mr. Shepherd, who sat across from her in the carriage.

"It appears as though we are in for a bit of a wait," said her mother, not sounding surprised in the least.

"Lord Drayson's arrival has caused quite the stir," added Mr. Shepherd. "Mrs. Bidding let it slip that the earl has done her the great honor of accepting her invitation and suddenly everyone wished to come."

Lucy sat back in her seat, much less comfortable than she had been before. Did Lord Drayson really plan to attend, even after her warning? Surely not. And yet . . .

She clasped her fingers to keep them from fidgeting. If he did come, perhaps Mrs. Bidding would not recognize him and Lucy's worries were all for naught.

The hope was a fleeting one. The earl was the sort of man to draw attention wherever he went. One glance was all it took for his handsome features to be seared into one's memory forever. It would take a miracle for Mrs. Bidding to not remember him.

The party was well underway and still no sign of the earl. Lucy began to breathe a little easier and even accepted a glass of something from a passing footman. She examined the amber liquid briefly before taking a sip and examining it again, this time with more interest. Whatever it was, it tasted wonderful, like raspberries and plums and candied cherries. Lucy took another sip and felt some of the tension leave her body.

She had worn one of her favorite gowns—a deep pink satin with a sheer overskirt. It danced around her feet, making her feel feminine and beautiful. She saved it only for special occasions or for those evenings when she wished to feel as confident as possible. Tonight was one of those occasions. Or, at least it had been. If the earl didn't plan to make an appearance, she could have easily worn her embroidered blue linen dress instead.

"Lucy, here you are." Patience Brooke tucked her arm through Lucy's as though they were the closest of friends, but she wasn't even looking at Lucy. She was standing on tiptoe, attempting to see over the heads of all the others, no doubt wanting to know if the earl had arrived. "Can you believe this crush?"

"I am certain Mrs. Bidding is quite thrilled by the number of guests who have come," said Lucy, attempting to extricate her arm in as subtle a way as possible.

"She ought to be, for this house will likely never see such success again. Lord Drayson need only experience one of the Bidding's soirées to learn that he ought never to do so again. Have you made his acquaintance yet? I hear he is quite dashing." Her fingers dug into Lucy's arm as she stretched even higher.

Lucy took another sip of the luscious liquid as she scanned the room for her mother.

A hush fell over the crowd, followed by murmuring voices, and Lucy's body immediately stiffened. She clasped the drink in her hand as she slowly turned her head toward the entrance, where the earl now stood, greeting Mr. and Mrs. Bidding. Dressed in all black, from his boots and pantaloons to his waist coat and double-breasted jacket, he did, indeed, look dashing. The only white that could be seen on his person was his collar and neatly tied cravat. He was definitely a commanding sight to behold.

At his side was a woman who was nearly as tall as Mrs. Bidding, carrying herself with poise and grace. Lucy could only assume it was his mother, the Dowager Countess of Drayson. She had heard he had arrived with his family. Next to his mother was a younger, slightly more petite, woman who appeared to be about Lucy's age. Her dark curls and light eyes appeared too much like the earl's for her to not be his sister. Both were dressed far more elegantly than all others in attendance.

While the countess spoke with Mr. and Mrs. Bidding, the earl searched the room until his gaze settled on Lucy. A touch of a smile lifted his lips before he returned his attention to his hostess. They spoke for a moment longer and the earl escorted his sister and mother away. He nodded at those he passed, spoke briefly to others, and stopped to introduce his family to a select few. Lucy could not seem to tear her gaze away as he, ever so slowly, made his way toward her.

"I believe he is coming this way," said Patience excitedly.

Mrs. Beresford materialized at Lucy's side and carefully pried the drink from her daughter's hand. She dropped her voice so that Patience could not hear. "Relax, my dear. You look ready to shatter to pieces."

"Why has he come?" Lucy breathed, trying hard to control her emotions even though she was trembling inside. What would Mrs. Bidding do? How would she react? Did she remember him?

"Only he knows his reasons," Mrs. Beresford whispered back, then lifted her head to smile and greet the newest family come to Askern. Lucy felt like her heart would pound right out of her chest.

"Mother. Harriett." said Lord Drayson. "I would like you to meet Miss Beresford, who made my first visit here so . . . memorable."

Lucy's face heated. She couldn't believe Lord Drayson would bring up such a thing at this moment. Lucy glanced around, noting a few questioning glances from those gathered around them, and immediately directed the earl a piercing look before dropping to a quick curtsy for the countess and her daughter.

"A pleasure," she murmured. "May I introduce my mother as well?"

Lady Drayson appeared unruffled by her son's remark. "It is lovely to meet you both. I hear you are to be married soon, Mrs. Beresford. May I offer my felicitations to you and Mr. Shepherd? He was good enough to extend an invitation to the wedding when he came to call a few days past."

Mrs. Beresford smiled. "It will be a small affair at our church, but you are more than welcome, Lady Drayson. As are you, Lady Harriett."

"I adore country weddings," Lady Harriett said, clasping her hands together in a somewhat dramatic gesture. "In fact, I adore everything having to do with the country. I find myself quite in love with Yorkshire already."

Lucy immediately liked the Drayson women. Despite their elevated stations, they did not seem high in the instep at all. And Lady Harriett's natural enthusiasm was such a contrast to her more subdued and dignified brother.

"Do you plan to stay long in Askern?" Lucy asked, unable to keep the question inside any longer.

Lady Drayson flickered a glance at her son before answering. "Our plans are somewhat undecided, I'm afraid. All of us were in need of a change of pace. We thought the Yorkshire air might do us some good, and here we are."

"It feels like a grand adventure," gushed Lady Harriett. "I believe I shall want to travel the world after this."

Lucy kept her smile pasted on her face even though she didn't feel like smiling any longer. The earl's mother and sister were adept at avoiding straight answers as well. Lucy looked at Lord Drayson, whose mouth, in contrast to hers, strained *not* to smile. No doubt he found it humorous to keep her in suspense. Perhaps this was his way of seeking revenge. Apparently, he'd returned to taunt, tease, torment, and stir up trouble for Lucy. It was the only explanation that made sense.

Lucy remained silent and allowed her mother to carry the conversation—at least until Patience returned with her mother in tow, who quickly begged for an introduction to the newest residents in town.

Patience did not waste any time engaging the earl in conversation. "Tell me, my lord, what has brought you to such a humble village as Askern?"

A flicker of annoyance crossed Lord Drayson's face

before he composed himself and bowed over the lady's hand. "I heard rumors that all other women paled in comparison to those found in Askern, so I had to come to see for myself."

Lucy fought the urge to roll her eyes.

Patience smiled coyly. "Have you decided such rumors are true or false, my lord?"

"True, of course. For I am now standing before the loveliest women I have ever beheld." His gaze strayed to Lucy as he spoke. Though there was a twinge of humor in his eyes, there was also warmth.

"Lord Drayson," Patience said. "I can already see you are quite the rogue."

His attention returned to Patience. "How can you accuse me of being a rogue when I speak the truth, Miss Brooke?"

"If you'll excuse me." Lucy took the opportunity to escape and went off in search of another drink, hoping it would sooth her pounding heart. Along the way, she was stopped by some friends, but the moment they asked about Lord Drayson, Lucy pled a headache and slipped out a side door, walked through the adjoining library, and onto the darkened terrace, where she could breathe a little easier.

It was a chilly evening, so Lucy wrapped her arms around her chest in an effort to stay warm as her gaze strayed across the gardens. In two weeks' time, her life would change yet again. It would be a good change, but another change nonetheless. From the moment her father fell ill, it had been one alteration after another. The absence of a loved one, the move to the dower house, her mother's return to sewing for pay, and Lucy's newfound love of roses. Her father's casket had been adorned with a pile of the flowers. They had looked so beautiful nestled there that Lucy had determined to grow a rose garden and bring more of that beauty into the world.

Her father would have liked that. He would have also liked that her mother had found someone new to share her life with.

Lucy looked up at the night sky that showed patches of glittering stars between the scattered clouds. "I miss you, Papa," she whispered, wondering if he could hear. Even if he couldn't, it felt good talking to him again.

"Mama is getting married in a fortnight, and I will be removing to Knotting Tree. It is an improvement from the dower house, but I am afraid it will feel more lonely. Mama has Mr. Shepherd now, and although I technically will have him as well, it won't be the same. The truth is, I am feeling a little lost as of late. I used to believe I could live out the remainder of my days as an eccentric spinster, but that isn't enough anymore. I want more than that, Papa. I want something that fills me up inside, like the life you and Mama had together—a life with a purpose and someone to share it with. Is that even a possibility for one as untamed as I? I simply feel so . . . empty. And cold." Lucy chuckled quietly at that, needing to lighten the disheartened mood she'd brought on herself.

In the whisper of the breeze that touched her cheeks and arms, her father seemed to answer. *Cheer up, my dear. A spirit that is down cannot see so clearly as a spirit that is up.*

How many times had he told her that whenever she had come to him downcast about one thing or another? He always had a gentle way of infusing her with hope and showing her the sunshine through the clouds.

"I love you, Papa," she whispered.

Lucy shivered and wrapped her arms more tightly around her. It didn't make her any warmer, so she grudgingly pushed away from the railing and walked back inside the darkened library. Not ready to return to the party,

Lucy lingered, breathing in the smell of aged parchment and leather. She ran her finger along the spines of a few books, wishing she could pull one out, curl up in the large armchair, and pass away the rest of the evening in a different world than the one she lived in. But she had been gone from the party too long as it was. Her mother would likely be looking for her.

A door opened from across the room and footsteps sounded. Without thinking, Lucy shrank into a shadowed doorway between two bookshelves, keeping herself hidden. With her back pressed against a door, she held her breath, hoping the intruder would soon leave.

The door closed, and Mrs. Bidding's voice sounded. "I realize your absence will be felt soon, my lord, so I shall get straight to the point."

My lord?

"I would appreciate that," came Lord Drayson's answer.

Lucy froze. Surely Mrs. Bidding did not intend to confront the earl in the middle of a soirée that *she* was hosting.

Lucy peeked out from her nook to see Lord Drayson perusing the bookshelves just as she had done moments before, with his back to Mrs. Bidding.

She did not appear happy. "Apparently, you are not a coachman after all, I see."

"Not any longer," he answered smoothly.

"How in heaven's name did you come to be—" She cut herself off. "Never mind that now. I told you I would get straight to the point and I shall. You have compromised Miss Beresford's reputation in the worst possible way, and I have brought you in here to ask what you intend to do about it."

He continued to scan the books. "I can think of worse possible ways I could have compromised her."

"My lord." The sound of her hiss echoed through the cavernous room. Lucy held back a smile, enjoying the fact that Lord Drayson didn't seem to find Mrs. Bidding the slightest bit intimidating.

He turned around to face her. "You have done me the honor of being forthright, and I shall do the same for you. Lucy has—"

"Miss Beresford," Mrs. Bidding corrected, shooting him a scathing glance.

"Very well," he returned. "Miss Beresford has been good enough to inform me that her reputation is still intact, which is a kindness we owe to you, I understand."

"You do indeed," Mrs. Bidding snipped. "I am no gossip. Not even Mr. Bidding is aware of the events that transpired."

"I am relieved to hear it," he said. "You are obviously a woman of great integrity."

"I am," she affirmed. "The question is, are you?"

"A woman?" His voice held a hint of a smile. "I hope not."

"A *man* of integrity," Mrs. Bidding hissed again.

"Ah," he said, clasping his hands behind his back. "In that case I would say I mostly am, yes."

"Then I shall repeat my earlier question," Mrs. Bidding said firmly. "What do you intend to do about Miss Lucy Beresford?"

"What, exactly, needs to be done? You said yourself that her reputation is still intact, and unless you plan to become a gossip, everything is as it should be."

"No, it is not." Her voice rose to a loud whisper. "I know what you have done, Mrs. Beresford knows, and so do you. Any man of honor would—"

"Would what?" he interrupted. "Offer marriage out of a

sense of duty? Forgive me, madam, but no real harm has been done, and that is not the way I plan to enter into matrimony. In answer to your question, I intend to do nothing about Miss Lucy Beresford."

Mrs. Bidding clenched her fists and cast him a glare that would have made her husband wither. "Then you cannot claim to be a man of integrity."

Lucy could remain silent no longer. The only reason Lord Drayson was made to suffer through such an interrogation was because of *Lucy's* lack of integrity. He did not deserve to be spoken to in this way, especially when his presence was the reason Mrs. Bidding's soirée was such a success.

"On the contrary, Mrs. Bidding," Lucy announced, stepping out from her hiding place. "Lord Drayson has only just proven his integrity."

Both heads swung to face her, watching her as she approached. Before either of them could speak, Lucy continued. "Lord Drayson has made his feelings quite clear on the matter, and I find myself in complete agreement with him. No one should ever be forced into a marriage they do not wish to enter into, so let us be done with this dreadful conversation. Lord Drayson, please consider yourself a free man in every possible way." Her voice trembled over the last few words. Despite her show of confidence, it injured Lucy deeply that the earl had proclaimed that he had no wish to marry her. But she refused to fall to pieces over it. Not here, not now, not ever.

As though by divine intervention, the door opened, and Mr. Shepherd walked in, looking every bit like a rescuer—*her* rescuer. He stopped short and took in the scene with intelligent eyes, his gaze finally landing on Lucy. "Is there a problem, my dear?" he asked.

"I am feeling a bit under the weather is all."

He continued to watch her for a moment, and as he did so, Lucy felt her composure began to slip. If he did not leave this instant, she would crumble into his arms and make a horrible scene.

As though reading her thoughts, he said, "Mrs. Bidding, several guests are inquiring as to the whereabouts of Lord Drayson, Miss Beresford, and yourself. It is creating quite a stir."

Mrs. Bidding uttered something that sounded a lot like a grunt. "Very well, then. I have done all that I can do anyway. Come, my lord, let us return to the party and find a way to silence the talk."

Lord Drayson hesitated, studying Lucy with an expression she couldn't decipher. He reached out as though to touch her, thought better of it, and let his hand fall back to his side. "I hope you feel better soon, Miss Beresford," he said. "The last thing I would ever wish is for you to be injured in any way."

Lucy watched him leave, feeling her heart heave and plunge. Why it hurt so much she couldn't say. Lucy had never entertained thoughts of a match between them, and yet hearing Lord Drayson speak so adamantly against the idea ached abominably.

Mr. Shepherd's warm and comforting arms enveloped her in an embrace. "I have no idea what was said in here," he whispered as he held her tight. "But you look as though you could use a hug."

The tears came then, squeezing from her eyes and dampening the fabric of his coat. Lucy wasn't sure when Mr. Shepherd had become a second father to her, only that he had, and she was fiercely grateful for it.

THE MORNING AFTER THE BIDDING'S soirée, Lucy awoke with a pounding in her head. With her palm cradling her forehead, she padded down the stairs, allowed Georgina to make her some restorative tea, and returned to bed until noon, at which point she awoke again feeling a little better. The dreariness from the day before still hovered over her, though, like a lost little storm cloud.

She dressed in a bright peach morning gown in an attempt to lift her spirits and hummed a cheery tune as she forced her feet to trot down the stairs.

"Lucy, is that you?" called her mother from the morning room.

Lucy popped her head into the room and immediately wished she had stayed in bed a while longer. Seated across from her mother was Lady Drayson and Lady Harriett. Lord Drayson stood casually next to the fireplace, with his elbow on the mantle, looking splendid in a dark jacket with a simple knotted cravat, tan pantaloons, and shiny Hessians.

He straightened when he saw her and executed a swift bow. "Miss Beresford," he said, sounding staid and proper and not at all like himself.

"Lord Drayson. Lady Drayson. Lady Harriett." Lucy dipped into a slight curtsy and mustered a chipper tone to her voice. "How wonderful to see you again." She prayed she sounded more genuine than she felt.

"Your mother was just telling us about the wedding plans," said Lady Harriett. "Do come and join us. She says you are to make the flower arrangements and claims you have quite the talent for it."

Unable to think of a possible way out, Lucy walked into the room and joined her mother on the settee. "I would not call it a talent, but I do enjoy creating arrangements."

"She's quite adept in the garden as well," inserted the earl. "She grows both flowers *and* vegetables."

Lucy cleared her throat, uncomfortable with the praise. "What your brother means to say is that I like to dig in the dirt."

"And wear it," he added with a grin.

Lucy smoothed her skirts, wondering what he was about. "As you can see, I am not wearing it now."

"No," he agreed. "You are wearing a lovely peach gown that looks quite charming on you."

Lucy had never felt more flummoxed. She glanced at the earl's mother, who was attempting to hide a smile behind her tea cup. Lady Harriett, on the other hand, practically giggled. "Who would have ever thought Colin could sound so romantic," she teased her brother. "I'm quite diverted by it. Please, go on."

Lucy lifted her chin in an unspoken challenge to the earl. "Yes, do go on, Lord Drayson, assuming you can think of another compliment to bestow upon me."

"I can think of several, actually." He pushed away from the mantle, crossed the room, and took a seat in the chair next to her. When he leaned forward to rest his elbows on his knees, coming a little too close for her comfort, Lucy immediately wished the challenge back.

"Let's see . . ." he mused, rubbing his chin in a show of thought. "You look lovely in every shade of color I have seen you wear, you make wonderful biscuits, you can drive the cart admirably—and after only a few lessons too. You hum on key, you are not afraid of hard work or dirty fingernails, you win grasshopper race wagers, climb trees, pick locks with a hairpin, steal a plow without a twinge of con-science—"

"I think that is enough compliments for one day," Lucy quickly said, her face flaming. Lord Drayson could go to the devil for all she cared at the moment.

Harriett laughed delightedly and clapped her hands. "Miss Beresford, I must tell you what I could not confide in you last night. The reason Mother and I travelled all this way was to meet you. You are quite famous in our household."

Had she meant to say *infamous*? Lucy thought, not knowing how to respond. She glanced at the earl, wondering what he had told his family and what they must think of her, and quickly decided she preferred not to know.

"Mother and Harriett were vastly entertained when I explained to them that I had lived the life of a butler, footman, and coachman for many days," he explained.

Lady Harriett seemed good-hearted enough, as did Lady Drayson. Perhaps they had found the situation more humorous than distressing. At least Lucy hoped they had.

"Did your brother happen to mention at what point his memory returned?" Lucy asked, thinking of the wager, the ghastly hat, and how long the earl had played her as the fool instead of the other way around.

Lady Drayson shook her head. "I'm afraid what little he has told us had to be extracted from him in a truly painful way—for us, I mean. He was not overly forthcoming with the details."

Harriett leaned forward and clutched her hands in her lap. "But you are not so secretive, are you Miss Beresford? Please say that you are not."

"Not at all," Lucy said. "Ask me anything and I shall answer with far more details than you could ever wish to hear."

Lord Drayson apparently decided it was past time to intervene, for he cleared his throat quite loudly. "Mrs. Beresford, might we offer some assistance for your upcoming nuptials?"

"I appreciate your kindness, my lord, but Lucy and I have everything well in hand."

Lucy was grateful to the earl for finding a way to redirect the conversation. She wasn't nearly as ready as she'd let on to share the details of their adventures together.

"The wedding *is* well in hand," agreed Lucy. "But I could use your help convincing Mama that she ought to stop fretting about me and take a wedding trip with Mr. Shepherd."

Lady Drayson set down her tea cup and looked at Mrs. Beresford in surprise. "You are not to have a wedding trip?"

Mrs. Beresford answered carefully. "We do not wish to leave Lucy at home alone."

Lucy tried her best to ignore the earl's snickering. "I will be surrounded by heaps of servants at Knotting Tree and couldn't possibly get into any trouble, Mama."

The earl coughed loudly, but it sounded suspiciously like he said, "Doubtful" while doing so.

Lucy glared at him while Lady Drayson tried to hide a smile behind her hand.

Mrs. Beresford attempted to rein in the conversation.

"The fact of the matter is that Mr. Shepherd and I do not have much time for a trip and are perfectly content to see ourselves settled at Knotting Tree."

"Why does Miss Beresford not stay with us?" suggested Lady Harriett, much to Lucy's dismay. "I will see to it that she does not come to any trouble."

"You?" The earl chuckled. "You are two peas in a pod, I think."

Before Harriett could dispute the accusation, Lady Drayson laid a hand on her daughter's arm. "What Harriett means to say is that we would be delighted to have Miss Beresford as our guest while you are away. It seems the perfect solution."

Absolutely not! Lucy wanted to shout. It was difficult enough to see Tanglewood Manor from afar. Living there would be akin to torture, especially if Lady Harriett truly did plan to question Lucy mercilessly about her time with Lord Drayson. Surely Mrs. Beresford would not agree to such a scheme. And yet she appeared to be considering it. Oh dear. Why had Lucy mentioned the wedding trip at all?

"Are you certain it would be no trouble?" Mrs. Beresford asked.

Lucy was about to insist that they could not ask such a thing of the Draysons, but then she spied the hope in her mother's eyes. She realized her mother really did wish to go on a wedding trip with her new husband. It was Lucy, and only Lucy, that held her back.

Lucy swallowed her argument, which felt like a cube of sugar grating down her throat, and allowed Lady Drayson to say, "Certainly not. It will be a joy to have her. That is, if you are in agreement, Miss Beresford."

Every instinct in Lucy urged her to say, "No, I am not in agreement," but she forced herself to nod instead. She could sacrifice a few days of discomfort so that her mother could have a wedding trip.

"I should love to join you at Tanglewood," Lucy managed to say.

The earl arched his eyebrow in a look of half surprise, half respect, as though he could read her thoughts and commended her decision. Then he settled back in his chair with a pleased expression on his face.

Lucy wished she could feel as pleased by the latest turn of events, but a large knot of dread formed in her stomach. She tried to push it aside and be happy for her mother, telling herself that she would simply do her best to stay out of Lord Drayson's path, but the knot wouldn't budge. Lucy could only pray that her heart would come away from the experience no more injured than it was now.

THE MORNING OF THE WEDDING day dawned with only a cloud or two marring the light blue of the sky. Lucy lifted her bedroom window, breathed in the sweet aroma of earth and vegetation, and listened to the happy chirping coming from the surrounding trees. This was a day she had awaited and dreaded at the same time. Her mother would marry a good man, a kind man, a man who had proven he would make an excellent husband and father, and a man Lucy had come to adore. But it was also a day in which she would say her goodbyes and accompany the Draysons to Tanglewood Manor for seven very long days.

At least Georgina would be coming with her. That knowledge gave her some comfort.

Lucy pushed thoughts of Tanglewood from her mind and tiptoed past her mother's room, quietly padding down the stairs. Last night, while her mother slept, Lucy and Georgina had crept outdoors with a lamp and had cut all the peach and orange roses Lucy would need for a surprise wedding bouquet. She and Georgina had stayed up late removing the thorns and chatting like old friends, discussing the new lives that awaited them at Knotting Tree. Georgina had been offered the job of either assistant cook or Lucy's lady's maid, and the sweet girl had promptly chosen the lady's maid position, much to Lucy's delight. Not only would Georgina carry a lighter load and earn a higher wage, but she would remain close to Lucy. It was a happy time for both of them.

Lucy found Georgina in the kitchen preparing what appeared to be a feast—bacon, eggs, sweet rolls, and marmalade. The room smelled divine.

"Good heavens, Georgy, how long have you been up?" gasped Lucy.

"I want Mrs. Beresford's weddin' day ter be perfect, is all," said Georgina.

Lucy dipped her finger in the marmalade and put it into her mouth, letting the gooey richness slide down her throat and into her belly. "You do realize Mama will likely be a ball of nerves this morning. I greatly fear this meal will be wasted on her."

"But not on you," Georgina pointed out with a smile.

"How right you are." Lucy said, helping herself to a plate. She sat down and savored as much as she could while eating as fast as possible. A beautiful day. A delicious breakfast. A glorious wedding. That is what Lucy would focus on today.

The roses fit together perfectly, creating a bouquet that was even more beautiful than Lucy had imagined in her mind. Clustered together, the various shades of orange and peach looked charming and simplistic, yet sophisticated and rich. She was tying the white satin ribbon around it when Mrs. Beresford walked into the kitchen.

"Oh, Georgy, the house smells divine," she exclaimed. "I'm afraid my stomach wouldn't let me stay in bed a moment longer."

Georgina shot Lucy a look of triumph and smiled at the

praise. "It's an excitin' day, ma'am. Only look at the flowers Miss Lucy made for you."

Mrs. Beresford finally noticed the creation and gasped, covering her mouth with her hands as she slowly approached Lucy. "Oh my goodness, how lovely," she said, touching the stems gingerly. "I had considered clipping some roses for a simple bouquet this morning, but decided that would be silly. I am an old woman getting married for the second time. Bouquets are for the young."

"Bouquets are for everyone, Mama," Lucy chided. "And did you really think I would allow you to walk down the aisle without one?"

"I should have known." Mrs. Beresford bent to press a kiss to Lucy's forehead. "Thank you, dear girl."

The wedding was everything Lucy could have wished for her mother. The church was filled to bursting, and Mrs. Beresford looked resplendent walking down the aisle wearing a deep peach gown with a sheer white overskirt trimmed in white Brussels lace. A strand of pearls adorned her neck, and a joyful smile adorned her face. Georgina had styled her hair in an elegant and sophisticated twist, and Lucy had tucked in a small handful of rosebuds.

Mr. Shepherd's gaze remained fixed on his intended, and Lucy wondered how it would feel to have a man look at her in such a way. When her imaginings conjured up Lord Drayson standing at the altar, staring down the aisle at her, Lucy forcibly returned her mind to the ceremony. Perhaps she should do as Mr. Shepherd suggested and take up writing. It would provide an outlet for all of her silly daydreams.

In what seemed like no time at all, Mrs. Beresford became Mrs. Shepherd, and the happy couple smiled and nodded, hugged and waved as they walked through the throng of people to the awaiting coach. Then it was off to the wedding breakfast with the Draysons, where Lucy picked at her food and said her final goodbyes to her mother and stepfather. Mrs. Bidding had been good enough to host the breakfast, and Lucy gave the woman a parting hug as well.

"Thank you, Mrs. Bidding. You have been kindness itself to our family."

"You are most welcome, my dear," said Mrs. Bidding with a blush. "I hear you are to stay at Tanglewood while Mr. and Mrs. Shepherd are away."

Lucy couldn't tell if the woman approved or disapproved, not that it mattered. "Yes, Mrs. Bidding. I do hope you will call upon me there. I shall feel quite lost without Mama and Mr. Shepherd."

"You may depend upon it." Mrs. Bidding patted her arm. "Ah, here is Lord Drayson now, ready to whisk you away to his home."

Lucy's eyes widened at the woman's choice of words. She made it sound rather indecent.

"Well, isn't he?" Mrs. Bidding said with a chuckle, then patted Lucy's arm again before leaving her alone with Lord Drayson.

Apparently Mrs. Bidding approved of her living arrangements for the next week. More than that, she seemed to find the situation rather humorous. Lucy could not understand it.

She turned her questioning gaze on Lord Drayson, whose eyes were alight with humor as well. He held out his arm to her. "Would you care to whisk away with me?"

"If you want the truth of it, no, I would not, but it seems I have no choice in the matter."

Lord Drayson lifted an eyebrow. "I think I prefer your lies over truth."

"In that case, Lord Drayson." Lucy slipped her hand through his arm. "I would very much love to whisk away with you." Interestingly enough, what Lucy thought was a lie felt much more real than the truth. Her hand sizzled where it touched his sleeve, and that rich and spicy smell she'd recently come to associate with him filled her senses.

In that moment, Lucy knew that her heart could not withstand a day anywhere near Lord Drayson. By the end of the week, it would surely be crushed, and Lucy would be left with nothing but prickly shards.

Much to Lucy's surprise, Lady Harriett did not deluge Lucy with questions about her time with Lord Drayson. Rather, she took her newest acquaintance under her wing, showed her around the house, and told her all about the family's charming estate in Danbury, along with story after story about the many scrapes she and her siblings had gotten into as children. It wasn't long before Miss Beresford became Lucy and Lady Harriett, just Harriett.

"I was dreadfully afraid of heights when I was young," said Harriett. "One summer, Colin promised that if I would climb to the very top of a tree, he would procure for me one of our neighbor's new puppies—one that Mama and Papa had already said I could not have. But I wanted the puppy so badly and believed that Colin could find a way to get it for me that I climbed and climbed and climbed. As the branches began to sway near the top, he yelled at me to come back down, but I refused. I had to touch the top so I could have my puppy.

"'I'll get you that puppy,'" he screamed at me. "'Just come down *now*.'"

"So I did," she continued. "And that very evening, he snuck the puppy into my bedchamber and informed me that he had fulfilled his end of the bargain. I now had my puppy, but it was my responsibility to convince Mama and Papa that it should remain mine. It didn't occur to me until later that he was too frightened to ask them himself. There he was, convincing me to face one of my fears while running like a coward from one of his own."

Lucy laughed, thinking her time at Tanglewood might not be as uncomfortable as she had imagined. Other than the carriage ride home from the wedding and a slightly awkward dinner, she had managed to avoid Lord Drayson completely. Or perhaps he was the one managing to avoid her.

Lucy frowned at the thought, then immediately accused herself of being a peagoose.

The pounding of horse hooves sounded from outside, and Lucy took a few steps to the window where she had a clear view of the scene below. Riding up the path on his black horse, Lord Drayson was accompanied by his bailiff, Mr. Graham. The two swung down from their horses and were thick in conversation. At one point, Lord Drayson glanced up and noticed her standing there. He doffed his hat, and Lucy immediately stepped away from the window and spun around, only to see a calculating gleam in Harriett's eyes.

That night, Lucy came to understand the look.

"Colin, I would like you to teach me the waltz," Harriett said the moment he had joined them after dinner.

"Pardon?" He looked at his sister as though she'd gone mad.

She instructed two footmen to move the furniture away from the rug and extended her hands to her brother. "The waltz. You and Mother are the only two who know it, and I need her to play the pianoforte. Please? If I am to have my comeout next year, I shall need to learn at some point, right Mama?"

Her mother set down her embroidery and gave her son a wearying glance. "You know that we will never hear the end of it if we do not humor her."

"She can beg until her voice grows dry," said the earl. "I will not be persuaded to teach her the waltz."

"What about Lucy?" Harriett said. "Will you teach her?"

Lucy's eyes widened at her new friend, wondering if Harriett had, indeed, gone mad.

"I do not believe Lucy wishes to learn the waltz," said Lord Drayson smoothly, easing his large frame into the chair next to her.

"Quite right," Lucy agreed, putting what she thought was an end to Harriett's ridiculous plan. "Waltzes are performed only at Almack's, and I very much doubt I shall ever set foot through those doors. And besides, I do not dance."

"What do you mean, you do not dance?" Harriett asked. "Do you not have dances in Askern?"

"Of course we do," said Lucy quickly. "I meant only that I have no talent for it. I am rather adept at treading on my partner's toes. Not even Lord Drayson could instruct my feet how to perform properly."

Harriett sat up straighter and smiled at her brother. "I do believe Lucy just issued a challenge to you, brother dear. How—"

"That was certainly not a challenge," said Lucy, horrified that it might be construed as one. "I was merely pointing out that I cannot dance."

"Nonsense," said Harriett. "You move about quite gracefully. I am certain that with proper instruction you can become a wonderful dancer."

"Harriett would know," said Lord Drayson wryly.

"I would," Harriett agreed, choosing to ignore her brother's sarcasm.

Lucy directed a pleading look at the earl. *She is your sister, will you please do something?*

His lips twitched a moment before he glanced at his mother, who seemed to be enjoying the exchange immensely. "Her voice will never dry up, will it?"

Lady Drayson smiled. "I'm afraid not."

He sighed, then slowly pushed himself up and extended a hand to Lucy. "Will you do me the honor of allowing me to teach you the waltz so that my dear sister will cease her prattling?"

"But she is the one who wishes to learn it," argued Lucy. "Not I."

"I believe I shall learn much better by watching," Harriett said quickly, proving that this had been her plan all along.

Panicked, Lucy gave it one last attempt. "But your toes, my lord."

"Have been trod on before," he said with a smile, hand still extended. "My nerves, on the other hand, can only withstand so much more."

Feeling as though she had been trapped into a corner with no means of escape, Lucy glanced at Lady Drayson for help, but the lady was already seated at the pianoforte, ready to play.

Lord Drayson wiggled his fingers. "Please, Lucy?"

Seeing no way out, she placed her fingers lightly in his and allowed him to pull her to her feet. He led her to the middle of the room, positioned her left hand on his shoulder, clasped her right fingers in his, and rested his left hand at her waist. Lucy's entire body trembled at his touch and her heart danced a waltz on its own.

The music began, and Lord Drayson explained the movements of the dance, saying something about one-two-three and moving forward and backward. Lucy tried to listen, she really did, but his scent invaded her nose, his voice reverberated in her ears, and his smile made her stomach lurch this way and that. And then he pulled her even closer and began stepping back, sideways, and forward. Lucy remained a half a step behind him the entire time. She tried to focus on the movements, but her gaze remained locked on his, and her feet moved wherever they needed to move to keep her upright.

Lord Drayson slowed his steps, and his voice finally broke through the fog in her brain. "Don't think so hard," he said quietly. "Simply listen to the music, feel its rhythm, and allow me to guide you."

He began counting again, and Lucy drew in a deep breath, trying to do as he said. Gradually, her breathing evened, the fog in her mind cleared somewhat, and she began to grasp the movements, which surprisingly, weren't overly difficult. Forward-side-back, then back-side-forward. And repeat.

As the song drew to an end, Lucy's mind had entered the doors of Almack's, and she was dancing in the center of the assembly room with none other than Lord Drayson. All eyes were on them. Some were curious, some envious, some disapproving, and some pleased, but Lucy didn't care about any of them. All she cared about was the feel of Lord Drayson's arms around her, the warmth in his eyes, and the touch of a smile on his lips.

"Would you care to dance another one?" his voice intruded into her thoughts, pulling Lucy back to the present, where her hands still clung to him even though the song had ended.

She immediately dropped her hands to her side and stepped away from him. "I believe I know it well enough now. Perhaps you will allow Harriett to take a turn."

The earl smiled. "For you, perhaps I will."

"Truly?" Harriett leapt out of her seat and grabbed her brother's hands before he could retract his offer.

"But only," added her brother firmly, "if you allow *me* to lead."

"What are you talking about? A man always leads," said Harriett. But as soon as the music started, she pushed her brother forward, sideways, and backwards, practically dragging him through the steps of the waltz. Throughout the dance, he directed dramatic and humorous glances at Lucy, appearing pained or bored or even scared. Harriett whacked his shoulder with each look, and Lucy's lips soon ached from the strain of trying not to laugh. It was a side of him she had not seen before, and she found she rather liked it.

That night, as Lucy lay in a soft and comfortable bed, staring at the embossed designs that patterned the ceiling, she thought that perhaps she wasn't as opposed to dancing as she used to think.

LUCY QUICKENED HER STEPS WHEN the pounding of hooves sounded behind her, wishing whoever it was would leave her in peace. It was her third day at Tanglewood Manor and the first time she had been able to sneak away without Harriett or Georgina in tow. Lucy wanted to check on her garden and perhaps harvest a few of the carrots to share with Tanglewood's wonderful cook.

The basket she carried swayed with each step, and as the horse neared, she glanced over her shoulder. The earl pulled Darling to a stop about twenty paces away and jumped from the horse's back. Lucy stopped as well and turned, wondering what he wanted now.

Only this morning he had waylaid her after breakfast to tell her about a book he thought she might like. A few hours later he had found her again, wanting her opinion on what flowers to plant in a certain area of the garden. Now here he was again, upsetting the peace she had only begun to feel.

The way Lucy reacted to him reminded her of a small morning glory flower. When the sun rose, the vibrant petals uncurled and blossomed, but when darkness came, it shriveled back into a pathetic little ball. It was the same with Lucy whenever Lord Drayson came near. She would immediately blossom, only to shrivel when he left. He was wreaking havoc with her peace of mind, and she wished so badly that she could return to Knotting Tree where she could avoid him completely.

"Where are you off to this afternoon?" said the earl as he approached, keeping his horse a safe distance behind him.

"I intend to harvest a few of my carrots and clip some roses, along with a few other things for a flower arrangement for your mother."

"*Your* carrots?" He quirked an eyebrow beneath the brim of his beaver. "Surely the labor of tilling the ground has earned me some stake in the harvest."

Lucy pretended to give it some thought before nodding. "I suppose you may have ten percent."

He chuckled. "If I help with the harvesting?"

Not wanting to encourage him to linger, Lucy pronounced, "Eight percent."

"Eight!"

"I'm afraid so," she answered, nodding solemnly. "I have seen you help with plants before. They have all wound up torn to shreds in a disorderly heap. I would not wish such a thing to happen to my—" she cleared her throat and corrected, "*our* carrots."

"I must protest," he said. "The only help I have given with regard to plants has been to cut the grass and rid the beds of weeds. Surely you did not expect gentle treatment of those."

"Of course not. It simply did not inspire any confidence in your ability to handle tender carrots or flowers with care."

He stopped abruptly and took hold of her arm, turning her to face him. "Lucy, if you do not wish me to help with our garden, simply say as much and I will leave you to it."

"I . . ." Here was her chance to tell him that she wished

him to *always* leave her to it. She needed him to stay far away from her heart, mind, and person so that she could find a way to move on with her life without constantly thinking of him or missing him or aching to be held by him.

But the words felt stuck in her throat, and in the end, all that came out was a strangled "No." She pulled her arm from his grasp and began walking again, hoping he wouldn't follow and yet wishing he would. Her emotions felt so muddled.

Unfortunately—or was it fortunately?—her wish was granted because he soon caught up. "What does 'no' mean exactly?"

"It means no," she repeated, the words coming easier this time. "I do not wish you to help."

"What about taking a drive with me once you have finished?"

"No." The word practically flowed off her tongue now.

"A riding lesson tomorrow?"

"No."

He caught her arm again and stepped in front of her to stop her progress. Lucy noticed that he'd left Darling to graze in the meadow several paces behind them. "Why do you try so hard to keep your distance from me?" he asked. "I thought we were friends, and yet you refuse to call me Colin, you do not want to stand up with me, ride with me, or allow me to help you with our garden, and you stiffen every time I come near, as though I am abhorrent to you. And yet you didn't seem to find me abhorrent when I was Collins. I cannot understand it."

"Friends, you say?" Lucy said, feeling her frustration rise to the surface and erupt like a stepped-upon hill of ants. "I do not think you know the definition of friendship if you think we are friends."

Rachael Anderson

His eyes widened, and he studied her for a moment before saying, "Pray enlighten me then. What is *your* definition of friendship?"

Lucy was losing patience. For an intelligent creature, he was being incredibly dim-witted. "Why are you here, Lord Drayson? What purpose do you have in coming all this way with your mother and sister? How long do you plan to remain, and what in heaven's name do you want from me? I have apologized for what I have done to you, and my mother and I have removed ourselves from the dower house. I see no reason for you to still—"

Lord Drayson's hands framed her face and his lips pressed against hers. Lucy gasped and froze, but once her initial shock subsided, the basket she carried dropped to the ground, and she began returning his kiss with vigor. Her mouth moved across his, and her hands clenched the fabric of his jacket, pulling him closer. His fingers worked their way from her cheeks to her hair, pulling several strands free from the pins.

Lucy kissed him as she had never kissed him before. It was as though someone popped the cork on her carefully guarded emotions and they came bursting out, one after the other. She wanted so much from this man while knowing she didn't deserve anything. Yet she continued to kiss him with all the energy she possessed. She kissed him until her breath was spent, and she had to pull away for air.

She buried her face in his shirt, feeling like a wanton for needing his arms around her more than ever. Against her cheek, his chest rose and fell as quickly as hers.

"That is the reason I returned," he said, keeping his arms locked tight about her.

Lucy slowly raised her face to his, noting that his eyes had become the color of storm clouds, looking down at her with something akin to uncertainty. Her mind felt so cluttered and thick.

"To kiss me again?" she said. "Lord Drayson, I—"

He clasped her shoulders, giving her a shake. "Deuce take it, Lucy, call me Colin."

"Not until you explain to me what the devil is going on," said Lucy, not caring about her language. She was tired of the rise and fall of her emotions, tired of guessing, wishing, hoping, and aching. She wanted to be free.

Lord Drayson closed his eyes, drew in a deep breath and let his hands slide down her arms to her hands, where he took her fingers in his, holding them securely in his own.

"I cannot explain what I do not understand myself," he said. "After I returned to Danbury, I could not rid my mind of your beautiful face. I wanted to see you again, make certain your reputation had not suffered because of me, and spend more time with you. I wanted to touch you, hold you, look upon you, and yes, kiss you."

"Why did you not write? Mother and I fretted for weeks, wondering if I had angered you, if we were to be turned out at any moment, if—"

"You think so little of me then?" he interrupted, his jaw taut.

Lucy's voice dropped to a whisper. "You came here to sell Tanglewood, and I used your injury to deceive you. I never had the chance to explain or see what you would think of me when all was said and done. Tell me, Colin, how could I not assume the worst?"

"Because I would never turn away . . . a friend," he said.

"Friend," she repeated, looking down at their hands. "You call me friend, and yet . . . Do you kiss all your friends, Colin?"

His finger came to rest under her chin, and he gently

lifted her head to meet his gaze. A smile hovered at the corners of his mouth. "Only the pretty ones."

He was attempting to tease a smile from her, but Lucy did not feel like smiling. She needed more from him than this. She needed his assurance that he would not crush her heart.

"What do you want from me?" she asked again.

He watched her for several heartbeats before answering. "I want time," he said quietly. "More time. With you."

Lucy drew in a shaky breath, unsure how to respond. She could either risk giving him the time he wanted—along with her heart—or cut her losses and walk away. It was her choice to make.

The trouble was, she had already given him her heart. She knew that now.

Lucy finally nodded slowly. Then she cleared her throat. "I believe I shall require your help with the carrots after all, Colin."

A small smile lifted the corners of his mouth. "On one condition."

"And that is?"

"That I get an equal share of the spoils."

"As they will all go to your cook, I suppose I can agree to those terms."

He chuckled and took a few slow steps backward before turning around to collect his horse. Lucy waited for him to return, and when he held out his arm for her to take, she accepted it without reservation. As they walked the rest of the distance to the garden, Lucy noticed that her feet felt lighter, her mind clearer, and her heart trilled with every beat.

Lord Drayson—no, *Colin*—had returned to Tanglewood because of her.

30

LUCY SELECTED A LAVENDER ROSE from the pail and began removing all the thorns and the leaves at the base of the stem. She placed it in a lovely glass vase before doing the same to two other roses. Lady Drayson and Harriett stood on either side of her, watching her movements.

"The arrangement will come together with greater ease if you begin at the center and work out from there," explained Lucy. "Also, I have found that odd numbers arranged in an asymmetrical way look best."

Lucy added a few white lilies to the mix, tucking them around and between the roses. To give it a touch of whimsy, she clipped and added some lovely greenbell. Then came several more roses, a few scattered lilies, and more greenbell. She would pause every now and again to fuss with a few stems, pull one out to clip it a bit shorter, and fuss some more. Once the vase was filled to her satisfaction, she drew back and smiled at her latest creation. She may not be handy with the needle or proficient on the pianoforte, but this . . . this she could do, and do well.

"I have absolutely no idea how you did that," said Harriett, studying the arrangement with something akin to wonder. "I will never be able to do the same."

"Do not sound completely hopeless as of yet, daughter," said Lady Drayson wryly. "Let us first attempt to mimic Lucy's skill and see if we cannot come up with something equally beautiful."

Harriett examined all the clippings Lucy had arranged in piles on the table. Everything from roses and lilies, to delphiniums, foxgloves, and geraniums, the table was an array of color and intoxicating scents. The gardens at Tanglewood were in full bloom, offering a large variety of flowers. Lucy had been in heaven that morning when she went about with a pair of shears.

"I do not know where to begin," said Harriett.

"Why not start with your favorite flower?" Lucy coached.

Harriett finally selected a deep pink orchid and held it up.

Lucy pressed her lips together in an attempt not to smile. "Orchids make wonderful filler. Perhaps select a larger bloom to begin with instead?"

"That would have been useful information to know before asking me to select a favorite flower," muttered Harriett as she set the orchid back on the table and selected a deep pink lily instead. She shot Lucy a saucy, *Does this meet with your approval?* look, lifting the stem for Lucy's inspection.

"That is lovely," said Lucy slowly, trying to think of a kind way to offer criticism yet again. "But if you would like to use the orchid in the arrangement, perhaps a less similar shade of pink would look better?"

Harriett rolled her eyes and dropped the lily, waving her hands over the flowers. "Perhaps you would be so kind as to suggest one for me."

"Well," said Lucy, trying not to enjoy that fact that for

once in her life she was more adept at something than another woman. "Why not this white lily instead?"

"Because that is what *you* used," Harriett said. "I do not wish to mimic yours exactly. I simply want my creation to be as beautiful as yours."

"Using only one of the same flowers will not make them too similar," said Lucy. "Not if you group it with some orchids, these purple delphiniums and perhaps a few of these apple tree stems."

Harriett studied Lucy's selections with interest and finally nodded. "Those could work well together, I suppose."

"Honestly, Harriett," said her mother. "You know very well they will look lovely. Lucy, you really are a wonder."

Lucy smiled and turned her attention to Lady Drayson's arrangement. "I like how you paired the foxglove with morning glory and anchored them with classic roses. I think you were bamming me when you said you had no talent with flowers."

"If this does indeed turn into something beautiful, I will owe it all to you. I, like Harriett, have never known where to begin or how to go about it. You have no idea how much your brief tutorial and example has taught and encouraged me."

"I'm glad to hear it." Lucy smiled. "Now I think I will leave you ladies to your creations and take my arrangement down to the drawing room."

"Please don't be gone too long," said Harriett, examining her arrangement with a frown. "I'm quite sure I will need your help shortly."

Lucy dropped into a curtsy and covered her heart with her palm. "I solemnly promise to make haste with my delivery and return as soon as humanly possible."

Harriett lifted an eyebrow. "No need to be so dramatic, Lucy. I shall be perfectly fine until you return."

Lucy laughed as she carried her arrangement from the room. In the past several days, she had come to feel very much at home at Tanglewood. Lady Drayson was kind and gracious, with a dry wit that could send Lucy into a fit of the giggles. And Harriett was like a gale wind bursting forth at all times. She was lively, frank, and the most wonderful friend Lucy could have ever hoped to find.

And then there was Colin.

Lucy's heart quickened its pace at the mere thought of his handsome face and intriguing eyes that seemed to change color depending upon his moods. Lately, they had been the color of a striking blue iris. He had become quite adept at finding opportunities to seek her out and even steal a kiss whenever possible. They walked the grounds, harvested more vegetables from the garden, laughed over dinner, and danced another waltz. He had even procured a sweet bay pony for her, and Lucy could now ride the animal. She'd progressed to the point where she could pet and nuzzle it with no fear that her nose would be bitten off. She had even given the pony a name.

"I believe I will call her Dear," she said to Colin as they left the stables following her first ride.

He threw his head back and laughed, then wrapped his arm about her shoulders as he guided her back to the house. "Dear and Darling . . ." he mused with another chuckle. "I greatly fear we will be the laughingstock whenever we go riding together."

Lucy had loved the sound of that word. *Together.* Her heart had warmed at the thought, for there was no one else with whom she would like to be together with.

Lucy set her arrangement on a table and fiddled with a few of the stems one last time before taking a step back to examine it from a distance.

Two warm and welcoming arms wound around her waist, and a light kiss tingled the skin at the nape of her neck. Lucy smiled and folded her arms over Colin's, lifting her face to his so that her cheek rubbed against his.

"Mmm," she murmured. "I hoped that if I were to sneak away you would ferret me out."

"I am becoming rather good at that, aren't I?" He turned her around until she faced him. Then he cupped the sides of her face and pressed a kiss to her willing lips.

Lucy allowed the kiss to go on for a few moments before forcing herself to pull away. "Sir," she whispered, laying her palm on his chest to keep some distance between them. "It is one thing to steal a kiss in a private corner of the gardens and quite another to indulge in such a public place as the drawing room. What if someone were to walk in?"

"They would probably exit rather quickly to avoid further embarrassment. And if you call me 'sir' one more time, I shall drag you to the middle of town and kiss you breathless for all to see."

"But then you would be obligated to do the honorable thing by me, and we both know how much you dislike the idea of having matrimony forced upon you," Lucy teased. "And I shouldn't like it anymore than you."

He heaved a sigh and gave her fingers a quick squeeze before tucking her hand through his arm so that he could lead her from the room. "I despise it when you insist on being sensible."

Lucy laughed, feeling a closeness to him that she would have never thought she could feel with another person. Around Colin she was complete. All seemed so perfectly in order with nothing missing from her life.

He led her past a maid and back up the stairs to where Lady Drayson and Harriett continued to fret over their arrangements. Lady Drayson's looked quite stunning, and Harriett's . . . well, perhaps another lesson would be in order.

"Did a stampede of cattle come through and trample your flowers, Harriett?" said Colin in his loving, brotherly way.

Harriett glared, and Lucy tried not to smile as she released Colin's arm to see if she could do anything to salvage the arrangement.

"It doesn't look so bad," said Lucy, fiddling with a stem here, trying to right a toppled stem there, and wondering how it came to be in such a sorry condition.

"It is dreadful, isn't it?" said Harriett in a mournful, self-pitying way.

"Dreadful is putting it mildly," said her brother, earning another glare.

"Now Harriett," Lady Drayson said patiently. "This is the first flower arrangement you have attempted. Lucy has put together a great many, I presume, and I have more experience as well. You cannot expect to do it perfectly on your first attempt."

"It is true," Lucy agreed. "If you could see all the flowers I have ruined in the past, you would not feel nearly so bad."

Harriett brightened. "There is hope then?"

Lucy tried to erase the doubt from her expression as she glanced at Harriett's creation again. "There is always hope. Perhaps tomorrow we may try again."

Harriett smiled and lifted an eyebrow at her mother. "Do you think we might exchange her for Colin, Mama? I would greatly prefer it."

"Then who would you spar with, darling?" said Lady Drayson wryly. "The cat?"

"Lucy could easily spar with me," said Harriett.

"Not so well as your brother," said Lucy. "And I

certainly could not ride with you. I have seen the two of you race across the property, and I fear I will never be up to such a feat."

"I disagree," said Colin. "Give it some more time, and you will be racing alongside us."

The warmth in his gaze sent Lucy's heart fluttering, and she very nearly rose to her tiptoes to place a kiss of gratitude on his cheek.

"Colin," said Harriett. "Will you not tell us the point at which your memory returned? Lucy has confided to Mama and me about your little wager, and I should very much like to see you wearing that ghastly hat."

Colin arched an eyebrow at Lucy. "Perhaps I am not the one who should wear it."

Harriett fiddled with one of the lilies in her arrangement until it, too, began to droop. She frowned at it before lifting her gaze to her brother. "If that is the case, then you would not have a reason to withhold the truth."

"Perhaps I'm not anxious to put Lucy through the shame of wearing the ridiculous hat."

Unperturbed, Harriett continued, "But you only just suggested that Lucy should be the one to wear it."

"I have not suggested anything of the kind. Nor will I."

A slow smile spread across Harriett's face as she watched her brother. "I do believe you are trying to protect your dignity," she said. "You know as well as I that Lucy won. You so obviously keep it a mystery because *you* don't wish to be shamed. Would it help, brother dear, if I were to affix my lovely flower arrangement to the brim? Would that make you more inclined to confess?"

Colin's eyes strayed to Harriett's sorry arrangement, and his lips twitched. "Why confess when it is so more fun to know something that you, *dear sister*, do not."

Harriett's eyes narrowed, Lady Drayson chuckled, and Lucy grinned. In those moments it was easy to forget that she was not part of the Drayson family and that things could not continue as they were forever.

LUCY'S FEW REMAINING DAYS at Tanglewood sped by like a high-speed curricle race. They were filled with such happiness that she almost wished her mama and Mr. Shepherd would extend their wedding trip for many more weeks. But it was not to be, for all too soon Lucy was gathered with the family in the drawing room for their final evening together.

"Lucy, your floral arrangement is still so fresh," commented Lady Drayson from where she sat on the sofa. "You must have a special touch. Mine began to wilt the day after I created it, and yesterday, I finally gave up and asked a footman to throw it out."

"I have no such touch," said Lucy, taking a seat across from her on the settee. "It is probably because I instructed Katy to dump out the old water and fill it with fresh water every day. I have found that clean water begets longer-lasting flowers."

Harriett sank down next to her mother and arranged the skirt of the lavender gown she wore before folding her hands primly in her lap. "I am discovering that our dear Lucy is very good at giving us proper instructions only *after* the opportune moment has passed."

Lucy laughed. "I do apologize. Truly. I had meant to tell Katy to do the same for your flowers, but it slipped my mind."

"I have noticed that you have been a little distracted of late," said Lady Drayson with a humorous glint in her eyes. "I wonder why that could be."

Lucy's face heated. She had no idea how to respond to such a comment. And Colin was no help at all.

"I will happily take full responsibility for any and all distractions." He gave Lucy's shoulder a light squeeze as he walked around the back of the settee and took a seat next to her. The past two nights he had chosen to forgo his port and had followed the ladies to the drawing room instead.

Harriett's feet began to dance out a rhythm on the floor. Her lovely gown swished around her ankles in a pretty show of her boredom. Lucy recognized the signs immediately and held back a smile. Her friend could not sit still for long.

"What shall we do tonight?" Harriett asked. "Perform on the pianoforte? Take a walk around the gardens? Discuss how lovely the weather has been today?" Her expression brightened, and she clapped her hands. "Oh, I have the most wonderful idea."

"Why do I find myself suddenly afraid?" said Colin, draping his arm across the back of the settee. The sleeve of his jacket grazed Lucy's bare neck and sent a swarm of gooseflesh down her back.

"You should be afraid," said Harriett, "for my plan involves a wager, and we all know how dreadfully unlucky you are with those."

"You know nothing of the sort," he said.

"What sort of wager?" Lucy's curiosity was piqued. Harriett's ideas, though out of the ordinary, almost always made for a lively time.

"Actually, it is more of a contest than a wager," said Harriett. "As this is Lucy's final evening with us, let us make it last and say that the person who is able to stay awake for the longest amount of time is the winner."

"Oh, heavens child," said Lady Drayson. "Why on earth would you wish to do such a thing?"

"Because it will be fun. And the winner shall get. . ." She pressed her lips together in thought before brightening. "To name any wish they please."

Colin snickered. "And who will grant said wish?"

"The losers, of course."

"And if said wish is not grantable?" he asked.

Harriett shrugged. "Then the wish will not be granted. So the winner had best keep that in mind and make sure to ask for a grantable wish."

Lady Drayson pressed her fingers to her temples as though she already felt a headache coming on. "I have a feeling this is to be the longest night of my life."

"Who wants to play whist?" Harriett beamed.

And so it began. The four of them played whist for hours until Lady Drayson cried off and returned to the sofa to rest her mind and her eyes for a bit. At that point, the cards were put away, and Lucy, Colin and Harriett began a game of riddles. Twice, Lucy's eyes grew heavy, but a slight nudge from Colin's elbow jolted her back awake. Why he bothered, Lucy could not understand. She felt sure that Harriett would be declared the winner.

But Lucy had underestimated Colin, who never seemed to tire. At some point during the wee hours of the morning, Harriett's head finally flopped against the wings of the large chair where she had curled up. Her mouth parted slightly and a light snore escaped, making Lucy giggle. Poor Lady Drayson had been asleep for hours. Harriett had propped a pillow under her head and lifted her feet to the sofa, so that she could sleep more peacefully in a reclined position. Colin had tucked a rug around her as well.

Blinking against the dryness in her eyes, Lucy stood and stretched her arms overhead, feeling utterly exhausted. "I declare you the winner, Colin. Shall we see if we can help your mother and sister off to bed?"

Colin's hand reached for hers, and he tugged her back down next to him.

"Since you have declared me the winner," said Colin. "I have earned a wish. And it is my wish that I have you all to myself for a few moments longer before I have to return you to your mother."

Lucy was more than happy to grant his wish. She smiled and snuggled into his side, murmuring with pleasure when his arm wrapped around her. He kissed her lightly on the forehead and settled back.

"Have you missed your mother?" he asked.

"Of course," she answered. "And Mr. Shepherd as well, if you can believe it. He has become a father to me. While I miss my natural father a great deal, and always will, Mr. Shepherd is quite wonderful, is he not?"

"Yes," Colin answered. "And I must admit, Yorkshire is rather lovely, especially this time of year."

"I am glad to hear you say as much." Lucy smiled, forcing her eyes to stay open. "I couldn't imagine living anywhere else. It's the only home I've ever known."

The earl said nothing more, so Lucy snuggled in a little closer and murmured, "What about you? Do you miss your father?"

A few moments passed before he answered. "I do miss him. Or rather, I miss the relationship we could have had if I had been a better son. We were not so close as I would have liked, but I did value his opinion on certain matters. I feel as though he left me a great weight to manage, and I wish I would have cared a little more to learn from him."

Lucy twisted to look up at him, but his eyes had a glazed look, as though he were far away from the drawing room at Tanglewood. There was a rawness in his expression, a vulnerability that Lucy had never seen before. Even when his memory had fled him, Colin had always exuded confidence, assurance, and strength. But now, whatever weight he carried could almost be seen, and it saddened her.

"Is there anything I can do?" she asked quietly, running a finger over one of the lines near his eyes.

He captured her hand and kissed it, and the vulnerability was replaced with warmth. "You can stay exactly as you are."

There is something you are not telling me, Lucy thought, wishing that he would. She wanted to pry whatever had caused those worry lines out of him, ease it from his shoulders, and figure out a way to lighten his burdens, but he said nothing more. He merely clasped Lucy's hand and leaned his head against the back of the sofa and closed his eyes. Lucy studied the angles on his face, his rigid nose with a slight bump in the middle, his textured lips, and every line. There were smile lines and worry lines, thinking lines and teasing lines. Lucy recognized all of them. She had fallen in love with each one.

What would happen to their "friendship" once she returned to Knotting Tree? Would it begin to fade? Would this closeness they shared eventually become a great distance? Or could Lucy dare to believe that this was merely the beginning of something wonderful? Was it possible for her, impoverished daughter of a vicar, to have a future with Colin Cavendish, the fifth Earl of Drayson? It felt so right, being with him. So normal. So comfortable. So . . . perfect.

Lucy couldn't help but think that the Draysons had once, long ago, called Tanglewood their home. Was there any hope at all that it could be their home again?

With such thoughts on her mind, Lucy closed her eyes and drifted into a wistful sleep.

BRIGHT LIGHT INVADED LUCY'S wonderful dream. She closed her eyes against it and rolled away from the window. Another drape flew open, and more light entered the room. Lucy groaned in protest.

"Are you ill, Miss Lucy?" Georgina's anxious voice sounded from somewhere, invading yet again. Lucy very nearly told poor Georgina to go to the devil until she caught herself in time and moaned instead.

"I'm fine, Georgy. I'm simply wishing you would go away." Lucy squinted out of one eye to see her maid readying her gown. Apparently Georgina wasn't going anywhere.

"I'm afraid I can't, Miss Lucy. Mr. and Mrs. Shepherd 're 'ere ter collect you. Probably best not ter keep 'em waitin' too long."

Sleep forgotten, Lucy bolted upright. "Mama is here? Already?"

"Aye, Miss. 'Tis nearly noon."

Noon already? Lucy could scarce believe it. She shoved the covers aside and slid from her bed. "Gracious, Georgy, why did you not wake me sooner?"

"I tried, Miss," said Georgina with a grin. "But you said somethin' about leavin' you be with Lord Drayson, so leave you be I did. Seemed ter me like you was in the middle of a sweet dream. 'E carried you ter your bed last night, you know."

Lucy's eyes widened as the memories of the night before returned to her mind. She glanced down at her nightdress with wide eyes. "How did I come to be wearing this, Georgy?"

"Lord Drayson awakened me, Miss. You was 'alf asleep, but I managed ter get you dressed proper-like."

Lucy sighed and enfolded Georgina in a hug. "Thank you for always being so good to me, Georgy. I am a perfect wretch to have barked at you a moment ago."

"'Tis nothin', Miss. Nah one likes ter be awakened from a 'appy dream."

"Which is precisely why I am so grateful you accepted the job as my lady's maid. Whatever would I do without you?"

"I might not 'ave a job much longer if'n I don't get you dressed soon."

Lucy capitulated to her maid's ministrations, trying to sip her chocolate and eat a few bites of toast in the process. Perhaps the food would help settle her stomach, which was currently a wad of nerves. Her time at Tanglewood had felt like a beautiful dream, but now that dream was about to come to an end, and she had no clue as to what her future held.

Not twenty minutes later, Lucy rushed down the stairs to greet her parents. Lady Drayson was already in the morning room, looking fresh and beautiful, as though she had not been made to stay awake so late the night before. Colin and Harriett were nowhere in sight.

"Mama, Papa." Lucy hugged each in turn, pausing in front of Mr. Shepherd. "I am free to call you Papa now, am I not? Mr. Shepherd is such a mouthful and Stephen is far too staid."

"Papa will suit me just fine," he said, returning her hug. Both parents glowed with a happiness Lucy could now understand.

She ushered them back to their seats. "You must tell us all about your trip. I am anxious for news."

Her mother smiled and took a seat on the sofa once again. "I am afraid we have already bored Lady Drayson with the details, so I shall wait to repeat myself until we have returned home."

"Your mother was just telling me about the ball they wish to host for you on Friday next."

"Oh, yes. The ball." Lucy sank down slowly beside her mother, wondering how she felt about it now. Her thoughts went to Colin and what it had felt like to dance in his arms. Perhaps a ball would not be so distasteful after all, so long as he would be in attendance.

"Try not to sound too thrilled, my dear," Mrs. Shepherd teased, patting Lucy's hands. To Lady Drayson, she explained, "For Lucy, balls are more of a thorn than a fragrant flower."

Lady Drayson laughed. "I understand completely. I never did enjoy them the way other young ladies of my acquaintance seemed to. They were always stifling affairs where I was forced to dance with more than one young man who either bored me to tears or trod on my slippers."

"And yet every young lady ought to experience at least one ball thrown in her honor, wouldn't you agree, Lady Drayson?" said Mr. Shepherd.

"Most definitely," answered Lady Drayson. "My own comeout ball was quite an enjoyable experience, I must say. It was there that I was introduced to the late Lord Drayson, which also happened to be the first and last ball he ever attended." She laughed. "I quite lost my heart to him that night, but I was such a timid thing back then that he didn't spare me a second thought. I had to do some sleuthing and put myself in his path numerous times before he finally began to notice me during my second season."

"Truly?" Lucy said, delighted at the story.

"Truly," she answered with a soft smile. "Those were wonderful times. I envy you, Mrs. and Mr. Shepherd. Most people do not get a second chance at love. One need not look far to see that you are both very happy together."

"Yes, we are," Mrs. Shepherd said, clasping her husband's hand. "Very happy. It was a lucky coincidence that I had to look only as far as the neighboring estate to find him. I feel very blessed indeed."

Lucy studied Lady Drayson with a new perspective. She seemed so strong and unwavering, and yet underneath that exterior, Lucy could see that she may not be quite so impervious as she let on. It tore at Lucy's heart.

Lady Drayson didn't seem to be one to dwell on sad things for long. She smiled brightly. "I think a ball is a splendid idea. Harriett and I would be thrilled to assist you in any way that we can."

"I would love your help," said Mrs. Shepherd. "I really have no notion how to go about it, and I'm afraid if I left it in Mr. Shepherd's hands, instead of dancing and merriment, our guests would be subjected to discourses on medicine, politics, or the various patterns in the weather."

"I believe you are spreading it on a bit thick, my dear."

"Perhaps." She smiled.

Lady Drayson laughed. "I must warn you that if you allow Harriett to be involved, there will be mountains of merriment."

"Mountains and mountains," Lucy agreed.

They discussed plans for the ball for a few moments longer before Mr. and Mrs. Shepherd rose to leave, thanking their hostess one last time for welcoming Lucy into their home.

"It was truly wonderful having her here," said Lady Drayson. "Our family has taken quite a fancy to her."

Lucy smiled, wanting the opportunity to say goodbye to Colin and Harriett before she left. "Is Harriett still abed?" she asked.

"I'm afraid so. Her maid attempted to rouse her and was struck by a large pillow as a result. But we will be sure to call on you tomorrow morning."

Lucy nodded, wanting to ask about Colin as well, but unsure if she should. He was likely still in bed as well. She twisted her hands together in a moment of hesitation before Lady Drayson seemed to guess what was on her mind.

"Colin would be here to say goodbye, but his bailiff arrived an hour ago with some urgent business. They have been shut away in the library ever since."

Lucy nodded again, struggling to keep a happy countenance. "Tell them both goodbye for me, and . . . thank you. I enjoyed my time with your family immensely." She gave Lady Drayson a parting hug and followed her parents to the waiting coach, where her small trunk had already been added to the rest of the luggage, thanks to Georgina.

Lucy climbed inside, settled into the seat next to Georgina, and watched Tanglewood grow smaller and smaller as they rode away.

TRUE TO LADY DRAYSON'S PROMISE, the family called at Knotting Tree the following morning. As soon as Lucy received news that they had come, she dropped her watering can on the marble tile in the conservatory and rushed to greet them. It had only been a day, but it seemed like weeks since she had seen them.

They were already seated in the salon with her parents when she found them. The men stood when she entered.

"Hello." She greeted them with a warm smile, her gaze lingering on Colin. He looked as handsome as usual, but his smile seemed a touch strained. She tried not to worry herself over it as she sat down in the chair next to his. "It is wonderful to have you here. It feels like an age since I have seen you last."

"I feel the same," said Harriett. "Yesterday was the dreariest of days. I awoke with a headache that refused to dissipate, Colin spent the entire day shut in the library with Mr. Graham, and Mother wanted to try her hand at arranging flowers again. I'm sorry to say that my second attempt fared even worse than before."

"I don't believe you for a moment," said Lucy, remembering how dreadful Harriett's first arrangement had looked. But Lady Drayson's subtle nod had Lucy reconsidering.

"Mother!" Harriett had noticed the nod as well and wasn't at all happy about it.

Lady Drayson's lips twitched. "I'm very sorry to have to say it, Harriett, but you are in the right of it. I believe you took your headache out on those poor flowers."

Lucy couldn't help the laugh that bubbled out of her mouth. She glanced at Lord Drayson to share the moment with him, but although he smiled, his eyes had that faraway look about them, as though his mind was focused on far less trivial matters than a ruined bouquet.

Lucy wanted to pull him aside and question him, force him to share his burdens with her, but she knew he would not appreciate such a scene. When the talk soon turned to the ball, Lucy joined in with the other ladies to plot and plan. But all the while, she stole glances at Colin and tried not to worry. Where had the teasing gone? The warmth in his expression? His excuses to be near her? Already, it felt as though he was drifting away.

Perhaps it is merely a difficult day for him, and tomorrow will be different, she thought hopefully.

But tomorrow was not much different. Or the next day. Or the next. With each new day that came and went, Lucy felt the distance between them lengthening. Her worst fears were being realized, and she felt powerless to stop it from happening.

The few times Lucy and her mother called at Tanglewood to discuss the upcoming ball, not once did Colin grace them with his presence. According to Lady Drayson, he was always away on business, and Lucy could only wonder what sort of business took him away so often. It was a side to him that he had never really shown Lucy. But now it seemed to be consuming him. Was something wrong? Had an investment failed? Was he having financial difficulties?

Please talk to me, she thought when she caught a glimpse of him riding away as she was coming.

Lucy's entire being ached to understand the reason behind his distance, but try as she might, nothing understandable came to mind. Had his feelings toward her changed so drastically in so short a time?

The day of the ball finally came, and Lucy was quite on edge. It was a day most young ladies dreamt about, but she couldn't shake the dreadful feeling that hovered around her heart, reminding her of the day the doctor had visited their home for the last time and explained that there was nothing more he could do for her father. It felt like a vicious storm was on its way, and rather than face it head on, Lucy wanted to hide away in her bedchamber and not come out until the skies had cleared.

Lady Drayson and Harriett called in the morning to see to the final details of the ball. They were to create a few flower arrangements and add the finishing touches to the ballroom that had not been used once in all the years Mr. Shepherd had lived in Askern. For a few hours, Lucy was able to forget her worries and get lost in the merriment of arranging flowers with the Draysons. Harriett still couldn't pair flowers together without it looking misshapen or lopsided, but with a few adjustments, Lucy made her arrangement look informally beautiful, like Harriett.

"It is quite frightful, isn't it?" Harriett said. "Perhaps we should display it in a dark corner of the library where no one will be subject to its imperfections."

"I think it is charming, and I shall display it in the ballroom along with the others," said Lucy. "As it is my ball, I should get whatever it is I wish."

"You are perfectly right." Harriett took Lucy's hands and gave them a squeeze in a rare gesture of affection. "You really ought to get whatever it is you wish tonight. And I hope and pray you shall. I hope we all shall."

If only life could be so magical, thought Lucy. Close your eyes, speak a wish, and suddenly what you wanted most appeared. But if it were that easy, Colin would be here now, taunting Harriett about her flowers and telling Lucy that he planned to instruct the orchestra to play a waltz so that they could shock the entire village by dancing it together.

But he was not here, and . . . Lucy refused to dwell on it a moment longer. Despite the feeling of dread, she would attempt to make this a wonderful, memorable night for herself and all those attending.

"Only wait until late summer, when Queen Anne's lace is in bloom," said Mrs. Shepherd. "Last year, Lucy created the loveliest arrangement I have ever beheld with that flower. It looked like a large ball of delicate lace."

Rather than brightening at the prospect, Lady Drayson and Harriett appeared saddened.

"If only we could see such a creation, Mrs. Shepherd. Unfortunately, we will not be here in August," said Harriett. "Has Lucy not—" Harriett stopped abruptly when she caught sight of Lucy's wide eyes.

"Oh my goodness, you do not know," Harriett whispered, her eyes wide as well. Almost as suddenly, her jaw tightened, and she frowned at her mother. "Colin has not told her yet. Can you believe that? My brother is a fool of all fools. Even Prinny himself—"

"Harriett, that is quite enough," spoke her mother firmly, and Harriett clamped her mouth shut, still frowning. Lucy's heart pounded as she waited for someone—anyone—to explain.

Lady Drayson bit her bottom lip for a few moments before exhaling a sigh. "Colin should be the one to tell you this, my dear, but I shall not keep you in suspense until that time comes."

Harriett scoffed and muttered, "It should have already come."

Lady Drayson directed a warning glance at her daughter before continuing. "It seems a buyer has been found for Tanglewood. He would like to take up residence immediately and has asked that we be removed from the house in two week's time."

The room began to wobble and tilt. Lucy's fingers clutched the table as she struggled to breathe. Tanglewood was to be sold after all. The Draysons would be leaving. Colin would be hers no longer—not that he ever was hers, but there had been a few blissful days when she thought he could be. Lucy drew in a sharp intake of breath as the reality settled around her.

Why had he kept this news from her? Why had he not prepared her in some way? Why had he given her the world, only to snatch it away at the first opportunity?

Her body trembled even as her eyes began to sting. She wanted to throw her arms around her mother and sob until her heart stopped throbbing, but she refused to make such a spectacle of herself in front of the Draysons. And yet she could not remain standing about either, feigning indifference about something that she was not indifferent to at all. She did not have the strength for it.

So Lucy did the only thing she could. She ran.

Voices called for her to stop, but she quickened her feet instead, running and running until she had reached her bedchamber where she found Georgina laying out her gown for the evening. It was there she flung herself onto her bed and burst into tears.

Colin sat hunched at his desk, attempting to read through the contract Erasmus had drafted, but his mind would not focus. It had already been signed by the buyer—a Mr. Jonathan Ludlow—and only awaited Colin's signature to be official. And yet he could not bring himself to sign his name just yet. Unbeknownst to Colin, Erasmus had scoured the country to find a buyer willing to allow the Beresfords to remain on the property. By the time such a buyer had been found, Mrs. Beresford had already become Mrs. Shepherd, and an occupied dower house was no longer an issue—not that any of it mattered at all to Mr. Ludlow.

The man wanted the property regardless. In fact, he wanted any property that was in a rundown state. If Tanglewood could not be his in two week's time, he would go looking elsewhere. Colin had already put him off for a fortnight and wished he could continue to do so, but Mr. Ludlow had finally given him an ultimatum. Sign today or do not sign at all.

Colin leaned back in his chair and sighed, rolling the pen between the palms of his hands. Through the open window at his side, he could see the dower house in the distance. He pictured Lucy kneeling in her gardens, wearing her worn straw bonnet and smiling—always smiling. One word or look from her was all it took to induce Colin to smile or laugh or have the strongest urge to shake her senseless. She had wriggled into his mind and heart to the point that the thought of losing her made him ill.

She was the sole reason he could not bring himself to sign his name to the contract just yet.

A loud rap sounded on the door before it burst open.

His mother breezed into the room, skirts swishing, and the moment Colin saw her stern expression, he knew he was about to be read a lecture.

"Colin, you are my son and I love you, but you are behaving like a nodcock," she said.

Colin had no idea why he found her comment amusing, but he smiled faintly, then steeled himself for what was to come. Any conversation beginning in such a way could not bode well for him.

He gestured for his mother to take the chair opposite his desk, which she did. Then he lifted an eyebrow to indicate he was ready for her to continue, which she also did.

"I have tried to stay out of your affairs, but I'm afraid I cannot any longer. After your behavior toward Lucy at Tanglewood, I was certain that you had at least some sort of understanding with her. Is that not the case?"

Colin pressed his lips together a moment before answering. "No. At least not yet."

His mother gaped at him. "What in heaven's name are you waiting for? Father Christmas? And why on earth would you agree to sell Tanglewood at such a time?"

"I have not signed the contract yet. The situation is . . . complicated."

His mother's expression hardened and her jaw became taut. "Perhaps you can *un*complicate it so that a simple female mind like my own can understand."

He let out a breath and barely refrained from rolling his eyes. "That is not what I meant, and you know it, Mother. I only meant to say that this is my problem, not yours."

"Like all of your father's business dealings became *your* problem and not mine when he died?"

"Exactly."

She shook her head as though her son was very much in

the wrong. "Colin, you have always been fiercely independent, and while it is a great asset to your character, it is also a flaw. From the time you were a babe, you have never wished for my—or anyone's—help with anything. You preferred the sofa to your nursemaid's hand when learning to walk. You would drag over a stool to help you reach high places instead of asking an adult to reach something for you. You learned to eat on your own, shoot on your own, and ride a horse on your own."

"Your point, Mother?" Colin was not finding her lecture nearly as amusing now.

She slowly rose from her chair and bent forward, planting her palms on the desk as she met her son's gaze. "My point is this. From the moment you took over your father's holdings, you have kept me out, insisting that it was now your burden to carry and you would handle matters yourself. You were so adamant that I stepped back and allowed you to do so, thinking you would eventually come to your senses. But I can no longer stand back for I have lost all patience with you."

Colin pressed the end of the pen against his chin and frowned. It seemed he was getting reprimanded for attempting to be a gentleman and not burden his recently widowed mother with the troubles associated with business. Not only had she needed time to grieve, but a man didn't burden his mother—or wife—with such things. It was Colin's responsibility—and his alone—to see that the family's holdings stay strong throughout the remainder of his life and for future generations to come.

"Mother, I don't understand what has you so upset," he finally said.

She stood to her full height, which was rather tall for a woman. Colin would have stood as well, but he had a feeling that she wished to tower over him in this moment, so he remained in his seat.

"If you had bothered to ask my opinion about Tangle-wood, not only could I have informed you that a lovely family called the Beresfords were living in the dower house, but I could have told you the reasons as to why."

The pen froze between his palms. "You knew?"

"Of course I knew. It was my idea."

"What?" Colin had never felt more shocked in his life. Why had she not said as much before now? Never mind the fact that he hadn't asked. She could have volunteered the information.

"Your father had the habit of consulting me on all important matters, which I appreciated. We had been discussing the possibility of selling Tanglewood for quite some time and had finally decided to move ahead with it when we received news that Mr. Beresford had died. I knew his wife, having no connections of her own, would be left with nothing. So I told your father that even though it didn't make financial sense, we should consider holding onto Tanglewood a while longer and offer the dower house to the Beresfords. He agreed and left London that very day, arriving in time for the funeral."

His mother walked around the desk and placed a hand on Colin's shoulder, giving it a squeeze. "There is a reason a man and a woman complement each other. A woman thinks with her heart and a man with his head. When the two come together to work through difficulties, more perspectives can be evaluated and a better solution can be found."

Colin let out a slow breath as he considered his mother's words. They were wise words, spoken by a wise woman. In that moment, he realized that he had never looked up to his parents in the way he should have.

He covered his mother's hand with his own and gave it a gentle squeeze. "I am sorry for not consulting you about Tanglewood. Truly, I am. I had no idea you had any knowledge of . . ." He wasn't sure how to word the rest of the sentence, so he let it dangle.

"Anything beyond tea parties, menus, and fripperies?" his mother finished for him with a smile.

"Apparently I am a nodcock."

His mother laughed. "I have a feeling you will be cured of that very soon."

Colin fingered the paperwork on the desk before sliding it toward his mother. "The contract for the sale of Tanglewood," he said. "It's a good offer and one we would both be nodcocks to turn down for we will likely never see such an offer again. But, as I have already informed you and Harriett, he wants us gone soon."

He glanced up at his mother. "What are your thoughts on the matter?"

Lady Drayson eyed the paperwork but did not pick it up. At long last, she slid it back toward him. "I believe you are asking the wrong woman that question. Perhaps once you discuss it with the right one, everything will look a little clearer."

Colin swallowed, forcing himself to voice his greatest fear aloud. "I do not want to ask her to choose, Mama, and yet . . ."

"Choose she must?" Lady Drayson finished for him.

He nodded and swallowed again. "If we had more time. If . . . well, what if it isn't me?"

His mother lifted his chin with her finger and looked at Colin with eyes that seemed far wiser than they had only moments before. "What if it is?" she said quietly. With a slight smile, she kissed him on the forehead and left him alone with thoughts that were a little less muddled than they had been before.

Colin set the pen on top of the paperwork and stood. It was past time to dress for Lucy's ball.

HER EMOTIONS SPENT, LUCY submitted to Georgina's ministrations to dress her for the ball with a countenance devoid of any feeling. Her heart and mind had run through the entire gamut, and all that remained was a vast emptiness, which was actually preferable to the excessive weeping she'd indulged in earlier. Georgina had done her best to console Lucy until her mother had arrived to do the same. But it wasn't until Mr. Shepherd entered the wretched scene that Lucy had finally seen reason.

He had walked to the bed and gently lifted Lucy's tear-stained and undoubtedly blotchy face, and with a tender look in his eyes, said, "Your story is not near to being over, my dear. There is still much to be written. Chin up, and let us see how it will all turn out, eh?"

His words had somehow given strength to her shattered heart and had finally stopped the flow of tears. Her new papa was right. Her story was not over. It had simply hit a very large rut in the road and had broken down for a bit. Lucy had landed in ruts before and had always managed to find a way out. She would do the same with this one.

As she looked at her reflection in the glass, Lucy studied the white on white embroidered linen gown. Slightly out of style, it had a lovely square neckline and puffed sleeves over longer, sheer sleeves. Her parents had given it to her on her seventeenth birthday, right before her father fell ill. Only weeks later, she had tucked the gown away in the back of her wardrobe to make room for mourning clothes. Though she'd attended a few country balls since that time, the dress had remained untouched. It had never felt right to wear it when her father would not be in attendance.

But tonight, it had felt more right than the new gown Mr. and Mrs. Shepherd had presented her with after their trip. Though the rose silk was far lovelier than any gown Lucy had ever owned, she had passed it over for the white embroidered one that her parents had given to her with so much love years before. It were as though her father's comforting arms now surrounded her, giving her the strength she would need to make it through the night. She could almost hear his voice whispering in her ear. *Wear it, my darling girl. It's time.*

Georgina had styled Lucy's hair in an elegant twist that erupted into a mound of curls that spiraled down from the crown of her head. Lucy had never looked finer, and she wrapped her maid in a quick hug. "Thank you, Georgy. You have worked wonders with the red puffs that used to be my eyes."

"You look beautiful, Miss. I 'ope you 'ave a grand time."

As ready as she could ever be, Lucy stepped down the stairs to join her mama and papa in the receiving line. All the guests faces were a blur as they passed by, and Lucy couldn't remember a thing she said to anyone, only that the Draysons had not yet arrived. Would Colin even come?

When it was time to take her place for the opening dance with Mr. Shepherd, Lucy's face ached from the strain of feigning a smile.

"A smile is not a smile unless it can be seen in one's eyes," Mr. Shepherd teased as the music began for the cotillion.

"You think I ought to drop the act entirely?" Lucy asked, grateful for the lightness of his tone. For a brief moment her smile almost felt genuine.

"Certainly not," he said. "You may not be able to fool me or your mother, but you are doing a splendid job of duping the rest. Even Mrs. Bidding seems to believe you are quite thrilled to be the belle of the ball."

The steps of the dance carried them apart for several paces, and when they were together again, Lucy asked, "Mrs. Bidding was not curious as to where the Draysons are this evening?" Lucy couldn't deny her own curiosity on the matter.

"I'm sure she believes, as I do, that they will be here shortly. Perhaps a wheel has broken on their carriage, stranding them somewhere between here and Tanglewood."

"Or a highwayman has detained them," suggested Lucy.

"Or they spotted a rabbit hopping by, and Lord Drayson has decided to hunt it."

Lucy almost giggled at that. "Or perhaps they stopped in at the dower house to snack on some of my carrots. They are quite delicious, you know."

He chuckled. "Carrots, indeed. Ah, there is that genuine smile I do so love."

Lucy felt lighter after that and found herself enjoying the rest of the cotillion. When the music came to an end, she felt much more ready to face whatever came next, even if it was most unexpected.

A rather tall, elegantly dressed gentleman stepped in front of her and bowed over her hand. "Again we meet, Miss Beresford. Mr. Shepherd." His hair was a nondescript brown, but styled like a wild and unruly Bedford crop that had been allowed to grow beyond what was fashionable, and yet it seemed to suit the hardness Lucy noticed in his rather striking green eyes. She recognized that look immediately. It was probably very similar to the look in her own eyes.

How could Lucy not remember meeting this man earlier? She glanced at her papa for help.

Mr. Shepherd tried to hide his amusement at her obvious bafflement. "How do you do, Mr. Ludlow? I hope you are enjoying yourself."

"I shall enjoy myself more if this beautiful young lady will agree to dance with me."

Feeling more than a little confused, Lucy allowed him to lead her onto the floor, wondering when she had met Mr. Ludlow—the receiving line, perhaps?—and what he had already told her about himself.

"In the event you may not remember," he said, correctly interpreting her expression as they walked across the dance floor, "we met at the door. I am here from London to see about a property."

"Oh," was her only response. Nowhere, in Lucy's sea of memories, could she place his face.

"Lady Harriett extended the invitation," he continued. "As I told your parents before. I do hope that you are not displeased that a stranger has come to your ball."

Feeling utterly ridiculous for not recalling her introduction to him, Lucy lifted her chin and smiled. "As you are a stranger no more, Mr. Ludlow, you are perfectly welcome. Please forgive my deplorable manners."

"No apologies necessary, Miss Beresford." He smiled as well, and a charming dimple appeared on his left cheek. The hardness about him remained, however, and Lucy found herself wondering about his past and how he came to wear that look.

The music began, and he took her hand in his. Lucy was about to ask which property he had come to investigate, only to recall that Lady Harriett had issued the invitation and therefore the property was likely none other than . . .

Her eyes flew to his as her feet began the steps of the dance. "You are to be the new owner of Tanglewood." It was said as a statement, not a question.

Mr. Ludlow lifted an eyebrow in a show of surprise before he joined hands with another partner. When the steps brought them back together, he said, "It was my mention of Lady Harriett that gave it away, wasn't it?"

Something about his tone bothered Lucy. In fact, everything about this man suddenly bothered her. However handsome Mr. Ludlow may be, it was not his face Lucy wished to see at dinner parties or dances or other gatherings from now on. She especially didn't want to see his face anywhere near Tanglewood, not when it would take the place of another, much more dear face.

Why have you come? she wanted to demand. *Why can you not withdraw your offer and return to wherever it is you came from? You are not welcome here.*

The steps carried them apart again, but Lucy could feel his gaze following her movements, and when they rejoined, she wasn't surprised when he asked, "Is something amiss?"

Yes, she wanted to shout. *Everything is all wrong, and it is all your fault.*

Even as she thought the words, Lucy knew how preposterous they were. It was not Mr. Ludlow's fault that Tanglewood was for sale. The fact of the matter was that Colin did not have to sell if he did not wish to. But he *did* wish to, and therein lay the real problem. He wished to sell, leave, and never return. Perhaps Lucy had merely been a diversion to keep him entertained until a buyer could be found.

And now she was dancing with said buyer.

"Perhaps we should sit the rest of this dance out," Mr. Ludlow suggested as he clasped hands with her again. "You are looking a little pale."

Lucy very nearly accepted his offer when the Draysons were announced. Colin was almost a head taller than his mother and sister and most of the surrounding people, so it was easy to spot him. He made a quick perusal of the room before his gaze rested on her. She stumbled over several steps of the dance as she watched him draw closer and closer. The only reason she was able to remain in the dance at all was because of Mr. Ludlow's firm grip on her hands.

Lucy pried her gaze away from Colin and focused on her partner instead. The hardened look about him reminded her that she needed to be the same. She would keep calm. She would stay strong. She would remain impenetrable.

A coolness settled around her, and when Mr. Ludlow asked again if she would like to sit down, Lucy said firmly, "I would like to dance, sir."

He smiled, showing his dimple. "I believe you are an enigma, Miss Beresford."

"How so, Mr. Ludlow?"

"I have never seen quite so many expressions on one's face throughout the course of a dance."

Lucy clapped hands with another partner, circled around him, and returned to Mr. Ludlow. She immediately rounded her eyes in a wide-eyed expression of fright, and he burst out laughing.

Next came crossed eyes, followed by a distasteful, scrunched up nose, the batting of her eyelashes, and finally, a coy, bashful sort of look. "If only I had a fan to hide behind," she murmured as the dance came to an end.

Mr. Ludlow chuckled as he led her from the floor. "I

must say that was the most diverting reel I have ever danced, Miss Beresford. I shall never forget it." He bowed low over her hand, and when he rose, he added, "I am very glad we are to be such close neighbors."

"You speak as though the contract has been signed, Mr. Ludlow," intruded a voice that sent unwanted thrills down Lucy's spine. Colin stepped next to her and directed an icy stare at Mr. Ludlow.

"Has it not?" came Mr. Ludlow's response.

"No, it has not."

"You have changed your mind then?"

"I have not yet made up my mind one way or another," came Colin's answer. "But when I do, you shall be the . . ." he paused, glancing at Lucy, "*second* to know."

The hardened look was back in Mr. Ludlow's eyes, but instead of responding, he bowed over Lucy's hand again. "It has been a pleasure, Miss Beresford. I do hope I shall get an opportunity to stand up with you again."

"I would like that very much," said Lucy. Then he turned around and was gone, leaving Lucy alone with Colin in a crowded room. She frantically searched for her parents, Mrs. Bidding—anyone—only to have her view blocked by Colin moving in front of her.

"May I have this dance, Miss Beresford?"

She could not run, she could not hide, and she definitely could not slap his face like she wanted to do most. "No, you may not," she said instead.

He looked beyond her and quirked an eyebrow. "Perhaps you wish to dance with Mr. Mead instead. He is headed this way with a rather determined look in his eye."

Lucy hesitated. Dancing with Mr. Mead was like dancing with an excited puppy. He bounced, he trounced, and he always left her with a wet kiss on her hand.

"Very well," she said, ignoring Colin's arm as she led the way to the dance floor. When she turned around to face him, there was no Mr. Mead in sight. Her mouth dropped open, and she glared at Colin.

"You lied," she mouthed.

"I have evened the score," he mouthed back.

The music began and she handed him a limp hand that she pulled away the moment she switched partners. When they came together again, Colin asked, "How is your garden?"

"Good."

"And your riding?"

"Good."

"The ball?"

"Good."

"Have you read any interesting books lately?" he tried again.

"No."

"At last." He grinned. "A different answer than 'good.' I call that progress."

Lucy left him and took another's hand. Almost immediately her arms began bouncing up and down, and she glanced at her new partner to see that Mr. Mead had joined the dance. Well of course he had, she thought dryly. Lucy vowed then to never attend another ball as long as she lived.

When she took hands with Colin again, he pulled her slightly closer than necessary, and her traitorous body shivered in response. She would not be undone by him, she would *not*.

"It is a good thing we did not meet at a ball," he said. "I would have found you very dull indeed."

"Perhaps we *should* have met at a ball," she snapped back. "Only think of all the disappointments we could have avoided."

His lips lifted into a half smile. "Ah, there is the spark I have come to love."

Lucy had never been more grateful to exchange hands. She ripped hers from Colin's and practically latched on to Mr. Mead, not caring that he shook her about. How dare Colin speak of love? How dare he walk into her ball, ask her to dance, and expect her to behave as though he had not split her heart in two?

It took every ounce of strength within her to take his hands again. How long would this blasted dance continue? As the last notes finally faded away, Lucy released the earl's hand and left him standing on the dance floor without a word. She strode quickly through the crowded room, needing some air. A few people called out to her, but she pretended not to hear. She needed to be free from people, the noise, the sounds, and especially Colin. Thankfully, she knew this house well and quickly located the hidden side door where she could escape to the library, and on through that to the darkened conservatory. She had discovered this beautiful glass-encased room within a day of her arrival at Knotting Tree. It wasn't quite the same as being outside, but it was a close second.

She breathed in the luscious aroma of vegetation and sank down on a marble bench, dropping her head to her hands. What a coward she had been. Though she had lasted through to the end of the dance, the moment the music ended, she had picked up her skirts and fled. Eventually she would have to return, but how could she possibly do so with her head held high?

"May I join you?" a voice said from the darkness. Lucy lifted her head, but she did not have to look behind her to see who had spoken. She would recognize that voice anywhere.

He must have taken her silence for a yes because he sat

down beside her. After a few moments, he spoke quietly. "As I told Mr. Ludlow, I have not sold Tanglewood yet."

"What are you waiting for?" Lucy asked. "Simply sign the papers and be done if that is what you wish."

"I do wish it," he said. "Tanglewood has been nothing but a drain on our holdings during the past several years. Besides the manor house, all the tenant homes are in serious need of repair. It will take a great deal of money and time to restore it to a respectable state, and for what purpose? My family's home is in Danbury. It is a beautiful, fully restored estate that is quite lucrative, and it also happens to be close to several other holdings in which we are invested. I have no idea what Mr. Ludlow's reasons are for desiring Tanglewood, but he wants it. He wishes to make something of it and has the means and the time to make it happen. He has also offered a large sum that is worth more than Tanglewood at the moment. I would be a fool to pass on his offer."

Lucy felt her spirits sink lower with every word he uttered. How could she have ever held out hope that he would want to make Tanglewood his home? It seemed such a silly, juvenile hope now.

"I do not understand what the problem is," said Lucy.

"Do you not?" he whispered, angling his body toward her. "*You* are the problem. You and only you."

Lucy's eyes snapped to his in confusion. How could *she* be the problem? Granted, there had been a time when she had been a very big problem, but she and her mother had since moved out of the dower house, and Lucy had not stood in his way since.

One of his fingers grazed hers, as though testing it. When she did not flinch or draw away, he slid his hand under hers and curled his fingers through hers.

"I have fallen in love with you, Miss Lucy Beresford," he said. "More than anything, I want to ask you to be my wife."

Lucy gasped. For a few moments she did not breathe at all, and then her breath came in and out in short bursts, as though she had just raced across the meadow and could not catch her breath. Had Colin just asked for her hand? Or hadn't he? She didn't quite know, but she felt a burst of joy that gave her reason to hope.

He sandwiched her hand between both of his. "As I explained to you earlier, it does not make sense for my family or me to remain in Askern. But perhaps, together, we can find a way to make it work, if that is your wish. If not"—he swallowed—"then by asking you to be my wife, I am asking for you to leave your home, your family, and all you hold dear and come with me to Essex. I have been wrestling with this for weeks, telling myself it was not fair to ask such a thing of you, attempting to figure out a way to remain here, and feeling like there was no good resolution. So here I am, unloading my problems to you while hoping and praying that you can aid in the solution of them. You—"

"I most certainly can help," Lucy blurted. "It is quite a simple solution, really. Sign your name on that dratted contract and ask me to be your wife. Or have you already asked me? I am a little unclear on that point."

He studied her a moment, his brows furrowed. "Of course I have, but I do not think you realize what I'm asking. Your mother—"

"My mother has Mr. Shepherd now," said Lucy. "And he has her. And I will always have them both no matter where I live. You say that I will be leaving all that I hold dear behind, but that is not the case at all. You have become far dearer to me than anyone else in this world, so why in heaven's name would I choose to remain behind when you are offering me a great deal more? Can you not see that? I choose *you*, Colin. Always you."

He let out a breath that sounded more like a strangled chuckle. "I did not dare hope," he said. "I knew you cared for me, but then you said you could not imagine living anywhere else. I thought if we had more time, I might convince you that—"

"Colin, you have just asked me to be your wife, and I have given you my answer in as straightforward a manner as I know how. I believe it is long past time for you to kiss me and put an end to this silly conversation. And in the future, I hope you will think to ask my opinion sooner rather than later."

He chuckled. "Given the force with which you speak your mind, I suspect I will not need to ask it."

"And I shall continue to speak my mind," she answered. "Now kiss me, or I shall have to resort to kissing you, and we both know how unseemly that would be."

"Because you never behave in an unseemly way," he teased, framing her face with his large, warm hands.

"If I am to be the wife of an earl, my behavior must always be above reproach, mustn't it?"

He kissed her then, and Lucy kissed him back. In that moment, everything felt exactly as it should.

"Don't ever change for anyone, my love," Colin whispered against her lips. "I prefer you exactly as you are."

A door opened somewhere, but Lucy did not care and neither did Colin it seemed. He continued to kiss her quite soundly until a shrill voice rudely interrupted their happy moment.

"Lord Drayson, Miss Beresford!" gasped Mrs. Bidding. "You must stop this at once!"

Colin smiled against Lucy's lips before he slowly drew back and pulled Lucy to her feet beside him. "Is there a problem, Mrs. Bidding?" he asked.

"My lord," she said, her eyes narrowing. "I may have looked the other way before, but I can do so no longer. I must insist you go to Mr. Shepherd at once and do the honorable thing by Miss Beresford."

"You are quite right, Mrs. Bidding. If you'll excuse us, we shall go straightaway." Colin began to lead Lucy past a shocked Mrs. Bidding, only to hear her say, "We?"

Colin glanced over his shoulder. "Yes. We."

"Always we," Lucy agreed. "Thank you so much, Mrs. Bidding, for finally making Lord Drayson see reason. I must admit, I had quite lost hope. Now I owe all my happiness to you."

"Oh, well . . . of course, my dear. Anything for you." Mrs. Bidding had never looked more pleased.

As Colin led Lucy from the room, he whispered, "I thought you were through with telling tales."

"That was not a fib," said Lucy. "That was creative truth-telling, and it is a perfectly acceptable thing to do."

"For the daughter of a vicar, you have very loose standards. Breaking vows, inventing lies, picking locks, stealing plows, allowing yourself to be thoroughly compromised—not once but several times—and now bending the rules of truth and deceit to suit your wiles. I find myself quite shocked indeed."

"Prepare yourself then," warned Lucy. "For the most shocking thing is yet to come."

"Dare I ask what that could possibly be?"

"Certainly," she said. "I would very much like you to convince the orchestra to play a waltz, ask me for a dance, and continue to dance with me the remainder of the evening."

His eyes widened in a dramatic show of astonishment. "How will our reputations withstand such scandal?"

"They shan't," teased Lucy. "So you see, it is a good thing we will be removing to Danbury."

Colin laughed. Then he stopped and gave her one more kiss before they reentered the ballroom and went in search of Mr. and Mrs. Shepherd. They were both delighted that Lucy and Colin had finally figured things out. Hugs were extended to both, and when Mr. Shepherd made a public announcement, the room broke out in cheers and applause. Lady Drayson and Harriett rushed to congratulate the couple as well.

Several minutes later, when the orchestra began to play a waltz, Lucy glanced over in surprise to see Colin—*her* Colin—walking away from the musicians and toward her with a devil of a smile on his face.

Harriett recognized the tune and leaned in close, whispering in Lucy's ear. "I believe that you have agreed to marry quite the scoundrel."

"It is a good thing I am rather fond of scoundrels," said Lucy, allowing Colin to take her hand and bring it to his lips.

"If you are not otherwise engaged, Miss Beresford, might I have the honor of this dance?"

"You certainly may." Lucy smiled as he swept her into his arms, held her much too close, and swirled her around and around and around. She used to think balls were horrid, tepid affairs where one had to always be on one's best and dullest behavior, but how wrong she had been. If only Lucy had put a little more faith in her new papa's wise counsel. How right he had been when he said her story was not near to being over yet.

Indeed, it was only just beginning.

Dear Reader,

Thanks so much for reading! I hope it gave you a break from the daily grind and rejuvenated you in some way. If you enjoyed this book, be sure to check out the next two books in the series, *The Rise of Miss Notley* (Tanglewood 2) and *The Pursuit of Lady Harriett* (Tanglewood 3).

If you're interested in being notified of new releases, feel free to sign up for my New Release mailing list on my website at RachaelReneeAnderson.com. (You will only be emailed about new releases.)

Also, if you can spare a few minutes, I'd be incredibly grateful for a review from you on Goodreads or Amazon. They make a huge difference in every aspect of publishing, and I am always so thankful whenever readers take a few minutes to review a book.

Thanks again for your support and best wishes!

Rachael

TANGLEWOOD SERIES

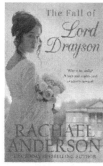
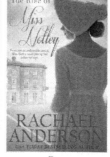

Book 1   Book 2   Book 3

ACKNOWLEDGEMENTS

I have to start off by thanking my friend, Kathy, at BookwormNation.blogspot.com for encouraging me to stretch my wings by trying out a new genre. I am so grateful for all your kindness and support.

Kathy Habel, from IAmAReader.com, what would I do without you? From beta reading to marketing, you have helped me with every single one of my books. You have been an answer to many prayers, and I will always feel indebted to you.

Letha, what an awesome sister you are! Thanks so much for talking me through some of the more sticky parts of my plot. I am so thankful for your creativity, humor, and willingness to help me out whenever I have a need.

As usual, I have to thank Karey White for being the best kind of friend there is. You have listened, encouraged, and listened some more. You also happen to be the most brilliant editor ever. Bless you for your goodness and friendship.

Braden Bell, thank you for your thorough, honest critiques. You have taught me so much about character-ization, plot structure, and so many other things.

Andrea Pearson, thank you for your keen eye, honesty, and valuable feedback. I'm so thankful for your friendship.

Joanna Carnejo, thanks for giving the book one final proofread and for catching the things you did. Someday I hope to be able to return the favor.

Jeff, a hundred million thanks for being the husband, father, supporter, confidant, and friend that you are. I love you.

I must also thank my heavenly father, for loving me enough to challenge, inspire, and bless me.

ABOUT RACHAEL ANDERSON

RACHAEL ANDERSON is a *USA Today* bestselling author and mother of four crazy and awesome kids. Over the years she's gotten pretty good at breaking up fights or at least sending guilty parties to their rooms. She can't sing, doesn't dance, and despises tragedies, but she recently figured out how yeast works and can now make homemade bread, which she is really good at eating. You can read more about her and her books online at RachaelReneeAnderson.com.

Made in the USA
Lexington, KY
11 May 2018